MONSTERS ALL THE WAY DOWN

RYAN MCSWAIN

This is a work of fiction. Names, characters, places, and events are either the products of the author's imagination or used in a fictitious manner. Any resemblance to actual persons—living, dead, or worse than dead—or actual events is purely coincidental.

First edition.

Published by Pithos Publishing
4401 Derrick Place, Amarillo, Texas 79121
www.pithospublishing.com

Cover design by Rory Harnden, rrry.me

Source photography courtesy of The Library of Congress and Dustin Schmieding

Author photo by Dustin Taylor

Proofreading by Catherine York

ISBN: 0990460770
ISBN-13: 978-0-9904607-7-0

For my wife, who makes me believe I can win.

PHASE I

1

"OF COURSE IT'S GOING TO HURT."

The technician, whose shiny name tag labeled him as Bill, pushed a tiny gadget against Brennan Wade's index finger. Brennan heard a tiny click and felt a sharp jab as it did its job, and a dark bubble of blood oozed from the tip of his throbbing finger.

"I'm glad you guys were able to fit me in on such short notice," Brennan said. "I start work on Monday, and no one called to tell me they needed a DNA background check until today."

"No problem at all," Bill the Tech said. "Glad we could help. What's the job, if you don't mind me asking?"

"Security at Dallas Love Field Airport. I really need this job. Glad I'm not going to lose it because someone else dropped the ball."

"No kidding. At least there was no harm done, right? And it looks like you're a good bleeder, Mr. Wade."

Bill the Tech collected the sample with a tiny glass straw. *It's called a pipette*, Brennan's mind reminded him, digging deep into old knowledge. He had last used a pipette in a college chemistry course, but he was past thirty years old now and college felt like a long time ago. Seeing the pipette full of his own juice made him uneasy.

He became aware of the intense smell in the medical lab. It was the familiar smell of alcohol and hospital rooms, and it made him feel queasy. It reminded him of a class trip to a veterinary hospital when he was a kid. The veterinarian, wearing the same white coat Bill the Tech now wore, held up a plastic model of a dog's heart. It was brown, with red and blue accents. She took a large chunk out of the front of the fake heart, and it was infested with worms, molded in bright white plastic. She explained how the worms lived off the dog, and the room started spinning around little Brennan.

Bill the Tech looked concerned. "Mr. Wade? You okay? Do you need—"

That was all Brennan heard. He slid out of the chair and onto the cold floor, pulling his stack of forms with him like a paper waterfall. He dreamed of a dog-headed man in an unkempt tuxedo stabbing him with one of his doggy claws. Brennan noticed the dog man had snot in his nose, but it wasn't snot it was a worm and—

"Mr. Wade!"

Brennan's eyes blinked open and closed as he tried to remember where he was. His lips were blue and a towel was under his head. He had been out long enough Bill had panicked and called for help. Brennan looked up at a circle of concerned faces. A young man in scrubs got down on his knees and yelled into his face, "Mr. Wade! Can you hear me?"

Before Brennan could answer, the man started resuscitation. He performed three chest compressions before a woman pulled him off. "Stop that, you idiot! He's awake!"

"Oh, shit! I'm so sorry!" The young man jumped to his feet and the woman sent him to get Brennan a cup of water. Brennan took a second to peek at his pants—thankfully, he had not wet them.

Bill the Tech helped him sit up. "Sorry about that," he said. "The guy is new. This happens all the time around this place. He'll get used to it."

Brennan groaned and was pulled to his feet. "I'm sorry," he said. "That hasn't happened to me for a long time."

Bill laughed. "Seriously, don't worry. It really does happen more than you'd think. Sit down for awhile and you'll be fine."

"Did I screw up the test?"

"No, no, no, we're good. I'd rather not stab you again. It's obviously not your thing."

Brennan tried to smile. They asked him to sit in the break room until he felt okay to drive home. He didn't have the heart to tell them his car had been repossessed, and the half-hour spent in the break room made him miss his bus.

He waited for the next bus in a fast-food burger place. He considered getting something cheap to eat, but the alcohol smell hit him again and he thought better of it. An annoyed cashier handed him a child's size cup of water for free, and Brennan sat in a sticky booth with a window facing the bus stop. He glanced down at his worn sneakers and wiggled his right pinky toe, which stuck out a small hole in the side of the shoe.

I probably look like shit, he thought. A glance at the window confirmed he did indeed look like shit. He looked like it was his first day out after a week sick with the flu. His skin was still pale, and his dark hair looked like he'd slept on it. *Which I kind of did*, he thought.

Brennan hoped no one at the lab would tell the airport about his little accident. He imagined arriving for his first day of work, and everyone knowing he had passed out giving blood. In his mind he saw a guard—a spitting image of the jerkass who bullied him in junior high—fanning himself frantically with his hand. "I got the vapors!" the jerkass wailed in a high-pitched southern voice, and all the guys in blue coveralls laughing. *Labs aren't allowed to give out that kind of information, right?* he thought. *There have to be laws against it, like when you tell something to a priest.*

To pass the time, Brennan played his secret game. He called it *Get Out Alive*, and the rules were simple: he imagined everyone in the room wanted him dead and he must plan an escape. Brennan played this game several times a week, and he privately felt he was good at it.

The restaurant was far from crowded, with just enough people to make it interesting. Including the six or so workers behind the counter, there were almost two dozen people. About ten of the customers stood in line or waited for food, and the rest sat at booths and tables.

Threat assessment: the primary problem was the man a few booths down who looked like he might be an off-duty cop. *Don't forget you're still wobbly from fainting,* he told himself. *The goal is just getting out of the restaurant.*

First option, shove through the people waiting to order. Move quick, arms up and head down. Hit the line where the kids are standing. They'd go down like bowling pins. Then it's two old women at the door. Pros: the obstacles won't be a big problem. Cons: that is still a lot of people, and if they react fast enough, the others could overpower me by weight of numbers. If they hold me up at all, the off-duty cop would have plenty of time to pull his hypothetical gun or knock me over the head with a chair.

Second option: pick up a chair that isn't occupied or bolted down. Hit the armed guy in the face with it and throw it through the main window. Then I jump out. Pros: less people to deal with. Cons: I might not be faster than the maybe-a-cop, the window might not break, and I'd probably cut the hell out of myself on the busted glass.

He could not decide which option would be better, but the second sounded more exciting. He felt a twinge of regret as the possible cop threw away his trash and left.

The last bus arrived after the sun went down. Brennan made the long series of exchanges necessary to reach his apartment. As the bus reached Brennan's stop, he bumped into a bearded man in a cowboy hat, causing the man to drop the magazine he was reading. The cowboy looked a bit taller than Brennan, but that could have been his boots.

"Sorry about that," Brennan said. He scooped up the wadded magazine and returned it.

"No problem," said the cowboy. He sounded rushed. "You have a nice evening."

Brennan exited the bus, and watched it drive off. *Funny that I live in Dallas, Texas,* he thought, *but it's still weird to see a cowboy hat on a city bus.*

It was Friday, so he had one last weekend to enjoy his unemployment. He entered his apartment and flipped on the light switch. Nothing happened, which was no surprise to Brennan. He tripped over a stack of thrift-store vinyl records, but made it to his bed. Still clothed when he hit the mattress, he soon drifted off to dream of plastic hearts and white worms.

Standing on a cracked sidewalk across the street, the bearded man in a cowboy hat stared at Brennan's dark window and smoked a cigarette; blue smoke curled in the air around his head. He dropped the cigarette in the wet gutter, extinguishing the burning cherry with a soft hiss. His eyes never left the window.

On the other side of town, a computer compared the digital representation of Brennan Wade's DNA against a database of millions. The machine made a soft beep when it found a match.

2

BRENNAN WADE ARRIVED at Dallas Love Field Airport on Monday at 7:30 A.M. They had not given him his uniform yet, so he wore his nice-but-not-too-nice outfit. He sprung for new shoes.

They told him over the phone his first day would consist of training videos and the final pile of forms. Brennan could not imagine what else he could possibly tell them about himself, unless it was what he had dreamed about the night before (which he could not remember) or what had eaten for breakfast that morning (he had skipped it). He decided to leave those spaces blank if they came up.

Lugging the manila folder bulging with the latest round of paperwork, he found the employee entrance. He walked up to the receptionist's desk, but someone he had not met before was sitting there. The desk's nameplate still read "Martha," but the middle-aged man with a striped clip-on tie did not look like a Martha. Brennan said so.

"She's sick," the man at the desk said. "Cancer."

"I'm sorry to hear that." Brennan's mother once told him to always make friends with the secretaries anywhere he worked;

they were the ones who did everything. So he held out his hand. "I'm Brennan Wade. Nice to meet you."

Clip-On Tie Guy did not answer the greeting or the handshake. He did not look up. "Says here you're starting with security today. Have a seat, and I'll send you back when they're ready for you."

"Hey, thanks. Nice tie, by the way." Brennan left the receptionist looking down at his tie while Brennan picked a seat out of a line of identical chairs. The orange and yellow fiberglass chairs looked like they came out of a laundromat from the 1970s.

He sat down, holding the manila folder in his lap and feeling like he was waiting to see the principal or the Wizard of Oz. His throat was dry and his stomach turned, letting out a growl he swore shook the pencils in the cup on Tie Guy's desk.

Tie Guy evidently heard. "Need a doughnut?" he asked, gesturing to some plastic-looking pastries in the corner. They looked like toy food a kid played with in a pretend kitchen.

Brennan was hungry, but he was too jittery to eat. "I'm good, thanks. Just nervous. First day, y'know?"

Tie Guy looked at him sympathetically. "How about some water?"

"Ah, man, that would be great. Thank you." Brennan walked up to the desk as Tie Guy poured him a Styrofoam cup from a pitcher. "Thank you, sir," he said.

"Don't call me 'sir,' I'm not that old. Call me Jim."

"You got it, Jim," Brennan said, and this time when he held out his hand, Jim shook it.

Brennan had plenty of time to finish his cup of water. He wished he had brought a book or a magazine. Would that have been all right on his first day? He had been through so many first days he did not know anymore.

"You're not packing, are you?" Jim asked.

"What?"

"Did you bring your own firearm with you?"

"Oh, okay, no," Brennan said. He did not own a gun. "I told them I wasn't licensed to carry yet, but they said that was okay. Was I supposed to—?"

"No, no, that's good," Jim said. "No personal weapons. That's why they had to fire the guy you're replacing. Turned out he was showing up every day armed to the teeth." Jim laughed, and Brennan did his best to laugh with him.

Jim went back to whatever he was doing at his desk, and twenty minutes passed. When he finally spoke, Brennan almost spilled his third cup of water. "They're ready for you, Mr. Wade. Go down that hall and take the last doorway on the left. Keep walking until you get to the security manager's office. His name is Robertson. It's on the door."

Brennan thanked him and started down the hall. The second metal door had a small window crisscrossed with little lines, like the kind he had seen in the doors of public schools. *What the heck is that stuff?* Brennan wondered as it closed behind him with a click. The new hallway contained one door at the opposite end. Robertson's office was nowhere to be seen.

I bet I can figure this one out, Brennan thought, walking down the hallway. The cinder-block walls were painted a shade of yellow so pale it was almost white. The door at the end had no window, but was unlocked. It closed behind him with the same click. Yet another yellow hallway stretched before him, one door at the end.

Old Robertson must love this walk, he thought. *Lets him work off all those toy doughnuts.*

The next hallway was dark, but the florescent lights sputtered to life as he entered. *Motion sensors,* he thought. When another windowless door clicked behind him, the harsh fluorescents revealed he was in yet another hallway with one door on each end.

Ridiculous. That jerk Jim sent me the wrong way. He turned to go back and double-check the directions, but the door had locked behind him.

An involuntary sigh escaped him. He examined the doorknob, but there was no keyhole. And there was no place to slide a card or type in a code. *The doors must work on a remote system,* he thought. *Sounds like a security thing, so maybe I'm going in the right direction, after all. Good ol' Jim didn't steer me wrong. But good ol' Jim might have warned me about the Willy Wonka architecture in this place.*

He walked through several more empty hallways before he started to worry. How many doors had he passed through? He had lost count. *For all I know,* he thought, *at the end of these hallways is a broom closet, where I'll die using a mop as a pillow. But what else can I do?* He opened the next door.

After a few more empty hallways, panic set in. He wished he had caved in and bought one of those pay-as-you go cell phones. *But how was I supposed to know I would end up trapped in hallway hell?* He looked into the next hallway—pale yellow, one door, standard height, smooth ceiling, tiled floor, twelve-and-a-half paces long—and refused to enter it. He knew the door would click and he would scream. So he ran back to the last locked door and gave it seven knocks in rapid succession.

"Jim! It's a real funhouse in here! Great joke on the new guy! Could you please open the doors?"

No answer.

"Fine! Martha was way better than you, anyway! And your tie looks like shit!"

Man, you need to calm down, or you're going to get fired before you even meet the boss, he thought. *Unless I die of starvation in a piss-yellow hallway before they can fill out the paperwork.* He regretted not filling his pockets with stale doughnuts.

First things first, he decided. *No more locked doors between me and outside. Between me and freedom, hot diggity dog.*

The new shoes went first, because those would be the least embarrassing things to be missing if this was all a misunderstanding. He propped open the door with a shoe, then walked to the next door and did the same with his other shoe. Then his socks. Tie. Belt. Watch. Keys. Wallet. Starched dress shirt.

He stood there in his undershirt and pants, facing door number one million, and contemplated removing his pants. The headline might make the cover of the employee newsletter: '*Sex Pervert Meets the Boss.*' That would be a great story for the next office party. Brennan doubted he would get to attend this imaginary office party, of course, or any party ever again.

He heard a loud click behind him.

He spun on his bare heel, but it was too late. He faced a blank door that was no longer propped open. All of his doorstops—including his driver's license and three maxed-out credit cards—were gone.

"Son of a bitch!" He ran to the door and pounded on it with both fists. *I'll break the fucker down,* he thought, slamming into the door with shoulder. *Break them all down! I'll feed Jim his tie, eat all the doughnuts, and then I'll find a job at some little ma and pop place without any goddamn circus tricks.*

The door refused to budge. He could not even dent it. His hands would break long before the door gave way. *How do they break down doors in the movies?*

He remembered and stepped back. He braced himself and kicked beside the doorknob as hard as he could with the sole of his foot.

That put him on the floor, gripping his foot like a cartoon character who had kicked an anvil disguised as a football. He swore gibberish under his breath while pain shot up through his heel. *Why'd I have to leave the shoes?*

He looked around for another way out. The walls were cinder block. When he picked at the tile on the floor, he found it was glued tight, and it felt like there was concrete underneath. The ceiling was too high to reach.

He spotted a security camera, a little gray box suspended on a short metal arm, nestled up in a corner. Brennan asked himself, *Was there a camera in the other hallways?* He jumped and swatted at it, careful not to land on the foot he had used to kick at the door. On his fourth try he grabbed onto the camera and pulled it down. There were no wires. Brennan looked into the lens and yelled, "What is wrong with you people?" He squeezed the camera and was surprised at how easily it gave way under his grip. Looking closer, he saw it was a cardboard shell with plastic accents—a prop.

Brennan threw the toy camera and watched it bounce down the hall. He opened the next door and stepped through.

Confused, Brennan entered an enormous room. He stood in an airport terminal, but it was in shambles. Piles of broken drywall and torn cables were piled against the walls. A few flickering florescent tubes lit the expanse from high above. Windows were covered with paint and cardboard.

He walked toward what looked like a route out of the terminal, careful not to slip in a puddle of standing water. He rounded a corner and gasped. There was a gaping hole stretching across the entire floor. Rusted pipes and sputtering wires jutted out of the dirt, and the chunk of tile he tossed into it disappeared. It never hit bottom. *A bottomless pit*, Brennan thought. *Like in a fairy tale.*

That was enough. *This is wrong*, he thought. *This isn't real.*

He heard something move behind him. A bag was pulled over his face, muffling his scream. Something solid hit the back of his head, and Brennan saw a flash of light.

3

WHEN BRENNAN CAME TO, the bag was still over his head and he felt groggy and nauseated. His arms were strapped behind him. He tried to move them, but he stopped at the sound of jingling metal and the pain of something cutting into his wrists.

Oh my god, I'm in handcuffs, he thought. *What happened?* Cold panic grew in his gut, and his heart beat like a snare drum. The pain in his head was dull and steady.

He took a quick inventory. His ankles were also cuffed, and he felt the pressure of straps over his shoulders, chest, waist, and thighs. Aside from the pounding in his head, his body was unhurt. The inside of his hood smelled like dried spit. He thought, *If I've been drooling, I've been out for a while.*

Murmuring voices told him he was not alone, and there were at least three or four men seated around him.

"Where are we going?" Brennan asked no one in particular. His words were answered with sudden movement all around him, and he heard metallic clicking sounds, which he guessed were guns being readied. No one answered him.

"Can you at least loosen the straps on my chest? I can barely breathe over here."

He heard a whispered exchange. An agreement was reached: "No can do, buddy," said a familiar voice.

Brennan let out a short, dry laugh. "Jim? Jim the receptionist? You gotta be joking."

There was no answer.

"You aren't really a secretary, are you? I bet you're not even a real Jim," Brennan said.

"Today I'll be Jim," Jim said.

"You got me good there, Jim. How'd you do the thing with the hallway? You should sell that to the carnival, man, you'd make a million bucks."

He heard a whispered question. *These guys are great at whispering,* he thought. He could not tell which direction it came from. *How big is this van?* he thought. *Or is it a train?*

"It was the water, right? Something in the water."

"And the doughnuts," Jim answered. He seemed to be about six feet from Brennan, directly across from him. "Who the hell doesn't take a doughnut?"

"Good point," said one of the other men; they laughed.

Brennan grunted. "Sorry, Buddy Jim. Those doughnuts were crap. Looked like I'd chip a tooth on one."

"What're you talking about, Wade? That's how people *like* their doughnuts. Makes it look like they're out of a magazine."

Brennan laughed. "No way. I could've made a tastier looking treat with my Easy-Bake Oven."

Another voice chimed in. "You had an Easy-Bake Oven? I had one a' those."

"Shut the hell up," Jim told the baking enthusiast. "Loose lips."

Whatever they were traveling in, the ride was smooth. No bumps, no turns. There was the sense of motion, a steady hum, and the slightest vibration.

"Tell me why you gave me that stuff," Brennen said. "That was screwed up, man. If you wanted to knock me out, why didn't you just give me something to knock me out?"

He heard someone snickering. Jim said, "Fine, numbnuts, you tell him why." The man was silent. Jim said, "Go on, go ahead. It'll keep him calm, and it's not like you're telling him anything he don't already know."

There was the sound of paper rustling. Easy-Bake Oven Guy read, "'Suspect is highly tolerant of depressants, including alcohol and barbiturates. Suspect eluded capture after ingesting, according to the bartender, "All the cheap liquor we had in the place." Suspect has also eluded capture when unarmed, through improvisation and extreme violence.'"

Jim added, "Some animals know when they're being hunted. Flies and vinegar. So we decided to improvise, too. We pumped you full of enough hallucinogens to soak every asshole at Woodstock. Locked you in a closed-off section of the airport where you couldn't hurt anybody and gave you a little unseen direction. Then we let you wear yourself out. Could not have gone better. Hook and line. The bit where you used your stuff to prop open the same two doors over and over again? That was classic. You can't plan that kind of a thing."

Brennan finally recognized the hum. They were on a plane, and he had been out for an unknown amount of time. *We could be anywhere by now*, he thought. "Listen. I don't know who you think I am, but my name is Brennan Wade. I came in this morning for a security job. I've never hurt anybody. I've never done anything worth this treatment. I'm actually a pretty boring guy."

Jim said, "That's not exactly true, is it, Wade? You have one assault on record."

"Fine, yes. Okay. But that was a misunderstanding, and I was acquitted. We all had too much to drink, and this guy started messing with this girl I was talking to. This girl I wanted to talk to. I tried to—"

"Yeah, it says that here, too. Intracranial bleeding? You really messed the guy up."

"He slipped and hit his head on a stool. I'd never been in a fight before. I thought that guy was gonna kill me. I didn't know how bad he was hurt until later."

Brennan heard a few people laughing. "Wade, cut the shit," Jim said, "That's the only thing with your name on it, but we've got more files on you. Library of Alexandria. I know you can't see them through your happy head-sack, but I'm holding one up, and it's thick, buddy. Phone book thick. And it's all yours, fucko; we know it is. We're about to close more cases than the entire run of Columbo."

"Are you crazy? You've got the wrong—"

"Don't talk to me about crazy, you sick fuck!" Jim yelled. "Tell me this. Where were you living, summer, 1992?"

"Flatland, Texas. I was—"

"And were you in Kansas City, Missouri, in the spring of 1999?"

Brennan rolled the date around in his head. "Yeah, but—"

"Shut up. California, December, 2002?"

Brennan stayed silent. His breath felt warm and damp inside the sack.

"Don't worry," Jim said. "We know you were there. And that's just three. There are bread crumbs everywhere you go, Wade. And there are plenty more incidents we'll tie to you. The shoe fits."

Brennan squirmed in his chair, shaking the chains of his restraints. The cuffs sliced into the skin of his wrists. "I don't know what you're talking about. You have to believe me."

"Stick with that, asshole. It'll make a great defense. Never works. If at first you don't succeed. Oh, hey, we're landing. Don't forget to fasten your seatbelts. Tray tables."

The plane came to a stop. They unstrapped Brennan roughly and secured him to a gurney.

"Try anything and it's goodnight, Gracie," Jim whispered by his ear while jabbing a gun barrel against his temple. Brennan nodded stiffly.

Outside the plane, he could feel the sun through his clothes. Between the heat and his fear, sweat covered his body. He felt sick to his stomach, but he did not know if it was a side effect of the drugs or ordinary hunger. He had not been eating well recently, and he had no idea how long it had been since the funhouse hallway treatment.

They wheeled him into a building, and the sudden rush of cold air felt like walking into a shopping mall in the middle of summer. Still in restraints, he could hear the wheels rolling on a concrete floor. Small sounds echoed like in a cave.

His keepers argued over who had to fingerprint him. He was still strapped to the gurney when they did it, and his arms, wrists, and fingers were all bent back a bit more than they needed to be for the process.

"Anybody gonna read me my rights?" Brennan asked.

Jim laughed. "Buddy, we pumped you full of experimental drugs on a whim. You think we're the kind of people who read you your rights? As of this morning, you might as well not exist."

After a short ride, someone unstrapped Brennan from the gurney.

"Forward," Jim said.

Brennan shuffled his restrained feet accordingly. The door clanged shut behind him.

"Put your back against the bars," Jim said. One of the jailers removed the handcuffs and other restraints, which made a terrible clangity clang clang as they were pulled through the bars.

Brennan fumbled with the hood. By the time he got it off his head, Brennan Wade was alone in his cell.

4

BRENNAN LAY FLAT ON HIS BACK on a rough concrete floor. There was no bed, no cot, no flea-bitten mattress. There was just him in a dreary hole of a cell. There was not even a bucket.

The cell itself was about ten-feet square, about the size of the bedroom in his crappy apartment in Dallas. Three of the walls and the ceiling were the same pitted concrete as the floor. Bars made up the other wall of his cube. Except for the fact the bars looked brand new—there was no rust, and fresh mortar held them in place—he might have believed he was stuck in a jail cell from the old west. He wished someone on a horse would tie a rope to the bars in the window and pull the wall down like in the old black and white movies his grandfather used to watch. But this window had no bars; it was only a tiny slit.

The cell door had an electric lock with a keypad facing the outside. *A bit anachronistic for playing cowboys and Indians*, he thought. The lock's smooth casing revealed no screws to fantasize about removing. Try as he might, he could not reach the buttons or pry the casing apart.

No one bothered to tell him how long it had been since he was captured, so he started a new internal count as the sun went down. He knew it was night because of the tiny window in the wall opposite the bars. The window was a good nine-and-a-half feet up the wall, and it had no glass—he could tell by the occasional outdoor sounds coming through it.

Starting at mid-morning, a tiny, slow-moving line of sunlight appeared on the ceiling. It disappeared that evening, leaving him in total darkness. It was cold at night—surprisingly cold considering the mild temperature during the day. His concrete hole remained cool enough, and if he stood on tip-toe, he could feel occasional bursts of dusty air from the window-slit.

A narrow hallway ran past the wall of bars, leading off in both directions. It went on forever, for all Brennan knew, and the thought of another round of that nonsense made his head swim. He saw no one and no one spoke to him. Occasionally, he thought he heard breathing or even footsteps down the hall, but the echoes were in competition with his mind to see who could play bigger tricks. While strapped to the gurney, he had no idea how many turns they had made or how deep he was in whatever hole they had dumped him.

But the sunlight gave him hope. At least he was not already buried under the ground.

On the first day, his head continued to ache. The headache, coupled with the drugs they had given him, left him nauseated and dizzy. Every few hours he stood up and leaned on the bars, straining to see as far down the hallway as he could. It was like when Brennan was a kid and looking in the hallway mirror. He would try to see the parts of the mirror rooms that he could not quite reach, trying to stretch his eyes around the backward corners.

He managed not to vomit on day one, but other bodily functions were another matter. No bucket ever showed up, so he designated one corner as his toilet. At least he guessed right and used the lowest corner so nothing ran back into the middle of the room. If he had used the corner by the hallway, the slope would have left him sleeping in filth. It was amazing how suddenly the definition of good fortune could change.

Brennan had never been arrested before. He had never sat in the back of a police car, and definitely had never been through booking, but he had seen it in the movies. He knew this was not right. He had met some jerk cops before, like he had known nice ones, but none of them would have handled things like this. *They drugged me and threw me in a goddamn dungeon for Christ's sake*, he thought.

So they're not cops. Who does that leave? Army? The government? He had heard about the crazy things the CIA did to people, things like MK-Ultra and extraordinary rendition. He supposed it possible these were government people acting on mistaken information. "Like that's never happened before," he said, and laughed to himself. Maybe a file had gotten mixed up, and someone named Brennan Waid-with-an-A-I was out there chopping people up. *Maybe I can sue the shit out of somebody for this*, he thought.

The alternative was much worse. If these guys were not government, then he was already dead.

On day two, Brennan tried being a bastard. He yelled down the hall in long shifts, waited for his voice to come back, and then yelled again. He yelled about being an American citizen and having his rights, and he yelled about hitting their asses with a lawsuit. He yelled about sleeping on a concrete floor. He yelled about the need for proper toilet facilities. He yelled an order for a pizza if anyone was buying. He spent a solid half-hour on Jim's ugly tie and felt proud of himself, or at least as proud as he could feel when he took another pathetic shit in the corner.

It first hurt to urinate at sundown of day two, and that scared him. He had told himself his mouth was dry from all the yelling, and tried not to think about the fact he had been without food and water for at least forty-eight hours. But when he felt the stinging pucker as he urinated, he admitted to himself it was serious. *If I don't figure something out*, he thought, *I am going to die, no doubt about it.*

So he started urinating into his wadded-up undershirt. He

had heard you could live off your urine for a short time. He had no idea if this was true, but he had to do something. When they finally came to dispose of him—if they ever did—he wanted them to see he had put up a fight. The dark urine tasted salty as he sucked the last few drops out of his make-shift sponge.

On day three his stomach was in knots, and his headache came back with a vengeance. He barely moved the entire day, reasoning that if he conserved his energy he might live long enough to make it out.

But that's crazy, he thought. *Nobody does this to someone they plan on letting go.* He began to think his best hope was someone coming in and finishing him off. *One-two, back of the head. Three-four, left for dead.*

As the sun set, he listened at the outside wall. He heard no cars, no people, no anything. Not even birds. Wherever he was, they had dumped him where no one would come for him. If not for the slim evidence to the contrary, he would suspect they had taken him to the moon. He cursed himself for his lack of relationships. The first person to realize he was gone would probably be his landlord, and rent was not due for a month. And his landlord was an okay guy; in the past he had let the rent slide a few weeks.

When night fell on day three, Brennan lay on the floor and wondered, just wondered, if he could hang himself from the bars with his pants. "Only as a last resort," he said out loud. He tried to remember the right type of knot to use, but he could not decide if he could manage it without a rope.

Then he left the cell. He was back in his apartment, in his own bed, and he was listening to old records scrounged for a quarter or a dime apiece. He could hear where the record skipped as Robert Johnson sang about the crossroads. He could smell the cheap white paint that never dried all the way. He could feel the bedpost he tapped his foot against.

"Wade."

The word was so faint that if he had been exhaling, he would have missed it. He stood up in the darkness and walked to the bars, bending his eyes as far as he could in either direction. But there was nobody. It was just another echo trick, or one last joke courtesy of his airport drugs. He cursed and lay back down. When he stared up at the ceiling, he noticed a change.

On the ledge of his window slit, he saw a tiny bump, like the microscopic imperfection in a razor's edge. *That wasn't there before*, he thought. He was sure of it. He had been staring at the unbroken line of the window ledge for three days.

He stood up slowly, his knees creaking. *Are they watching me?* he asked himself. *They might be. They must be.* At this point, he believed them capable of anything. But he had to know.

Gritting his teeth, he crouched. Ignoring the pain in his head and gut, he sprung up as hard and quietly as he could, reaching for the window. He missed, landing softly. A puff of dust exploded silently under his feet.

He readied himself and tried again. This time, his hand brushed against something flat and thin. On the third try he brought it down with him.

It was a dagger of broken glass, sharp enough he had already sliced himself on the edge. Blood welled up on the tips of three fingers, but he didn't care. This was the key, this was his hope. It came from the stars outside to save him.

He took his once-white undershirt and sliced off one of the arms. He wrapped it tightly around the broader end of the shard. Gripping the makeshift handle, he tested the weight of his weapon in his hand. Then he took his time wrapping the rest of it in the remnant of his shirt.

Brennan lay back down on the floor, cradling the precious bundle. He waited for his chance.

5

AN ETERNITY AFTER Brennan found the piece of glass, he heard the footsteps. The sound was unmistakable: click-clop, the sound of expensive shoes on concrete. He did not bother standing and trying to see the trespasser. The odds remained too much in favor that he was imagining the sounds.

The footsteps stopped, and he strained to hear the words exchanged between two men. He could not make out all the words, but the key point resounded: "Get the fuck out of here."

Different footsteps, solid and quick, faded into the distance. Then, click-clop, the expensive shoes approached. Brennan realized he lay shivering on the floor. No, not shivering; he shook violently. He bit down on his dry tongue to stifle a shout.

He heard musical tones as his visitor entered a code into the lock. *No keys rattling here, this is a modern operation,* he thought, biting his shriveled tongue again. He allowed himself a peek at his visitor.

There stood Jim the Tie Guy, Jim the Fake Receptionist, Jim of the Expensive Shoes and Bags Over Your Head. He still wore the same God-awful tie, and he gripped a police baton in his right hand. Moonlight caught the baton, and for an instant it lit up like a florescent bulb.

"Stand up, you son of a bitch," Jim said.

Brennan stayed where he was. For all he knew, Jim was not really there.

"I said stand up!"

Brennan's body jumped. At that, Jim flinched. It was a barely perceptible widening of the eyes, and Jim recovered immediately. Only a man who had stared at concrete, bars, and a sliver of sunlight for three days would have noticed, but Jim flinched. *He waited until I'm half-dead, and he's still scared to death of me*, Brennan thought. *Who the hell does he think I am?* Brennan felt his guts tightening inside him.

Brennan spent his high school years living with his Grandpa. The man had not been his real grandfather, but Brennan did not care as long as Grandpa cared about Brennan. Brennan worked with him out on his land, fixing things that fell apart. The whole situation suited Brennan just fine.

The old man had a tool he called a come-along. It was the only time Brennan ever saw one, but he remembered it clearly: a lever connected to a chain, and each time you pulled the lever, it tightened the chain. They used it once to pull up a fence, Grandpa bullshitting the whole time, and Brennan knew his grandfather could move the whole world with a come-along and enough bullshit to fuel it.

That was exactly what it felt like inside him now—like the slack being taken out. Each crank of the lever pulled him up higher.

Jim paced back and forth along a small line. "Says in your file you tried for law school, but didn't have the grades. Then it says you tried for a police academy, but lacked the balls." Jim took a step forward. "You're an idiot and a coward, and you are very, very sick. You prey on the weak, and you're going to tell me what I need to know."

"What is it you need to know?" Brennan asked. It felt like someone else spoke for him. *The old ventriloquist act*, he thought. *S'alright? S'alright.*

"You know what I'm talking about."

"Okay, all right," said Brennan. "I didn't want to say, but I like it when a girl has her leg in a cast."

Jim kicked him in the ribs.

Brennan gasped as the wind burst from his lungs. After a few deep breaths, he continued. "I don't know why. Something about the way they have to hop around. The way the crutches push their boobies out. I don't know."

Jim kicked him again. "Get up, Wade."

Keep pulling that lever, Brennan thought, allowing Jim to pull him to his feet. *Keep shoveling in that bullshit.* Brennan's hand slipped around the piece of glass in his waistband.

Jim kneeled and whispered in Brennan's ear, "Who do you work with?"

"Ain't got no job, Jim, you know that. You took my application. Times are tough all over. Unless you're telling me I got the job at the airport."

Jim scowled and raised the baton. The fog lifted from Brennan's mind and vision. A red siren went off in his mind. Time slowed.

Brennan grabbed Jim's wrist in a vice. With his other hand, he jammed the piece of glass into Jim's chest, below his collar bone. Their momentum carried them into the wall. The impact snapped off the end of the glass dagger, leaving the tip inside Jim. The back of Jim's head bounced against the concrete wall, and the baton flew from his hand. Brennan drove his knee into Jim's stomach, and Jim doubled over.

Brennan pushed him to the ground and planted a knee into his back. He pressed the sharp edge of the remaining glass shard against Jim's neck. A drop of blood bubbled up.

"Jim, I need you to be quiet. It's very important for you to be quiet," Brennan whispered. He pushed Jim's face into the cold floor. Brennan decided it was time to make use of his mistaken identity. "You know what I'm capable of. If you make as much as a peep, that'll be all she wrote, am I right?"

"Yeah," Jim wheezed.

Brennan dug the glass a little deeper into Jim's neck as he picked up the fallen baton. "I said no peep, Jim. Understand?"

Jim nodded.

"I'm glad we understand each other, Tie Guy. I'm really glad that we do."

"My wife bought me this damn tie, you bastard."

Brennan lifted the baton over his head. "That should tell you something right there." He hit Jim in the back of the head with the baton as hard as he could.

It was hard enough. Dropping the baton and the glass dagger to the floor, Brennan checked Jim's shoulder. The bleeding did not look life threatening. He left Jim unconscious but breathing, minus his dark slacks. Jim's fancy shoes were too small, but the laces came in handy for tying Jim up. Brennan wadded up his piss-stained undershirt and stuffed it in Jim's mouth as a gag, holding it in place with Jim's tie. It turned out not to be a clip-on after all. *Goes to show you,* Brennan thought. *You can never be sure about anything.*

Jim had left the cell door unlocked, and Brennan shut it for him on the way out. The bleak hallway led into a large room, unfurnished and almost completely empty. Brennan picked up a thin jacket left behind by one of Jim's associates, but saw nothing that could identify his kidnappers. He expected to be stopped every step of the way, but no one waited for him. There was no one anywhere; the place was deserted. *Everyone in the world has been raptured except for those two old sinners, Brennan Wade and Jim the Tie Guy,* he thought.

The final door led to a dark, sandy wasteland. He turned to examine his prison, a nondescript bunker in the desert. Jim's watch said it was 2:10 A.M., which gave Brennan hope no one would find Jim or notice his own absence until morning.

A handful of cars sat in front of the building. Empty spaces between them and tracks in the dirt gave a hint to the dozen or so vehicles that were missing. Jim must have sent everyone out for a break while he gave Brennan his little interview. *Overconfident much, Jim?* Brennan thought. *Or maybe some information can't be shared with the hangers-on.*

He considered seeking out the car that matched Jim's keys, but thought better of it when he saw the motorcycle. It was a crotch rocket for sure, but Brennan did not recognize the make or model. *Hell, I haven't ridden a motorcycle since high school,* he thought. *But what have I got to lose?* He approached the bike and saw the keys waiting for him in the ignition.

Brennan clenched his fist around Jim's keys, and he threw them into the dark as hard and as far as he could. He then dug Jim's Old Timer pocket knife out of his pocket and slashed the tires of the few cars left parked around the building. He doubted it would buy him much time, but it felt good. *It feels fucking amazing,* he admitted to himself. He considered leaving the pocketknife in the last tire as one more fuck you to Jim, but it was a nice knife. He slipped it back into his pocket.

He climbed onto the bike and worked through his mental checklist to start it up. The bike roared as it came to life, and Brennan followed the tangled mess of tire tracks back to the highway.

6

THE FIRST MILEAGE SIGN read 110 miles to Las Vegas, so it surprised Brennan to find out he was in New Mexico. He skipped the first gas station he saw, but stopped at the second. If the tired clerk noticed Brennan had been through hell and lost his shoes along the way, he didn't mention it. *'No shirt, no shoes, no service' has been repealed,* Brennan thought. *Chaos reigns in the world.*

Brennan headed straight to the bathroom. Inside he gulped down as much water as he could from the faucet. After he started feeling sick, he wiped his mouth and pulled out Jim's black leather wallet. Inside he found a few hundred dollars in cash and a grainy photograph of a smiling woman lying in a white hammock. There were no credit cards and no identification. He drank more at the faucet and exited.

He went to the register and laid some money on the counter for gas. On his way out the door, he spotted something hanging next to the New Mexico snow globes and dream catchers. It was a backpack with a water bladder inside and a tube to bite down on and suck out the water. He paid for the backpack and a gallon of water to dump into it. After fueling the bike, he continued on his way, sucking water from the tube like it was his umbilical cord.

Brennan drove as fast as he could without losing control of the bike. He ignored the speedometer as best he could, but he spent most of his trip well over a hundred miles per hour. *Don't think about how fast you're going,* he told himself. *Think about it and you're nothing but road pizza.* He arrived in Santa Fe before 4:00 A.M. and found a twenty-four-hour Wal-Mart. There were only a handful of people in the entire store to stare at his dirty bare feet.

Inside, he grabbed a change of clothes (complete with shoes this time), a jacket, sunglasses, a stocking hat, and toiletries, then went through a self-check aisle.

Before sunrise he ditched Jim's clothes at the bottom of a dumpster and rinsed off in another gas station bathroom. A week ago the bathroom would have looked disgusting, but after his cell in the desert, it was the Ritz.

Cars began to appear on the roads, and Brennan felt his time was running out. He rode until he found a rougher part of town. It was after 6:00 A.M. when he found what he was looking for: a used car dealership that looked like a front for something else. A large man in a muscle shirt was unlocking a garage door when Brennan approached him from behind.

"Good morning," Brennan said, making the man jump. "I need to sell a motorcycle."

The man turned around. He looked bigger up close. "Sneaking up on people isn't healthy."

"Sorry. Next time I'll wear a bell. Got a minute to look at my bike?"

Seeing the motorcycle, the man's eyes widened for an instant. "What do you want to get out of it?"

"Quick cash," Brennan said.

The man nodded as his expression grew somber. "I'll give you a thousand dollars right now for it."

"I was hoping for three."

Scowling, the man said, "For that much, I'd want to know where it came from. I'll go fifteen."

"Lowest I can go is two thousand. We both know you'll get more out of it than that."

"Fine. Be right back." The man entered the garage and returned with an envelope. He handed it to Brennan, who checked the contents and handed over the key.

"Now get the fuck out of here," the man said.

A city bus took him to an enormous gas station near the outskirts of town. He purchased a soda and leaned against an out-of-order payphone until the right opportunity came along.

An older car weighed down with skis and snowboards pulled up to the pump at the edge of the lot. Two men and a woman, all college age, climbed out. The woman, wearing big fur boots, and the taller of the two men went into the gas station. The other man, wearing an orange University of Texas sweatshirt, swiped his card and started pumping gas. Brennan took a quick look around and made his move.

The college kid gave Brennan the once-over as he approached.

Brennan nodded toward the skiing equipment. "Plan on doing some skiing?" he asked.

The college kid smiled. "Yeah, but the mountains here are crap this year. We're heading up to Colorado. Find the real stuff."

"Nice," Brennan said. "Tell you what; maybe you can help me out."

The man squeezed the last few drops out of the gas nozzle into the car. "Oh, yeah? How's that?"

"I'm trying to get to Colorado myself. I'd pay you two hundred bucks up front to get me there."

The man's traveling companions returned, eying Brennan suspiciously. "Give me a second," The guy in the sweatshirt said; he walked over to talk with the other two.

There was a short but heated discussion, and then the girl turned to Brennan. "Make it two-fifty?"

Brennan nodded. He pulled the bills out of his pocket and held them up. The guy in the sweatshirt said, "Buddy, two-fifty will get you there with all the cheap-ass beer you can drink."

Brennan smiled. "Water will be fine for me, thanks."

7

SIX-AND-A-HALF HOURS LATER, Brennan waved to Michael, Terry, and Sharon as they drove away. He knew they would tell their friends back at school about helping out Ben Willard, a soldier on his way home to see his poor momma. Depending on whether they wanted to sound kind or crafty, they might leave out the part about the money. He wondered if any of their college friends would notice their passenger shared a name with Martin Sheen's character in *Apocalypse Now*.

They listened to The Sleeping Prophets, some indie band Brennan had never heard of, for the entire drive. He caught himself humming one of their tunes as he considered the list of destinations hanging above the ticket windows. Denver was a big city. Going there and getting lost among its people was an attractive idea, but he was still only a state away from his concrete cell in the desert. He needed to widen the gap before he could sleep with anything approaching comfort.

It was a long time since he had bought a bus ticket, and he was relieved no identification was necessary if he paid with cash.

He chose a bus to Kansas City, Missouri, a destination with the right balance of leaving-right-now and far-enough-away. It was also on his list of places he needed to go based on the airplane conversation.

He bought a turkey and Swiss cheese sandwich from the snack shop inside the bus station. The sandwich was vacuum sealed in a plastic wrapper and had an expiration date in the alarmingly distant future. Brennan had wondered what kind of a person bought gas station sandwiches. *Apparently it is the kind of man who is wrongfully accused of murder and on the run from a death squad*, he thought.

Much to Brennan's surprise, the sandwich had a satisfying flavor, and he washed it down with a gulp of water from his backpack. *How did I go without one of these water things for so long?* he asked himself. *This is the single greatest invention in the history of mankind.*

The bus ran late. The longer it took, the harder it became for Brennan to take his eyes off the doors. He moved to a seat in a corner that gave him the best view of all entrances and exits. Huge windows faced the busy street and he scanned the crowd as it flowed past. Every person who walked by could be looking for him. Every person who actually opened the glass doors and entered the building made Brennan's heart play a drum solo. *Oh my God, it's already a game of* Get Out Alive, he thought. *I've waited too long. They're already on to me. I should run now. Steal a car or another bike and take off.*

Across the bus station's waiting room was a bearded man in sunglasses reading a paperback novel. Brennan shot several quick glances and decided there was a good chance the man was only pretending to read. Brennan thought he caught the man's eyes behind the sunglasses, staring him down.

One of the station doors opened, and Brennan looked to see a smiling young couple enter with a little boy. When he looked back at the bearded man, the seat was empty.

He jumped out of his skin when they announced over the loud speaker his bus was ready for passengers. Feeling sick, he stood up and walked over to the bearded man's empty chair. He found an empty pack of menthol cigarettes and the man's paperback—a collection of stories by Joseph Conrad with a shiny label reading, '*Featuring* Heart of Darkness *and* The Secret Sharer.'

Heart of Darkness was the basis for the film *Apocalypse Now*, the movie from which he lifted the name he gave to the college students. It had to be a coincidence—a thin one at best—but dizziness and nausea hit him as he stared at the book. He left it on the chair and made his way to the bus.

8

AS SOON AS BRENNAN ARRIVED in Kansas City, he bought a laptop and a bag to carry it in. He found a coffee shop with free wireless internet and sat down in a booth next to an electrical outlet. Taking a deep breath, he went to work.

Butterflies went to war in his stomach as he connected to the shop's wireless network. He did not check his email, and avoided anything else that might lead back to him. With only a vague idea how anyone was traced on the internet, he decided to err on the side of bat-shit paranoid. His searches contained three sets of words: Flatland, Texas, summer, 1992; Kansas City, Missouri, spring, 1999; California, December, 2002. That was all Jim had given him to go on. Brennan hoped Jim had not intentionally leaked the information.

In the summer of 1992, Brennan was fifteen. Flatland, Texas, had a population of about 200,000 people, by far the smallest of the three locations mentioned. So he started by checking *The Flatland Courier*'s website. Nothing popped up. He also struck out with Kansas City, and he had no idea what happened in California during December, 2002.

Too bad Jim didn't actually charge me with anything or ask for a confession, he thought. If he knew what crime he was suspected of committing, he might have a chance of proving he was innocent.

Sucking down another free refill, he considered the facts, or at least what currently passed for facts. In his mind, there were two possible reasons for this cluster fuck. One was that they believed him responsible for stealing an unbelievable amount of money. But then why had Jim been afraid of him, and why had he kept commenting on what a freak Brennan was? White collar crime at that level was a respectable act, with nothing perverse about it. Another option was that they thought Brennan was a murderer.

So he hit the *Courier* again and read every headline from April 1 to September 30, 1992. He looked for any mention of murder. There was a clerk shot in a liquor store robbery, but the suspects were named in the article and apprehended a few days later. There was a transient man convicted for killing two little girls. Brennan bookmarked that one, but it didn't feel like a fit. Why would they want him if someone was already convicted? Nothing else jumped out at him.

What if the paper didn't know it was a murder? He went through the headlines again, this time looking for accidental deaths. His high school caught fire, but no one was there when it happened. He remembered the fire; he and the other students went to class at local churches while the school was rebuilt. There were car accidents, but none of them were unusual. A roof collapsed while an office building was being renovated, killing one worker and injuring two others. It was a hot summer, and several people died from heat stroke. How was he supposed to clear things up if he didn't even know what he was suspected of? What was missing?

Missing, he thought. Brennan went through the headlines for what he hoped was the last time. He looked at anything related to a missing persons case.

He hit pay dirt with a story filed on Tuesday, July 14, 1992.

LOCAL TEEN MISSING
by Timothy Mouton
Elsie Paroubek of Flatland has been missing since Friday, July 10.

The fifteen-year-old was last seen walking home from the house of her friend, Vivian Glandel. The distance between the two houses is less than a half-mile.

Paroubek is 5'3", with a slim build and shoulder-length blonde hair. When she left the Glandel home, she was wearing a white tank top and cutoff jean shorts. She completed her freshmen year at Flatland High School this spring. She played volleyball on the junior varsity team and sang in her church choir.

The Flatland Police Department is pursuing leads. They ask that anyone with useful information contact them immediately.

The last person to speak to Paroubek before her disappearance, Vivian Glandel, is active in the search. "Come home, Elsie," Glandel says. "We miss you."

A photo was originally included with the story, but the link was broken. The photo was probably Elsie's school photo from the previous fall, dressed up but trying not to look too dressed up. Elsie had a beautiful smile. Brennan wished the picture was there so he could remember her face, but all he could remember was her smile.

Son of a bitch, he thought. *How could I forget Elsie?*

9

ELSIE PAROUBEK sat in front of Brennan during Chemistry throughout his freshmen year of high school. They were the only two students whose seats did not change over the course of the fall and spring semester. Brennan thought the teacher was doing his best to give Brennan a shot with Elsie.

It was Brennan's first year in Flatland. Elsie, of course, had been going to school with the other kids since kindergarten. She was beautiful and popular; Brennan was shy and awkward. Brennan could have hated her for all of that, but she was just too nice.

Brennan hated the subject of Chemistry, but he looked forward to the class. She always smiled so sweetly at him, and he always chatted with her as much as he could, trying to make her laugh and touch his arm. During the lecture, he would rest his foot between the bottom of her chair and the metal book holder beneath it, always aware of how close he was to her. It was a creepy thing to do, and he knew it. Every day Elsie did a cat stretch, bending so far back that the top of her head would come to rest on the top of his desk. She stayed like that for an eternity, her face upside down and grinning, her green eyes shining, her small breasts pointed at the sky.

Elsie always had a boyfriend, one after the other. By the time Brennan realized she was single, some new jock or cowboy would be slapping her on the butt in the lunchroom. What did they have that he did not? And why the hell did they break up with her? As he watched her crying to her friends, signaling another breakup, he could not imagine a reason good enough.

Brennan would sit at his grandfather's house, holding their only phone in his lap. He would dial the first six numbers of Elsie's home phone, and then struggle with himself until the alert tone started, emphasizing his failure in staccato bursts.

During a shift at the supermarket that summer, Brennan heard she was missing. Along with the fire at the high school, it was all the town gossiped about for a month. But everyone moved on eventually. Elsie's obituary ran in the *Courier* on July 17, one week after her disappearance. But there was no reference to her being found or an explanation for what happened to her. It only said, "Elsie Paroubek died unexpectedly," followed by a list of her surviving relatives. The service was reserved for close friends and family members, and they asked money to be donated to a local charity in lieu of flowers.

Brennan felt a pang of guilt—he had mostly forgotten about his crush by Christmas. He never thought of her again.

This has to be it, thought Brennan. *I can feel it.* What was the story on Elsie's missing week? He tracked down the relevant phone numbers and hoped some of them were still up to date.

He bought a pay-as-you-go cell phone and found a quiet corner of a city park. The first number on his short list was for the *Courier* itself.

A woman answered the phone on the first ring.

"*Flatland Courier.* What can I do for you?"

"Uh, can I speak to Timothy Mouton?" Brennan asked.

"Who?"

"Timothy Mouton, he writes for you guys? Or, I mean, he

wrote for you. I don't know. But I need to talk to him."

"Just a minute, please," said the woman. As he waited on hold, a Flatland radio station played for him. It was a commercial for a local feed store.

After a few minutes, the line clicked back on, this time with the gruff voice of an older man. "Hello? This the guy lookin' for Mouton?" Brennan could picture the man chomping on a cigar, the Perry White of the newsroom.

"Yeah. I needed to ask him about an article he wrote."

The man on the other side of the line sighed. "Look buddy, Mouton hasn't worked here in almost twenty years. He was my buddy when I was first starting out, but I haven't heard from him since he left. Mind telling me why you're lookin' for him?"

"I wanted to ask him about a story he wrote when he was still at your paper, about a missing girl? Elsie Paroubek?"

"Oh, yeah, the Paroubek girl. Damn shame. That was what, summer of '92? That's actually the summer when Mouton quit. Picked up and left town."

"He just left?"

"Yeah, damn shame. He was the closest we ever came to a real crime reporter on this rag."

Shit, Brennan thought. "Okay, how about the obituary for Elsie Paroubek from around the same time? Can I talk to whoever wrote it?"

The man laughed, "Buddy, if it was '92, that would'a been me. I was new and new guys get the shit work."

"Can you tell me anything about Paroubek's death?"

Another laugh. "You know how many obits I wrote a week back then? Plenty. I can't tell you a damn thing about a damn one of 'em."

"C'mon, help me out here. Is there anything you can remember?"

"Tell you what, if it was like most every other obit, I got a piece of paper from the family telling me what they wanted to say. I fixed it up, made it printable, and sent it off." The man on the other end of the phone paused as someone in his office spoke to him. "Look, buddy," he said to Brennan, "not that I don't appreciate bullshitting about the good old days, but I got a paper to run here."

"Yeah. Yeah, thanks. I appreciate the help."

"No problem, pal." Click.

Brennan was left with the last name on the list, Elsie's mother. As he dialed the number he had found in an online white pages, he wondered if it was the same number he had dialed countless times way back when. This time he did not hesitate on the last number. *It's not like Elsie's going to answer*, he thought.

It rang numerous times. As Brennan was about to hang up, a tired voice answered. "Hello?"

"Hello, can I speak to Mrs. Paroubek?"

"What do you want?" said the tired voice, and Brennan could almost see her, sitting alone in a dark room.

"I had some questions about your daughter, Elsie."

There was a loud click. Brennan called again, hoping it was a misunderstanding, but the phone only rang.

Brennan threw the phone into a metal trash can. "Shit-shit-shit-shit-shit," he muttered. *I really screwed that up*, he thought. *Apparently not everyone can move on.*

He had reached the end of his list. It was not until he was going through the stories again the next day he realized who he had missed. He almost choked on his soda. He found one more phone number to match one more name, and he bought another disposable cell phone.

Vivian Glandel was a real bitch in high school. She looked as hot as it got, and she knew it. Looks might not count for quite as much in the adult world, but in a high school she wielded an atomic bomb. Brennan could distinctly remember talking to her several times, always in a group of other students. Every time, she asked him, "*Who* are *you*?" She wasn't asking for his name, either; she was asking what right he had to exist and to waste her time. But it had been a long time, and even being a snob in high school had a statute of limitations.

A little girl answered the phone. "Hello?"

"Can I speak to Vivian, please?

"Sure." He heard her say quietly, "Mommy, it's for you."

"Thanks, sweetie," a women said. To Brennan: "This is Vivian."

"Yeah, Vivian, this might sound weird, but I was hoping I could ask you about Elsie Paroubek."

"And *who* is *this?*" she asked in the accusatory tone he remembered.

"Brennan Wade." *Shit*, Brennan thought. "We went to high school together.

"I don't remember you."

"I wouldn't expect you to. Listen, I was putting some stuff together." *Putting stuff together?* he asked himself frantically. *Why the hell would I be putting stuff together?* "I'm putting stuff together for the reunion."

"The next reunion isn't for years."

Brennan slapped himself hard on the forehead. "Yeah, but there's plenty to do. Just trying to stay on top."

"Fine," she sighed. "What do you need to know?"

"I was wondering if there is anything you can tell me about Elsie's death? I'm in charge of putting something together to honor the Flatlanders who are no longer with us." *Shut up, Brennan*, he thought. *You're laying it on too thick!*

Vivian said, "Oh, that's sweet."

I take it back. Way to go, Brennan! A joyous chorus sang in his mind.

"Okay. Somebody grabbed her after she left my house, and then they found her body about a week later."

"You're sure she was picked up? She didn't run off on her own?"

"I knew Elsie. She wasn't stupid. Someone grabbed her. And it doesn't matter—if she wasn't picked up then, someone got her later. Because…" She trailed off.

"Because what?"

Vivian whispered, "Okay, but you're not going to want to tell anybody this at the reunion. I know she didn't kill herself or anything. At the funeral, you know, the coffin was there. I sneaked a little peek inside."

"What? You're kidding."

"No, no, I'm serious. And they didn't even try to make her look nice, except for putting her in a nice dress. She was all sewn up. From the autopsy, I guess."

Brennan coughed at the thought. "That's terrible," he said. "But it doesn't explain—"

"And her head was gone," Vivian said.

Brennan grabbed onto the payphone as the dizziness hit him. "No."

"Yes, gone. There was plastic wrap and tape all over the neck hole. It was the grossest thing I've ever seen." But it didn't sound like it bothered her much at all.

Brennan didn't want to hear anymore. He said, "All right, thanks."

"You're welcome," said Vivian. "Anything to help with the reunion."

"Yeah, well—"

Vivian interrupted. "Now *who* did you say *this* was?"

Brennan hung up the phone.

10

"HEADLESS" was the detail that caused everything to fall into place. Brennan plugged it into his searches and found the articles he needed.

An unnamed individual found the corpse of a white male outside of Kansas City on April 4, 1999. The coroner reported it had been there since mid-March. The body was mutilated and the head was missing. It was never identified. Brennan had stopped in Kansas City during spring break that year.

Brennan bummed around California in the latter part of 2002. During that time three bodies turned up, all three missing at least their heads. Each one was found in an area where he had spent more than a week. Only one of the three was ever identified: Grace Budd, an elderly woman. Brennan did not recognize her. The story received some media attention, but it dissipated when no further leads or bodies turned up.

So here were five people Brennan had supposedly murdered. He knew Elsie. As far as he knew, the others were only connected to him by location. *And at least one by DNA evidence,* he reminded himself.

Over the next several days, he poured over everything connected to the five murders. He had already exhausted his leads with Elsie, and there was next to nothing about the Kansas

City corpse. Material about the California murders was more accessible, but none of it told him anything new.

Then he stumbled onto an online forum where users discussed unsolved crimes. In the archives he found a locked thread concerning the California murders attributing them to a serial killer they called the "King of Hearts." After a half-hour, Brennan realized this was a reference to the Queen in *Alice's Adventures in Wonderland.*

"Off with their heads," Brennan mumbled to himself. He sat in a doughnut shop with free internet and free refills on coffee.

A forum user by the name of C.A. Dupin posted a fair amount of information on the case. Dupin listed every known fact about the three victims.

Victim A was a Hispanic male in his late twenties or early thirties. The body was found stuffed into a storm drain in Sacramento. Dupin theorized this murder was done hurriedly or was interrupted, as the head was removed but the rest of the body was intact. The other bodies were missing at least their fingerprints. A jogger found the body on December 7.

Victim B, Grace Budd, was found in Los Padres National Forest, over one hundred miles from her home. She had a hip replaced in 1997, and the serial number on the hip positively identified her. She had last been seen on November 15. Her husband had died the previous year, and she lived alone. It was several days before a neighbor reported Budd missing. Authorities estimated she was killed on December 15. Her body was found by off-season hikers in the backwoods who spotted her grave after Rainfall uncovered her left leg.

Victim C, a female in her early twenties, was found in a cheap motel near Venice Beach. A man with a black hooded sweatshirt and sunglasses paid for the room in cash. Police worked on the theory that the woman was a prostitute. None of the women working in the area could provide her with a name, and the body's identity was never found.

Brennan shuddered. He pictured a man in a black hood opening the trunk of his car and three heads staring back at him: a grandmother, a man with a mustache, and a woman with bleached blond hair. *Who could do that to three human beings?* Brennan thought.

At least three. There could be dozens more. The killer intended for only one of those bodies to be found. He hid Emma deep in the forest. If those hikers hadn't found her, there was a strong possibility that no one would have ever found the body. He stuffed the Hispanic man into the drain in desperation, not by design.

Again, Brennan pictured the hooded man opening his trunk. This time the trunk was overflowing with heads—mouths gaping and eyes bulging. The man slammed the trunk closed and climbed in the car. More heads rolled in the floorboards as he sped away.

On the last page of the forum thread about the King of Hearts, Dupin wrote that he suspected the King of Hearts was still active outside California. He claimed he could back up his assertion. The post was written over five years ago, but Dupin had posted nothing on the forum since.

11

THE NEXT DAY, Brennan walked to the Kansas City Public Library. The size of it surprised him. Its parking garage across the street looked like an enormous book shelf with the spines of classic books, three stories high, displaying their titles. *A Tale of Two Cities* was painted so well that he reached out to touch it, half-expecting to feel leather. The library itself sported classic architecture—all white columns and glass. As he entered, the air conditioning hit him in a rush. Directly on its heels followed the vanilla smell of paper he remembered from his college days, back when he tried to study hard enough to get ahead but never succeeded.

Brennan had stayed the night in the only motel he could find that did not require a credit card. He also purchased and now wore the most non-descript piece of clothing he could think of: a gray hooded sweatshirt.

Trying to look as though he belonged in a library, he made his way to the front desk.

"Can I help you, sir?" asked a short, happy woman with glasses.

"Yeah, uh, I'm looking for old newspapers?"

"Microfilm. It's in the Media Center, down in the basement." The woman gestured over her shoulder. "Head down those stairs and follow the signs."

"Will I need a library card?" He had avoided the library up to this point for this precise reason.

"No, you just sign them out."

He thanked her and went down the stairs. He passed several old vault doors, which made him wonder if the building had once been a bank. At the media center, they handed over the cases for the *Kansas City Star* from 1999 and on. Brennan signed the check-out sheet as "C.A. Dupin." He spent a few minutes getting acquainted with the machine and went to work.

Brennan began his search one month before the Kansas City murder. He had no idea what he was looking for, but hoped he would know it when he saw it. The articles he had read online were worth examining again, as the online versions often lacked images. He quickly reread the initial article reporting the murder, and several following up on the investigation. His eyes widened as he hit an article written five weeks after the murder.

In a desperate attempt to find any information about the victim, the Kansas City Police released a photo of a tattoo on the man's forearm. The image was grainy, but Brennan could still make it out. The tattoo was a faded hand of playing cards: ace of spades, ace of clubs, eight of spades, eight of clubs, and the queen of clubs.

Brennan had seen the tattoo before.

He had just been dumped by his college girlfriend, Courtney. She wanted someone with more ambition, and—Brennan had to admit it—the sex had never been all that great. Passing through Kansas City alone during spring break in 1999, he camped out in a bar in an attempt to find female companionship. After striking out several times, he decided to get ripped instead. It ended up being a fun night.

He struck up a conversation with a biker down the bar. After a few rounds, they were old friends, although Brennan could not remember his name. Brennan complained about Courtney, and the biker guy agreed she was a bitch. The biker's wife had passed the year before—cancer—and he missed her terribly. Brennan asked about the man's tattoo.

"That there's the dead man's hand, my friend. Wild Bill Hickok, or Doc Holiday, or somebody, drew those cards right before he got shot."

Brennan said, "Man, that's fucking morbid."

The biker shrugged. "Maybe. But I look down at that, and I know my number's going to come up eventually. Maybe not today, maybe not tomorrow, but it's comin'. Then I'll be with my lady again."

In the library, Brennan leaned back and rubbed his tired eyes. *Maybe it was me*, he thought for the first time. *I was there. Maybe I killed him and I don't remember.*

He looked down at his hands. He had once put a man in the hospital. He did not even know the guy, but the man had slapped a woman, right there in public, and Brennan attacked him. Maybe it was self-defense, maybe an attempt at heroism, but he had seen red and gone over the top. *Could I go even further*, he thought, *completely over the deep end? Could these hands have cut off all those heads?* The feel of his knee jamming into Jim's gut popped into his mind.

Brennan would have left the library then and there, but he knew that once he left, he was never coming back. The man at the counter would forget him quickly enough, but not if he kept coming in and became a familiar face. If he was going to find another lead in the library, it had to be today or never.

Nothing else surfaced concerning the biker's murder. Brennan felt guilt well up in the pit of his stomach. Why couldn't he remember the guy's name? He wished he could do that much.

He skipped to December 2002. There was nothing there until the third California murder, the woman in the motel, and that was a small blurb from the Associated Press about a possible serial killer.

In a paper printed two weeks after the third California body was found, Brennan's eyes caught something, and he scrolled back to a letter to the editor. He would have missed it but for the reprinted photo of the Biker's tattoos accompanying it. The letter read:

> *I've been researching the recent California decapitation murders. I think the killer visited our fine city back in the spring of 1999. Remember the unidentified, headless victim with the card tattoo? Photos of the body are floating around the internet if you know where to look, as are photos from two of the recent murders in CA. I compared the cut marks on the necks of the victims, and I am convinced they were made by the same tool. When I tried to contact the police in CA they blew me off.*
>
> *I cannot believe they missed this important detail! To paraphrase Edgar Allen Poe's great detective, C. Auguste Dupin, 'It is just possible this mystery troubles them so much on account of its being so very self-evident.'*

The letter was signed "J. Cairns."

Brennan killed the machine and gathered the film canisters, dropping several in the process. It was all he could do to not sprint out of the library as he checked in the material.

"You guys got a phone book I could use?" he asked.

12

IT WAS RAINING HARD when Brennan walked up to the house. The front door was an attractive one, as was the modest house to which it was attached. Brennan knocked, hammering out three short bursts in rapid succession.

The sound of soft footsteps drifted through the door. Locks clicked and clacked on the other side of the wood. The door opened a crack, a chain dangling in the gap. A dark brown eye stared out at him.

"What is it?" a woman asked.

"Can I speak to a Mr. or Mrs. J. Cairns?"

"What about?" she asked.

"I need to talk about the King of Hearts murders."

The door closed quickly. Brennan's heart sank until he heard the chain thrown aside. As the door swung open, the woman was already turning a corner down the hall. Brennan remained in the doorway.

She called back over her shoulder, "Guess you found me. Don't stand there in the rain like an idiot. Come on in. Hang up your coat."

He wiped his feet on the old mat and entered, closing the door behind him. The entryway was sparsely decorated, and he hung his thin jacket on a thin wooden coat stand. A small ring around the bottom of the stand held an ornate umbrella with a crook handle, hand-carved from bone. He leaned his backpack against the wall and peered around the corner into a tiny kitchen. The sink shined and the counters were clean and bare. His host was bent over, hidden behind the open refrigerator door. Glass and plastic containers rattled against each other. Several pieces of paper were held to the fridge with magnets—the centerpiece was a child's drawing of the very house he was in, clearly labeled '*GRANMA'S HOUSE*' in crayon.

"Have a seat in the den. It's down the hall on the left. I'll be right out," she said as she fought with the contents of the refrigerator.

Brennan continued down the hall, passing several family photographs, and entered the large room that was obviously the den. Unlike the meticulously kept hallway and kitchen, the den looked like a library after the bombs dropped. Books of every size and color lined every inch of the walls, and many more were piled on the various tables and couches. A desktop computer hummed in the corner. He inhaled the faint smell of lavender.

He cleared a spot on a red leather couch and sat down. The leather squeaked under his weight. J. Cairns entered the room with two bottles and a plate of cookies. She was an older black woman with a clear complexion and intelligent eyes. Brennan guessed Cairns to be in her fifties. Her curly hair had been invaded by strands of white, and she was dressed comfortably in a red sweater and jeans. He imagined she had been quite attractive when she was young, and much of her beauty remained.

She balanced the cookies on a pile of books on the coffee table and handed him one of the open glass bottles. "I hope root beer is okay. I wasn't expecting company."

"Root beer is great. Thank you, Ms. Cairn."

"Please, call me Jennifer," she said, moving a stack of papers off a curvy wooden chair.

He extended his hand, and she shook it. "My name is Brennan Wade."

"Nice to meet you, Brennan Wade. Now, what brought you here to talk about the King of Hearts?"

Brennan explained how, while researching the murders, he found what she wrote. When he finished, she asked, "But how did you know I was the same person who had posted online?"

"The Dupin quote in the paper."

"Oh, that would do it, wouldn't it? I really left you a trail. It's so hard to resist quoting Poe. He was the first of us, wasn't he?"

"The first of us?" Brennan asked.

She grinned. "Yes, all of us mystery writers. Poe's Dupin stories started the ball rolling."

"You write mysteries?"

"Yes, but you wouldn't have heard of me. I write novels based on real crimes, and I'm published under a pseudonym. No one's tracked me down from that angle, not yet at least." She leaned over and knocked on the wooden coffee table.

She held up a paperback book. On the cover was the title, *Lock Your Doors: The Richard Chase Murders*. She flipped it over and handed it to him. On the back cover, an older black man in a police uniform stared up at him from the black and white photograph.

"No one wanted to read true crime by a secretary, even if she did work for the Kansas City Police Department for twenty-seven years. But a retired black police officer? It was just enough niche and just enough mainstream."

Brennan grinned. "I bet your picture would sell just as many books."

She rolled her eyes, and took back the book. "Flatterer. Tell you what. I don't do this for just anybody, but it shows some fortitude that you found me. See that box up there? Go get it for me."

Doing his best not to cause an avalanche, Brennan pulled the old copy-paper box off the top shelf. Meanwhile, Jennifer cleared off the coffee table, moving the cookies to an end table.

"Set it here," she said. She opened the box, which was full of manila folders. "Ta da!" Jennifer motioned to the box like a magician's assistant. "I've been working on a book about the

King of Hearts. It's been my pet project for years. I keep thinking I almost have something, but I don't have the right perspective yet."

He whistled. "That's a lot of stuff for five—for four murders."

She started taking files out of the box. Each one was stuffed with photocopies, handwritten notes on yellow legal paper, and photographs.

"Not necessarily. I saw a friend's files once on the Jack the Ripper murders—they filled a storage unit. But every one of these files represents a different King of Hearts victim."

Brennan stared at the table. "You have to be kidding. There've got to be fifty files here."

"Close. There are forty-two. In the basement I have a file cabinet full of the overflow. These are just the ones I'm currently working on. The one's I'm positive about."

The blood ran out of Brennan's face. "How many are there?"

"I have a list of over four hundred murders that could be connected to the King of Hearts."

Brennan's chest grew tight. "But—but that's impossible."

"I know it sounds impossible. These murders take place all over the world, and some of them go back as early as the '40s. I have one I'm still on the fence about from 1938."

Brennan breathed a sigh of relief, which he hoped Jennifer would misinterpret as him being overwhelmed. He did the mental math. He had a pretty strong alibi for the first forty years of this evil. He might be in the clear after all. "That's a long time to be killing. The guy must be in his seventies, at least."

"That's what I thought at first, too. But the murders went through the roof in the early '90s. Every murder in the file is connected by decapitation and a strong, usually successful attempt to hide the victim's identity. I think the original killer was joined by someone else at this point. Or replaced by him, I don't know. Either way, it helped him increase his output."

Brennan's ray of hope quickly dissipated. "That's crazy," he said.

Jennifer glared at him. "I know how it sounds. But I've put

enough work into this to see the big picture. I've made contacts all over the world, gotten into cold cases on the slim chance I would find something."

Brennan shook his head. "I'm sorry. It's a lot to take in. I thought I was looking at a few murders, not a billion of them."

"It's okay. This project is my baby. You can see why I might get a little defensive."

Brennan laughed. "I understand completely. I just don't understand who could do something so horrible."

Jennifer pursed her lips. "Evil is a funny thing. Not ha-ha funny, understand."

"It makes the universe seem like a pretty dark place."

"Could be," Jennifer said. "But I have a theory. Want to hear it?"

"I would love to."

Jennifer leaned forward and spoke in a hushed tone, as if sharing a secret. She said, "I think God lets bad people do bad things so he can bring in his own people to stop them. To help the rest of us."

Brennan looked at his feet as he considered this. "God sure seems to take his time," he said.

Jennifer shrugged. "I think sometimes it takes a while for the right person to show up."

"Somebody reminded me recently that I used to want to help people," Brennan said. "I wanted to be a lawyer, but I didn't have the grades. Then I decided to be a cop, but in the interview they told me I didn't have the headhunting attitude they wanted."

"Honey, I'm going to tell you something for free," Jennifer said. "Something I wish someone had told me a long time ago. It doesn't matter who you are or what you are. It doesn't matter what you've done or what you might do tomorrow. The only thing that matters is what you do right now."

He smiled. "That's a nice thought, Jennifer."

"I'd like to think so."

Brennan picked up a file. "Let's get back on track," he said, and the two of them laughed. "One thing is bothering me." He flipped through the file. "I mean, one thing is bothering me the most right now. How can there be this many unsolved murders—all sharing the same details—and no one knows anything about it?"

Jennifer sighed. "You know, I've asked myself the same question a hundred times. I know it sounds crazy, but it seems like someone would have to be covering it up. Someone with lots of pull." She frowned for a moment and then laughed. "Like I said, I know it sounds crazy."

"It doesn't sound crazy at all," Brennan said. He held up a file folder and nodded toward it. "I'm wondering why you'd share any of this with me."

Smiling, Jennifer said, "Because I know that look in your eye. I could see it when you were standing on my porch. The look that says you have to know, no matter what. I can't say no to that. Just promise me you won't go putting a book out about it before I do."

Brennan laughed. "I can promise you that. I'm just trying to make some sense out of all of this. You were the last lead I had, and I don't even know where to start with this pile of dead people."

"I might be able to help you with that," Jennifer said. She picked up a file and opened it. She skimmed the pages, but stopped short and closed it.

Jennifer bumped her root beer bottle with an elbow, knocking it off the edge of the table. Brennan picked up the bottle, but spilled root beer already fizzed on the rug.

"Shit," she said. She pronounced it "she-yet." She got up and started toward the kitchen. "Give me a second. I'll get something to clean this up."

Brennan wanted to lean back and relax, but instead he looked through the bodies. Each file was labeled in black marker with the victim's name—if available—and the location. Many of the files contained autopsy photos, which he skipped over.

Minutes passed, and Jennifer was still in the kitchen. Brennan picked up the last folder she had examined.

The tab on the folder was labeled '*Chicago 2003*' in black

marker. Brennan had been in Chicago in 2003. Beneath the date, in red pen, was the name '*Joan Runciter.*' There was a large asterisk next to the name.

The first piece of paper was a police report. It detailed the double murder of two female roommates. Both women were decapitated. A third woman lived in the same apartment, but had somehow escaped and called the police. A yellow sticky note was on the front page with the red words '*ONLY KNOWN PERSON TO SURVIVE AN ATTACK FROM THE KOH.*' Another sticky note below it read, '*Never returns calls.*'

"Good to know at least someone makes it out alive," Brennan muttered. On the last page of the report, Jennifer had written a Chicago address and phone number. Brennan memorized the information and turned to the last piece of paper in the folder.

It was a photocopy of a police facial composite of the murderer. He stared at it for several seconds before realizing who stared blankly back at him. It was his nose, his cheeks, his eyes. The words '*brown/black*' were written next to the portrait's hair, '*brown?*' across from the eyes. There was no doubt in his mind—this sketch was of him.

It was time to leave.

He stood up and walked into the hallway. The beautiful umbrella from the coat rack lay in the middle of the floor. The coat rack itself leaned against the wall, balanced on two of its legs. When he reached the kitchen, he saw Jennifer standing there, holding a sawed-off shotgun with both hands.

"Stay back!" she cried. Her eyes were wild.

He held his hands out in front of him. "I know how this looks, but—"

She waved the shotgun at him as he approached. He stopped moving.

Brennan said, "I didn't kill those people!"

Jennifer hesitated, and a look of pity entered her eyes. "Are you sure about that? Are you positive?"

Before he could answer, the front door exploded inward. A uniformed policeman rushed in, yelling at Brennan to hit the floor. *There has to be another way out*, Brennan thought. As he turned to run through the house, he ran right into two more officers who grabbed him and pinned him to the ground.

Brennan looked up at Jennifer, but anger and relief was all he saw in her eyes.

As someone read him his rights, he thought, *At least it isn't that asshole Jim.*

13

DETECTIVE JACK HART chewed his toothpick and sipped his third cup of station coffee. As he poured in a large helping of milk, he told himself that one of these days he needed to start drinking it black. He could save himself quite a few calories that way.

Jack had made detective early in his career due to several high-profile, undercover busts. In his twenties it had been tough going. For a long time everyone on the force treated him like a kid, but he felt he had finally reached the point in his career where he was respected by his peers and depended on by his superiors. He still loved waking up and putting on his affordable suit instead of a uniform, and he could not imagine a more rewarding job than closing cases and catching the bad guys. Hell, he would not admit to it in open court, but he even loved the paperwork. There was nothing like dotting all the Is and crossing all the Qs.

But today was what Jack's dad would have called FUBARed. Like any homicide detective, Jack had plenty of unsolved cases. It was tragic, but he understood—maybe better than most—how the world worked. Still, late at night, as he lay next to his wife, Rachel, there were certain cases he could not forget.

When he was still green, he and his partner Bryan Felix had

gotten the call on a notable homicide. A group of teenagers spotted the body outside of town while doing doughnuts in their truck. They were hesitant to report their discovery for nearly a day. They were trespassing at the time, but the condition of the body caused their main problem. The missing head and decomposition made the poor kids believe they ran over him themselves.

On the scene, Felix was as cool as ever. Hart felt proud for not losing his lunch when they examined the body, and he was the first to spot the only identifier that ever turned up: the playing card tattoo. They consulted an expert out of Nevada who reconstructed the image released to the newspapers. Privately, Hart called it The Case of the Dead Man's Hand. It was the most frustrating murder to ever come across his plate. They never identified the victim, and the murderer left no trace. If it weren't for the autopsy reports and crime scene photos, Hart could almost believe the whole thing had never happened. He wished he could have forgotten the file when they moved it down to the basement. Hell, even Felix had moved on. The lucky bastard had retired and left to go fishing every day in his boxer shorts.

It was crazy how fast the years flew by. Felix's spot was filled by Detective Kelly Jacobs. If Felix was cool, Jacobs was ice cold. Detective Jacobs was disarmingly attractive with an intimidating figure and striking features. Her looks did not go unnoticed at the station, which despite many changes, was still primarily a boy's club. Fortunately, everyone agreed Jacobs gave as good as she got. In their partnership dynamic, Hart came to think of her as the heavy.

Hart knew his wife, Rachel, suspected him of having an affair with his partner. The idea was appalling to Jack, who considered such an act akin to incest. He loved his wife and kids, and he would die before he did anything to jeopardize those relationships. Besides, he had heard about Jacob's social life, and it sounded like she preferred men of a more mature age and refinement.

Rachel barely stirred that morning when the phone rang,

waking Hart. After receiving a terrified phone call from his retired secretary, the former police chief had called in a favor to have several patrol cars pick up a suspect, supposedly for breaking and entering. The operation went smoothly, barring the appearance of an illegally modified shotgun that never made it to the evidence locker.

Jennifer Cairns, the retired secretary, handed copies of her files over to Hart that connected the suspect to a murder in Chicago. "He's your man for the victim with the aces and eights, too," she said.

Hart frowned. After a decade out of sight, the Dead Man's Hand Case was in the spotlight again.

"How do you know about that?" he asked.

"Sweetie, don't you worry about that; worry about this." She tapped one of the files. "If you need me, have your boss call me. Otherwise, I'll be on a long-overdue vacation." Before Hart could protest, she picked up her suitcase and was out the door. The chief said to not worry about Cairns, so he concentrated on the suspect.

Nothing was back yet on Wade's prints, and Jacobs was currently getting the rest of the information they would plug into the system. That was all child's play. But the thought of closing that damn case—

Somehow it felt wrong to Hart. If he saw this Wade kid on the street, Hart would not think twice about him. Nothing about the guy set off Hart's killer detector, and he trusted his instinct. After seeing the poor guy being processed, Hart had nearly laughed in Cairns' face.

Still, the police sketch from Chicago was an uncanny resemblance, and Wade's failure to explain who he was or what he was doing in Jennifer Cairns' house looked bad for him. Then there was the matter of what Wade was carrying around with him. Hart's brow furrowed at the thought, and he rolled his toothpick from one side of his mouth to the other. He grabbed the evidence bag as he opened the door to Interview Room B. He exhaled a deep breath as he prepared for his tough-guy, good-cop act.

14

AS THE INTERVIEW ROOM DOOR clicked shut behind Hart, Detective Jacobs raised her neatly trimmed eyebrow. "Please repeat that last part for my partner, Mr. Wade."

Brennan sat with his hand cuffed behind him and to the back of the chair. A fluorescent bulb flickered. He said, "You have to help me. I'm being framed for murder. Murders, I mean."

Hart leaned in close to Brennan. He chewed on the splintered end of a waterlogged toothpick. "Really. And how many murders are you being framed for?"

Brennan sighed. "Hundreds," he said.

The two detectives exchanged a look and laughed.

"I'm serious!" Brennan said.

Jacobs asked, "Are you also serious about being captured and held by this other group?" She glanced at her notebook. "In New Mexico?"

"Yeah. Yes! Jim never said who—"

"Jim?" Hart asked.

Brennan shook his head. "Jim's not his real name, he—"

Jacobs slapped the table. "Enough with the nonsense. You're a dead ringer for the suspect in a Chicago double murder, and from the sound of it we can link you to murders here and in California." Brennan had not told them about Elsie.

Hart cut in. "But we'll look into your story."

"Thank you," Brennan said.

"Don't thank us yet, buddy," Hart said. "As far as I can tell, you're either crazy, a murderer, or both."

The two detectives stood up, and Hart asked, "Need anything?"

Brennan tried to smile. "I'd love a cup of water, please."

"Sure thing," Hart said. The two detectives walked out, and Hart returned with a paper cup. He set it on the table in front of Brennan.

As Hart turned to leave again, Brennan said, "Um, sir?" and wiggled his shoulders. The handcuffs clanked behind him.

Hart shrugged. "Sorry, man, all out of straws. Oh, and one other thing." He set the evidence bag containing Brennan's laptop on the opposite side of the table. "We checked your browser history, hotshot." Brennan's heart sank even lower. Hart left the room, and as the door swung shut Brennan could hear Jacobs giggling in the hallway.

Brennan struggled in his chair. He braced his leg against the table and pushed, but the table and chair were firmly bolted to the floor. He only succeeded in knocking over his cup. Water ran off the edge of the table into his lap. As he glanced at what had to be a one-way mirror. *I hope that gives you one more thing to laugh about,* he thought.

So they wanted to find out if he was crazy. That was fine with Brennan; he was wondering the exact same thing. *At this point,* he thought, *it's not a question of if I'm crazy, it's more a question of just how crazy I am.* He had scared Jennifer Cairns half to death. She was ready to shoot him in the face for Christ's sake.

And that picture, he thought. *It was like going to the fair and paying the caricaturist to draw you. You get the picture, and there you are, riding in a goofy car or fishing or whatever, and ugly as hell. You want to say, "That's not me."*

But it was.

It was him, all right, a dead ringer. The face in the picture was the same face in the one-way mirror to his right. The eyes staring back at him were the same. He was not positive, but the haircut of the man in the picture looked to be the same way he wore his hair in 2003.

He changed the subject before his head exploded. He tried to play a game of *Get Out Alive*, but all options started with getting out of the handcuffs. He wished he'd paid better attention during the book report on Harry Houdini he had written in the seventh grade. But those were tricks, and the guy practiced and prepared for them ahead of time. Brennan did not have any handcuff keys hidden away. He did not have anything.

The cold water in his lap brought him back to his senses. He shifted around in the metal chair, but it did him no good. Brennan tried to remember the last time he had actually wet his pants. He decided he had to have been six or seven years old. The shame he had felt back then was intense, like a burning coal in his gut.

Eventually, Hart came back in the room. His eye darted to the spilled cup, and he smirked.

"What?" asked Brennan.

"The driver's license number you gave us, could you repeat it?"

"One. Six. Two. Six. Zero. Three. Five. Four."

"You positive? And you're sure it's a Texas license?"

"Yeah. Expires next year on my birthday. What's the problem?"

The detective leaned on the table. "You're not in the system. Neither are the murders you mentioned in California."

Brennan shook his head. "There's no way. I just read about them."

Hart said, "You're only here because Cairns used to work for the chief, and she said you might be the guy who committed the Dead M— the decapitation murder back in '99." He leaned over and stared Brennan in the eye. "I went back to check, and everything related to that case is missing. Everything—files, bagged evidence. Everything. We're making some phone calls, but I want you to tell me what you know about it."

Brennan straightened in his chair and said, "Look. I told you everything I know and you laughed in my face. Somebody wants me to disappear, or wants what happened forgotten, or I don't know what. I'm trying to figure things out, but it hasn't exactly worked out. The only hope I had was Cairns, and she wanted to shoot me in the throat. I have no idea what happened to your files."

"Wade, I can tell something is screwy here. The smart money is on you doing the screwing, but it might turn out you're the guy getting screwed." Hart pulled a bottle of water and a straw out of his pocket. He opened the bottle and stuck in the straw. "Either way, we'll get to the bottom of it. It's what we do." He set the bottle in front of Brennan.

Brennan thanked him, but Hart shook his head and said, "Don't hold out on us. My gut says to hear you out. But if you're in trouble, we need to know everything."

The florescent light flickered again. Brennan thought about Elsie. He said, "I've told you everything I know."

Hart looked at him, and Brennan had the odd feeling Hart was trying to read his mind. Whatever the detective was looking for, he didn't find it.

Hart said, "We'll get you into a cell for the night. Should be less than an hour. Need anything else?"

"You could let me out of these cuffs," Brennan said.

Hart shook his head. "Sorry, kid. You might look harmless, but there's a decent chance you're a five-alarm freak. We don't gamble with our safety around here." He got up to leave. "We'll be back if we need anything else."

"I'll be here," Brennan said, and was alone again in the room.

15

BRENNAN MUST HAVE FALLEN ASLEEP handcuffed to the chair, because he woke up to the hectic sounds of panic. The lights in the interrogation room were out, and with only a small window in the door, it was as dark as his cell in the desert.

Someone screamed. A thunderstorm of gunfire erupted, shaking the one-way mirror. Brennan's heartbeat thudded in his temples as he strained against the cuffs.

He could hear Jacobs taking charge and barking orders over the violent noise. She yelled, "Get that desk over here! Block the door!"

There was a man's voice Brennan did not recognize. "I can't get anyone on the radio. They must've jammed it, too."

Brennan wanted to yell to them, but he had no way of knowing what was between Jacobs and himself. He also had major doubts as to his importance to her at the moment.

Hart asked, "How many are there?"

"We dropped two of them, but there's at least a dozen," Jacobs said.

A woman was sobbing, past hysterical. "They killed them! They killed all of them!"

"Keep her quiet," Jacobs said. The crying quieted and stopped.

The pop-pop-pop of the guns became infrequent as Brennan considered the situation. The police officers could not use the radio. He guessed the invaders cut the land lines and jammed everything else. The survivors controlled a barricade nearby.

Brennan pulled at the cuffs as hard as he could. His shoulders stung, and the muscles in his back threatened to give out. The metal cut into his wrists, and his hands became sticky as the blood dripped down. He remembered a movie where someone dislocated their thumb to slide out of a pair of handcuffs, but he doubted it would work even if he could make himself do it; the cuffs were tight against his skin.

The shooting started again in earnest. Windows exploded and thick glass rained onto the ground. The gunshots grew louder and louder and then stopped entirely as a shadow fell across Brennan's face. Someone stood behind the door, but he could not make out anything through the tiny window. He gripped the handcuffs tightly to keep from screaming.

The door opened and Detective Hart stumbled through, clutching his side. He breathed in short, wet gasps. As the detective closed the door, Brennan could see a red stain spreading across Hart's white shirt.

"They're here for you," Hart said, and slumped behind the table.

Brennan didn't know what to say. "I—I'm sorry."

"Doesn't matter," Hart grunted as he pulled himself up to the table. He kneeled on Brennan's right, with his gun trained on the door like a hunter in a blind. Brennan noticed Hart's hands did not shake.

Without breaking his stare, Hart said, "I don't think this is a rescue attempt. I'm going to listen to my goddamn gut, and it says you're a victim in this, too." He sucked in air as he gritted his teeth against the pain, he said, "I wish I could say we'd get you out of this, but I'm all that's left and help isn't coming. We're sitting ducks."

"Is there another way out?" Brennan asked.

"No. They've got us pinned down. There are at least ten of them between us and the exits. They're armed with assault rifles and wearing body armor. It was a slaughter. Are these the guys you escaped from?"

Brennan said, "I don't know. Probably. It sounds like the way they work." He wanted to ask if Hart was okay, but there was no way to ask the question and not sound stupid.

Hart's elbow slipped out from under him on the table. He repositioned himself and said, "They have the files Jennifer Cairns gave me before she left town. I saw one of them leave with the box. I don't know if that means anything to you or not, but it must be important."

So closes the brief window where I might know something they didn't, Brennan thought. *Once they have a look at those, they'll head out to Jennifer's house and grab everything she has on the murders.*

The sound of footsteps echoed in the hallway. A helmeted man leaned into the doorway. A spider web appeared across his plastic face shield, and Brennan saw a third nostril spring up as Hart's bullet split the man's face. The body tumbled to the ground and shook.

Hart grunted in satisfaction.

Another armored man leaned around the corner. The muzzle of his gun flashed as he fired into Hart. Brennan saw a spark as Hart's last shot hit the metal door, missing the attacker by inches.

Brennan screamed as Hart hit the ground. Hart's already blank eyes stared up at him. Brennan pulled at the cuffs again, straining back hard in the chair and kicking his feet against the table.

The man lowered his gun and took off his helmet. "Brennan Wade. You're coming with us."

"Not a chance," Brennan said. "I just got used to eating again."

"I'm afraid you don't have a choice."

Brennan recognized his voice from the airplane: the man Jim had ordered to read the files. Brennan pictured the man as a nervous pencil pusher when he first heard him, but this man had a square jaw and cold eyes. "And once we make sure you're blamed for this massacre, you'll be better off with us. You—"

The gun clattered to the floor. Brennan flinched, but looked up in time to see the man's head teeter unnaturally to the side, blood spurting from the stump of his neck. The head bounced once when it hit the floor with the thud of a ripe cantaloupe. It rolled toward Brennan, stopping when it bumped into a table leg. The lips moved wordlessly as the headless body collapsed to the ground. Blood spread in a wide puddle on the floor.

Brennan frantically tried to see what had killed the man, but the hallway was so dark that he could not tell if anything was out there or not. For a moment he felt confused, like he had gotten turned around and was facing the one-way mirror again.

Something flew in the air toward him, landing in a noisy clank on the table. Brennan glanced down to find a key ring. A handcuff key stuck out from among the nickel and brass.

Brennan looked up, but the hallway still looked empty. "A little help, here?" he asked. There was no answer. He called out, "Not saying I'm not grateful, but what the hell?"

He pulled at his cuffs yet again. What good was a key he could not use? Hart's lifeless face stared at him from the floor, blood drying beneath the detective's nostrils.

Brennan leaned forward, straining against the cuffs, and managed to pick up the key ring with his teeth. It tasted like pennies. He closed his eyes and pulled in a deep breath through his nose. He turned his head to the side as far as he could and dropped the keys on his left shoulder.

There are so many reasons this won't work, he thought. With his chin, he nudged the keys until they fell toward his waiting hands. At the last second, he knew he had missed, but the key ring caught on his outstretched pinky finger.

With his bloody fingers, he felt for the thin handcuff key and the keyhole. Through painful trial and error, he discovered twisting his left wrist high behind his back allowed him to unlock the cuff. He groaned at the stiffness in his shoulders and freed his other hand. Brennan stood, rubbing his wrists. "I'm sorry," he said again to the lifeless Hart as he picked up the detective's gun. With his other hand, he gathered up the bag holding his laptop and gripped it to his chest.

Brennan stepped over the body of Hart's killer and out of the room. He swallowed a lump and called out a tentative, "Hello?" His rescuer was nowhere to be found, and no one else was in any condition to answer.

He found a horror show in the hallway. Two more dead invaders lay in a grotesque embrace. The police had holed up at the end of the hall, which opened into a wider area. They had blocked the door, but the armored men had advanced to a large window and mowed them down. A small woman lay facedown near the door. Brennan wondered if she was the one who had been so hysterical.

Creeping over the bodies a step at a time, he forced himself not to panic. In the larger office area, people sat dead in their office chairs. He found his backpack and other belongings on a desk. Sliding the plastic bag holding them out from under the desk's late owner, he said, "Sorry. I wouldn't do this if I didn't have to."

From Hart's count, at least five soldiers remained a threat. Brennan didn't know if whatever killed the man in the interview room had eliminated the rest of them, but he felt no desire to stick around and find out.

Clicking the unlock button on the keychain helped Brennan find the right car easily. He hoped the shitstorm coming as soon as someone found the police department covered his tracks long enough for him to ditch the vehicle. Looking back once more for any sign of who had saved him, he saw only a dead, silent building.

He hit the highway and headed east for Chicago.

16

JOAN RUNCITER carried two heavy grocery bags as she entered her apartment. She grunted and flipped on the light switch. Nothing happened.

"Damn it," she said to no one. "Of course I didn't buy any bulbs."

She stumbled over her cat in the dark, making it shriek. "Sorry, Solomon, but you can see better than me in here. Stay alert! Be vigilant!"

Joan heaved the two bags up onto the counter. Glass bottles rattled inside. She pulled out her cell phone, and the screen gave off enough light to rummage through the junk drawer. The cat continued hissing.

"Solomon, what'd you do with the matches?" Her hand closed over the matchbook. "Never mind. You're off the hook." She pulled out a match and bent back the book's cover. She pinched the flimsy matchstick between the two pieces of cardboard and gave it a quick pull.

Even though she expected the flame, its sudden appearance made her jump. She laughed at herself, and turned to find the enormous scented candle she kept around for such an occasion.

She ran right into a man waiting in the darkness.

The man silenced her scream with a palm pressed hard

against her mouth. The match tumbled to the ground and the room was dark again.

In a hushed voice he said, "Listen to me. I don't want to hurt you. I promise I don't. But I need you to be quiet. Nod your head if you understand."

Joan nodded. The intruder removed his hand and quickly gagged her with a strip of cloth. After finishing with the gag, he pulled several plastic cable ties from his pocket. Joan felt him begin to force her arms behind her back.

She wiggled one hand free, pivoted hard and threw back an elbow, catching her attacker in the ribs. She yelled into the gag. He cursed, dropping the ties.

The lights were still out as she rounded the corner out of the kitchen. Adrenaline and muscle memory carried her to the door. She grabbed the knob, but the door would not open.

She thought of the deadbolt. She gripped the thumb turn so brutally that it tore skin off her fingers. She made it as far as pulling the door open, only to be stopped by the chain lock.

The door slammed as the man threw his shoulder against it, and then Joan landed facedown on the ground, the man's weight holding her flat. He pulled her wrists together and bound them.

He said something she could not hear as he hefted her up. Tears threatened to stream down her face as he tied her to one of her dining chairs. He walked to the cheap chandelier hanging from the ceiling and screwed back in one of the bulbs. Harsh light and shadow shaped her attacker's face, and Joan screamed into the gag.

"We need to talk," Brennan said.

17

JOAN'S TEARS WERE SHORT-LIVED. Her mascara dried on her cheeks, and it provided an inky black frame for her glaring eyes. Her hatred for Brennan filled the room like the refracted air over a fire.

She must be playing Get Out Alive, Brennan thought. He cursed himself again for not thinking of a better way to question her, but her reaction told him there was no easy way. Someone put her through hell, and as far as she was concerned the bastard stood right in front of her. *I'm lucky she went for the door,* he thought. *If she had turned on me after knocking the wind out of me, she probably could have killed me with her bare hands.*

They sat in the living room of Joan's apartment, with Joan still tied to the chair with the zip ties he had purchased that morning, and with Brennan perched on a bar stool in front of her. The woman was slender, but he could see the strength in her frame. Her dark-brown hair was pulled back in a ponytail, leaving the bangs spread across her forehead. Her skin was pale and clear like vanilla cream. Brennan could see in Joan's enormous eyes that she was plotting ways to bludgeon him to death if given half a chance.

"Joan—Ms. Runciter—I'm sorry for the way this went down. I mean, for what I did. Shit, but not what you think I did; that wasn't me. I'm sorry for this." He nodded toward the zip ties. "But I have to talk to you. You're the only person who can help me."

Joan narrowed her eyes.

"I'm going to take the gag off of you now, but you have to be quiet. If you yell or anything, I'll gag you again and we'll be right back where we started until you can calm down. If you give me a chance to talk, I'll get out of here and we can get on with our lives. Okay?"

Joan rolled her eyes but she nodded. As Brennan took off the gag, he said, "I just bought the bandanas, you know. I thought that would be the most considerate way to gag somebody. With something new and clean."

"You," she said as Brennan backed away. "You jerk."

"Yeah," he said. "I'm definitely a jerk."

"It wasn't enough, was it? You had to come back and—" She fought the restraints, and the chair jumped around the floor. Brennan took a step toward her, and she stopped.

But not because she's afraid, he thought. *When I took her by surprise, she was afraid. But she's way past that now. The floodgates opened when she saw my face.*

"What do you mean, 'Come back?'" Brennan asked. "I've never been here before."

Joan laughed sarcastically. "Not back to the apartment, you ass. Back to finish what you started."

Brennan looked her in the face and tried to sound authoritative. "I need you to tell me what happened."

"Fuck you."

He rubbed his temples. "Fine. While you're stuck here, do you need anything? Some water or something?" Joan started to answer, but Brennan cut her off. "Other than being let go, I mean."

Joan looked like she was about to say it anyway. Instead she asked, "Could you put the ice cream in the freezer before it melts all over the carpet? It's in one of the bags I brought in."

"Yeah, sure," Brennan said. He went into the kitchen and dug through the bags until he found two pints of Ben & Jerry's. One was labeled Phish Food and the other was Cherry Garcia.

As he put the second carton into the freezer, he heard a loud thump.

Joan had tipped the chair backward, and was now lying on her back. She pumped her feet, trying to break them loose from the legs of the chair. When she saw him, she screamed, "I need help in h—," but he gagged her again. She screamed into the gag.

"You've got to understand, I didn't want to do this," Brennan said. He pulled out a coil of new nylon rope. "Look, I really do need your help. And you really are in trouble. Just not from me."

Brennan left her lying on the ground, but he tied her tighter to the chair. He took special care to strap down her feet. He pulled the chair back upright and pushed it until the back of it scraped against her dining table. He tied one of the chair legs to a table leg so she could not wobble off-balance again.

Brennan waited for her to stop screaming, then said, "We need to try this again. Will you tell me what happened?"

Joan's death glare never moved from his eyes, but she nodded. He removed the gag a second time.

She spit in his face. "You know what happened, freak."

"Doesn't matter if I know or not," he said, wiping away the spit. "You're going to tell me."

Brennan figured she would rather do anything than tell that story, but she shrugged. She leaned her head back and stared at the ceiling. Her voice sounded clinical and disconnected. "Fine. I was working in Haiti for spring break, helping with this one-week medical relief trip. It was the last time—

"Donna and Audrey were my roommates. We shared an apartment close to the school. They talked about going somewhere with a beach for spring break, but they were pretty broke. They decided to stay in town and have a good time. I called them once, and they'd been hitting parties, bars, and clubs every night.

"The night before I got back, they ended up at Jason's Tavern. We used to go there all the time, and we'd—" She paused, closing her eyes. "According to the bartender, they sat at the bar all night, looking good and turning down every guy who tried to hit on them. There was this one guy, though, who chatted them up for a while. He seemed into Donna, and Donna acted pretty into him, too. Donna didn't want to ditch Audrey, though, and the guy was cool about it. After a while, he left."

Brennan remembered all of this. He had gotten Donna's number that night and tried calling her a few days later, but no one answered.

Joan continued, "But after about fifteen minutes, the guy came back. He said he'd run into a great friend Audrey should meet, and Donna was all too happy to convince Audrey to go. The bartender didn't remember much else about the guy—it was the last Saturday night of spring break, right?—but he remembered the guy settled the ladies' tab with a hundred dollar bill and said to keep the change. The bartender thought that was pretty classy."

"No," Brennan said, "that didn't happen. I—"

"Shut. The fuck. Up," Joan said without opening her eyes. "You wanted me to tell, I'm telling. My overnight flight landed the next morning, and I made it back to the apartment pretty early. I picked up bagels for the girls.

"I unlocked the door and had just set down the bagels when I saw some guy sitting in the living room, watching cartoons. A black trash bag was on the couch to him. I asked who he was, and he said, 'Donna's friend.'

"I said something like, 'Right, good for you.'

"He said, 'I'll show myself out in a minute.'

"I said, 'Mind taking your trash with you?'

"He said, 'Sounds like a plan.'

"So I went into Audrey's room to check on her. She always had a rough time the morning after a night out. But she wasn't in her room, and neither was Donna. It was so weird; they never got up early on a Sunday. I looked back into the living room, but the couch guy was gone. He'd left the cartoons playing, though, and I can still see Sylvester trying to catch Tweety Bird by painting his clawed finger like a bird.

"I decided they must have left and told the guy to lock up

when he left. I left the bagels on the counter with a note in case they came back while I was in the shower, and went into the bathroom."

Joan's eyes were still squeezed shut, but tears still managed to escape. "And there they were, in the bathroom, piled in the tub. Everything was red. Donna's dress was torn, and one of her shoes was under the toilet. The shower curtain was pulled down, and Audrey's hand was still holding onto it. Their heads were gone."

Her head snapped down and her eyes flew open. "It was you, you son of a bitch. You killed my best friends and slipped out when I wasn't looking. You clogged the drain with their blood and went on your merry fucking way. I never figured out why you didn't kill me, too."

"What—what did you do after that?" Brennan asked. He felt sick.

"Do you think I could do anything after that?" she asked, laughing. It was the kind of laugh that kept climbing higher and higher. "My life has been a mess ever since. Sometimes I wish you'd killed me, too. But I guess now you've come to finish it off. Maybe I should be grateful."

Brennan blinked back tears. His voice caught as he said, "I wasn't there. I left. I never—"

"You think I'd forget?" Joan asked hysterically. "You and your fucking trash bag of tricks?"

He got right in her face. "I didn't kill your friends! I've never killed anyone! It wasn't me!"

"It was you! Your face! Your face is burned into my brain!" she screamed. "You're—"

A crash cut her off. The wood around the door latch splintered and the brass chain shattered, broken links flying. Standing in the doorway of the apartment was a man in jeans and a black shirt. His heavy boots shined.

He was a perfect double of Brennan. The man was evil, and his eyes were wild and cold.

The other Brennan said, "They figured out where you'd go. The whole place is surrounded. You can get out through the basement, but you've got to go right now. Take my car." He tossed a jangling key ring to Brennan. "And whatever you do, don't ditch it this time. You'll need it to get where you're going."

The stranger winked at Joan. "Nice to see you again, angel." Her eyes went wide, and the blood drained out of her face. He turned to leave, saying over his shoulder, "I mean it, Brennan, right fucking now or never."

And he was gone.

A silent second passed. Brennan spoke first. "Do you believe me now?"

"You-you or the other you?" Joan asked.

"Either one," Brennan said.

"No. Now cut me loose."

18

BRENNAN PULLED OUT JIM'S POCKETKNIFE and looked down at Joan. He was at a loss at how to proceed.

He had been half-convinced he was the murderer—much more than half, in fact. And he was, or at least someone exactly like him. He wanted to feel relieved, but the sense of guilt still stung in his guts.

The other man knew Joan. Brennan had no doubt this was the same man that ended the lives of Joan's friends and probably many, many others.

Then why the fuck would he help me? Brennan asked himself. But his evil twin could be telling the truth. Brennan's pursuers might be filling the building now, like rats filling up a barn at the first freeze. In a few seconds, he might have a bag over his head and vanish without a trace. *Again.*

After what they did at the police station, Brennan thought, *there's no way they'll leave Joan alive.* Beside his pesky desire to do the right thing, Joan was now Brennan's only hope to set the record straight. His drab life might not mean anything to anyone else, but it was all he had and he wanted it back.

Joan recovered from her shock faster than Brennan. "Cut me loose." Her nostrils flared. "Cut me loose! What are you waiting for?" Brennan leaned forward, but then he froze again, dropping the knife.

It was him, he thought. *It's been him all the time.*

The piece of glass in the cell. The motorcycle. The police station rescue. It was all this man who had stolen Brennan's face.

The man was a brutal murderer, but he had already saved Brennan from these people twice. This realization convinced Brennan what he needed to do. He scrambled for the knife and cut the plastic ties and rope binding Joan. The instant he finished cutting her feet loose, she was sprinting out the door, calling for help.

"Joan, wait!" he yelled. He grabbed his backpack from its hiding place behind the couch and pulled Detective Hart's gun from the front pocket. Clicking off the safety, he ran out the door after her. She moved fast and turned the corner before Brennan reached her.

He chased her through the gray hallways, numbered doors flying past him on both sides. As she turned the final corner and spotted the elevator at the end of the long hallway, a plastic number six lit up, indicating the elevator had arrived. A bell dinged. Joan stopped and Brennan skidded to a halt behind her.

The old elevator doors parted and slid out of view. Inside the elevator stood two men in SWAT team uniforms.

"Thank God!" yelled Joan. "You've got to help me! You wouldn't believe the—"

The man on the left said into his shoulder radio, "Targets acquired," and raised his assault rifle. Joan put up her hands. "Wait! No!" she yelled and dove against the wall.

The man squeezed the trigger and a bullet flew over Joan's shoulder, but then he jerked back. Brennan shot him again, twice in the chest. Brennan doubted it would kill the man in his body armor, but he hoped it would slow him down. *Looks like all that range practice for the police academy wasn't a total waste of time*, he thought.

As the second gunmen dropped to one knee, Brennan grabbed Joan and dove around a corner. Several three-round bursts rushed through the air where they had been. They were on their feet and running, a torrent of fear carrying them down the hall.

"Stairs!" Brennan said. "Where are the stairs?"

Joan pushed open a door. "In here, quick!" Brennan followed her inside. Bullets hit the door's frame as it slammed shut.

She had reached the first downward step when Brennan grabbed her. "No," he said.

"What are you, insane? We have to go!"

"He'll catch us."

"What are you going to do? Shoot him?" she asked.

"No," he said, "There were only three rounds, and I used them."

"What are you going to do?" she asked.

"Play a game of *Get Out Alive.*"

Joan's jaw dropped and her eyes clearly stated her opinion, but it was too late. Brennan grabbed her and pushed her against the wall behind the door. He looked around and saw a fire extinguisher in a recess beside the door. Grabbing it, he slid against the wall beside Joan.

The door flew open, and Brennan fired the extinguisher in the man's face. The stairwell was filled with fog, and the man was blinded, his face mask completely covered in white. He raised his gun, but Brennan brought the bottom of the metal extinguisher down hard on his hands. The gun clattered to the floor.

The man pulled his helmet off and it bounced down the stairs. A jagged scar ran from the corner of his mouth to his ear. He pulled back an enormous fist.

His eyes narrowing, Brennan's body worked automatically, like getting a knee tapped by a doctor. He leaned to the side and bent his legs, grabbing the man's wrist in one hand and shoving his other hand beneath the man's armpit. Brennan's legs sprang, and the man's momentum carried him over the rail.

Brennan watched him fall down the center of the stairwell. His hands flailed as he tried to grab at the rail as they rushed past, but there was only an empty clang as his hand slapped the metal. His body made a sickening sound when it hit the bottom.

Joan put her hand on Brennan's shoulder. "We have to go," she said.

Brennan picked up the rifle. The second gunmen, the one Brennan had shot, shouldered his way into the stairwell. Brennan emptied the clip into the man's chest. He fell writhing onto the floor. Without stopping to get the man's gun away from him, Brennan and Joan ran down the stairs.

After they made it down a few floors, Joan pulled him through a stairwell door and down a hall. "Another elevator is this way," she said. They nervously stood on opposite sides of the elevator doors, Joan holding the empty rifle and Brennan holding the small pocketknife. He had once seen a science-fiction movie about men fighting with knives on a desert planet—they held their knives blade down, so he did the same now. If the doors opened on more soldiers, he would put the knife in the first neck he could reach.

They tensed as the doors opened, revealing a terrified old woman. Brennan watched in disbelief as Joan pulled the woman out of the elevator.

"Get to your room," Joan said to the woman. "Now. Call the cops. Call the real cops. Don't leave your room until you're sure it's okay. Got it?" The woman nodded and ran. They entered the elevator and Joan hit a button, a bold B framed in a yellow-white circle.

The sounds of the moving elevator were soothing. Joan looked into Brennan's eyes. "How are we still alive?" she asked.

"I could ask you the same question."

Joan smirked. "And I could say I asked you first."

Brennan sighed. "I have absolutely no idea."

"Ever killed anybody before?"

Brennan glared at her. "I told you I hadn't."

"And now you have," she said. "You looked like a pro."

"It's been a little crazy lately," he said. "I guess I'm adjusting."

"Ah."

The elevator slowed, and the doors opened onto a wide basement hallway. Old toilets and stacks of sheetrock lined the walls. At the end of the hallway were the other elevator doors.

"Do you know the way out of here?" Brennan asked.

Joan shook her head. "I didn't think the elevator would even come down here without a special key or something. Sorry."

The other elevator dinged. Brennan sprinted down the hall, grabbing the heavy porcelain lid from the back of a cracked toilet as he ran. Seeing red, he raised the lid over his shoulder as the doors opened, screaming like he had caught fire. Inside the elevator stood two startled gunmen. They had barely started to lift their weapons when Brennan reached them.

He slammed the heavy piece of porcelain down onto the closest man's head. The man dropped to his knees. Brennan hit the other one in the side of the head and knocked him into the side of the elevator with a sickening crack, breaking the lid in half. Brennan hit the first man again over the shoulder with what was left of the lid, feeling the man's collarbone crack. Both men slid to the floor and were still.

"This way, you crazy freak," Joan said from somewhere far away. She ducked in one of the side doors. Brennan followed her in, and an exit sign glowed over a small upward staircase.

They burst out of the door onto the street. In the distance Brennan saw the front entrance to the apartment where more fake SWAT members piled into fake SWAT vans. Farther down the street were flashing lights and what looked to be legitimate police cars.

Brennan pulled the car key out of his pocket and clicked the unlock button on the key chain. The lights flickered on an old car across the street. It was painted black and quite old, maybe from the 1930s. They ran to the car, never taking their eyes off the vans down the street. Brennan started to open the driver's side door when Joan stopped him. "Let me drive," she said.

He looked at her, confused.

"You've been shot," she said and pointed.

He looked down and saw that his entire right side was drenched in blood.

"Oh my God," Brennan said, and he fainted.

PHASE II

1

"IT'S ABOUT TIME," Joan said.

Brennan groaned again at the sharp pain in his side. He lifted a clean white shirt and found his chest wrapped in thick white bandages. There was a red circle at the epicenter of the pain, where his blood seeped through the dressing.

Trees zoomed by outside the window. The sun was setting

His throat was dry, and the car smelled like smoke. "How long have I been out?" he asked.

"You've been out all day. I think we're in Florida."

"What are we doing in Florida?"

"I suspect we are going to get killed here," she said. "In Florida."

Brennan grimaced. He felt a lump under the bandages, right on top of the lowest rib on his right. A shooting pain flared up to his armpit, making him cough.

Joan glared at him. "Are you crazy? Don't touch that."

He put his hands in his lap. "Thanks for patching me up."

"I did the best I could with what I could buy from a gas station."

Brennan turned his head toward Joan. The sunlight lit up her hair like a halo. She stared intently on the road, nervously drumming her thumbs on the steering wheel. He noticed she had green eyes with hints of brown, like old glass bottles of Coca-Cola.

She shot him a quick look. "What?"

"Nothing." To avoid an awkward silence, he fiddled with the radio. Settled between two huge round gauges, it was tiny and looked original to the old car. The dashboard was chromed art deco, like the controls in Buck Rogers' rocket ship. When he turned the volume knob, there was static for a moment. Then the solemn twang of a Delta blues song filled the car.

"That's the only thing it will play," Joan said. "Try turning the station dial." Brennan turned the knob, and a tiny needle moved up and down the AM dial. The music was undisturbed.

"I know this song," Brennan said.

"Really?" She sounded genuinely surprised.

Brennan nodded. "Yeah, it's Robert Pete Williams—no, it's Skip James. 'Devil Got My Woman.' That's a weird one to hear out of nowhere, and this is the clearest recording of it I've ever heard." He gave the knob one more useless turn. "The radio must be hooked to something else." He sang along with the song quietly until James and his devil drifted away.

He didn't know the words to the next song, a number by Booker White. Joan turned the volume knob down. "You know," she said, "you're going to have to tell me what the hell is going on."

"We are on the run from armed goons who want to kill us."

"I know that, you idiot. I meant why do the armored goons want to kill us?"

"It's not going to make me look any better," he said. "And it won't make any more sense."

Joan shrugged. "Either way, I want to hear it."

"Fine," Brennan said, and he told her about the DNA test and the endless hallway at the airport. He told her about Jim and the three locations mentioned on the plane. He left out most of what he experienced in the desert cell, but he told her about the assisted escape and how he ended up in Kansas City. He told her about finding Jennifer Cairns and reading the file about a surviving witness. Then there was the massacre at the police department and how he made his way to her apartment in Chicago. "You know the rest," he said weakly.

She whistled. "You're right. That doesn't exactly clear things up."

"Told you," he said. "I have no idea what's really going on."

"So the fake SWAT guys were the same ones who grabbed you the first time?" she asked.

"Seems that way. But I don't know why they want to get me without the cops getting me."

"And the bastard who looks like you?"

Brennan thought back to the shard of glass, and the soldier's head bouncing off the floor in the police station. "As far as I can tell, he's saved my life three times."

"And murdered a bunch of people. Including my friends."

"I think a bunch is being conservative." He arched his shoulders as the pain hit again. "I'm sorry. We have to deal with this me-getting-shot thing. Has anyone been following us?"

"Not that I can tell."

"We should be far enough away, unless—wait, do you have your cell phone?"

"No," she said, frustrated. "It's in my purse back in the apartment. Along with my wallet, all my clothes, and my spoiled cat. Why?"

"It's probably a good thing. I bet they could find us if you used your phone. Do you have someone you need to call? Parents or something?"

Joan shook her head. "They died when I was in medical school, and they were the last family I had."

"I'm sorry."

"It was a long time ago," she said, looking thoughtful. "So how'd they find you? Were you considerate enough to leave them a note? Did you have a radio tracer-bug thing on you?"

He shook his head, "No, I ditched the clothes from the police station, and I looked over my laptop and stuff. Even though I wasn't looking for that kind of thing, I think I would have seen it. But now I'm paranoid, so I'll have to check again."

Brennan took a deep breath. "One of the detectives said they took Jennifer's files, which probably led them to you. He also said Jennifer left town, so I hope she made it somewhere safe." He frowned. "That's one more person who would be better off if she never met me. So yeah, I bet they followed the same trail I did."

Joan bit her lip. "You're probably right. Think we're far enough away yet?"

"What?"

"Far enough away to stop."

"Probably not, but I think we're as good as we're going to get. You've seriously been driving for fifteen hours?"

She rolled her head around, her neck popping. "Feels closer to fifty."

Reading road signs, Brennan said, "Pull off here, there's a motel. We—you can't drive forever."

The motel looked cheap and had external rooms. They parked, and Brennan unbuckled his seat belt and started to get out of the car.

"What are you doing?" Joan asked.

"Checking in. What are you doing?"

"I'm checking in. You're waiting in the car. You look like shit, Brennan."

Brennan fell back into the seat. "Fine."

"But I'm going to need money. I paid for your bandages with what you had in your wallet, but there's not much left."

His money stash was not with the stuff he got back from the police station. "Shit. Guess we're sleeping in the killer's car tonight."

"Check the car. Maybe there's some seed money," she said.

Brennan popped open the glove compartment, and his eyes widened. He pulled out a bundle of twenty-dollar bills several inches thick. It was one of several stacks. "Look at this. What is this?"

She grabbed the stack and pulled some out. "It's a shower and a bed. Past that I don't want to think about it. Watch which room I go to and follow me in about fifteen minutes."

Brennan watched her as she walked into the motel office. *She's handling this pretty well,* he thought.

It's not exactly her first rodeo. You need to remember Joan spent a day driving around and patching up a guy she's probably been seeing in her nightmares for years. It doesn't matter that it wasn't me, not really.

Joan exited the motel office. She held her hand to her chest so he could see it clearly and signed the numbers one, zero, and four. *She's definitely adapting,* Brennan thought. *She's as paranoid as I am. Maybe more so.*

While he waited, he inventoried what was in the car. He wasn't sure how much money was in the glove compartment, but it turned out a few of the stacks were all fifties. The compartment also contained several envelopes, each one holding a different set of identification with photos and descriptions matching Brennan. He rummaged through them: Leo Bluthgeld, Pete Fox, Bob Brady, Bill Asher and a dozen others. The center console contained an electric stun-gun. Brennan hefted it in his hand; it felt well-made and expensive. He pulled the trigger. He jumped as the gun produced a bright spark and a loud crackling sound.

He put everything away carefully and exited the car, making sure to lock it. He found room 104 and tried the door. It was locked, of course, so he knocked.

"Scoot back!" Joan said from behind the door. He backed up until he was standing in the street. She opened the door for him, and he went inside, raising his eyebrow at her as she passed.

She glared at him. "I had to be sure it was you and not…" She didn't have to finish for Brennan to know who she meant.

The motel room was huge. "It's handicap accessible," Joan said. "Sorry, I wanted the guy to think I was by myself, so I got a single."

"It's got a couch," Brennan said. "I'll be fine."

He started to sit on the couch, but Joan stopped him. "Wait just a minute," she said. She went into the bathroom and grabbed several of the towels to drape on the couch. "There you go. In case you spring a leak."

"Thanks," he said, sitting carefully. He flinched as his rib screamed at him again.

"Get your shirt off and let me change your dressing," she said.

He slowly pulled off his shirt, parts of it sticking to his bloody bandage. She unwrapped the bandage and whistled softly.

"That bad, huh?" Brennan asked.

"No, it'll be fine. Bullet went through clean, just grazing the bone." She redressed the injury. "But just to be sure—" She fished out a small bottle from her pocket and dropped it in Brennan's open hand. "Start taking these, one pill five times a day until they're gone. Take three the first time."

Brennan read the bottle. "These pills are for fish. Aquarium fish."

"I know. I got them at a big pet store in Alabama." Joan must have seen the face Brennan made, because she said, "You were out cold. You should probably get more sleep."

"But fish pills?" he asked.

"It's amoxicillin. The same damn thing you'd get from a doctor, without the mandatory police report for the gunshot wound. And here's some ketoprofen. Sorry it's not the hard stuff, but it should take the edge off the pain."

Brennan dry-swallowed the pills. "Thanks."

She looked around the room. "Are you okay here for awhile? I'm going out for supplies."

"Yeah, sure," Brennan said. "There's a stun-gun in the center console. In case you need it."

"Thanks," she said. "There's also an empty assault rifle in the back under a blanket."

"Ah," he said. "I forgot. Hurry back."

"You sure you'll be okay?"

"Yeah. I'll watch some TV. Not like I need any more sleep."

In three minutes he was snoring.

2

HE AWOKE TO THE SOUND of the shower water shutting off.

"Joan?" he asked, scanning the room from the couch.

"Yeah, it's me. Way to stay on red alert." Joan exited the bathroom, her body wrapped in a towel.

"My radar must recognize you as a friendly."

She sat on the edge of the bed; its ancient springs creaked. "You lost more blood than you think. It's good you got some rest."

"Best sleep I've had in a month." He groaned as he turned to face her. "Too bad it took getting shot."

"Thanks for that, by the way," she said.

"Thanks for what?"

Joan rolled her eyes. "Thanks for getting shot trying to help me out. I'm pretty sure that's a first for me."

Smirking, he patted the bandages. "No big deal. I do it for all the girls." Joan snorted and went back into the bathroom. He listened to her change and felt guilty for what a quick mess he had made of her life, however indirectly. *Except for the most recent disasters,* he thought. *Those are definitely on my head.*

She walked back around and tossed a clean white shirt at him, catching him full in the face. She was dressed in clean, utterly non-descript clothes. "Put that on and come outside. I want to show you something."

He sat up with some difficulty, but not as much as he expected. He pulled on his t-shirt and followed Joan outside to the parking lot. She stood behind their getaway car and checked to make sure no one was watching.

"What's going on?" Brennan asked. "Did I leave blood all over the seat?"

"Shush," she hissed. "The blood cleaned up surprisingly easy. But look what I found when I loaded our supplies." As she unlocked the trunk, white fog drifted out. It was refrigerated.

It must be running off its own power source, Brennan thought. The trunk contained rows of large, clear plastic cases. They hung from a motorized track, and a control pad apparently let the user move the rows back and forth, choosing which row sat in front. Brennan quickly guessed there were at least two dozen.

Most of them contained human heads.

A small yellow piece of paper was stuck to the middle of the front row. In bold black letters was written:

DO NOT
DITCH
THIS CAR

"Holy shit," he said.

Joan closed the trunk. "That's what I said. What do we do?"

Brennan leaned on the trunk, but then remembered what was in it and stood up awkwardly. "I don't know," he said.

Joan spoke quietly into his ear. "Are we going to drive around with a deathmobile full of heads?"

He turned to her, his face inches from hers, and said, "I don't think we have a choice. It's not like we can leave them in the motel room or toss them out the window as we drive. We could go out into the middle of nowhere and dig dozens of little head-sized graves, bury them all in a nice new hat, but what happens when this guy catches up with us? I think he's going to want his heads back."

Joan looked up at the stars. "Fine," she said. "But if we get pulled over, I'm some hitchhiker you picked up, and I have no idea about the horror show in the trunk."

"I'm pretty sure that getting pulled over," he said, "is what the stun-gun is for."

"Makes sense," she said. "Now come on. It's time to stitch you up."

Back in the motel room, with the door securely locked, Joan grabbed one of the shopping bags and started setting up on the motel desk. The first thing she pulled out was a plastic bottle of tequila.

Brennan nodded toward the bottle. "Is that for the pain?"

Joan grinned at him. "No. I need something to calm my nerves. But if you're nice, I'll share." She took a long draw from the bottle and handed it to him. He took a sip, coughed, and took another.

"Sorry, it's been a long time since I've done this, and I've never done it MASH-style." She cut a length of thin fishing line and washed it and a tiny needle with dish soap. "Can you grab me some paper towels, please? I think they're in that bag over there."

Brennan found the shrink-wrapped paper towels and handed them to her. "No, wash your hands and tear a few off. And I mean really wash those hands. Then line that ice bucket with the cling wrap and fill it with the distilled water."

He followed her instructions, and she rinsed the needle and fishing line in the water. She set the thread on a paper towel to dry. Pulling a plastic lighter out of the bag, she held the side of the flame to the needle, which she held with another paper towel.

"Great. Now fill this cup with the rubbing alcohol and drop the thread in there for about twenty seconds. Then wash your hands with the alcohol and get it out." She repeated the cleaning process on a pair of tweezers.

She lined up the sterilized instruments on a clean paper

towel, and set them on the small table beside the couch. "You may want to grab a sock."

"Why?"

"Because this is going to hurt like a bitch, and you're going to want something to bite down on. Get over here and lie on your stomach. Make sure the hole in your gut is facing me. And bring the tequila."

3

THE TWO OF THEM SAT SIDE-BY-SIDE on the couch in the drab motel room. The small plastic trashcan held their makeshift operating tools and bloody towels. The tequila bottle was nearly empty.

"Car wreck. Nobody's fault, really, just an accident," Joan said. "It was so weird to wake up the next day and realize my parents were both dead."

"I'm so sorry," Brennan said. "That must have been tough." His shirt was still off, but a clean bandage was wrapped around his lower torso.

"I held it together pretty good, I think. At least for a while. But then the mess with my roommates, and I lost my grip on everything. Med school is hell all by itself, you know? What little time I had to sleep, I saw them every time I closed my eyes. I drank some to feel sleepy, and then I drank to feel nothing. It wasn't long until all I had left was a pile of student loans I'll be paying off forever." Her eyes brightened. "Hey, at least people on the lam don't have to make loan payments."

"Way to find the silver lining," Brennan said.

Joan lifted the bottle to drink. Finding it empty, she let it slide from her fingers onto the floor. She gave it a kick with her foot, sending it rolling across the carpet. It hit the wall with a dull, empty thud.

"Enough about me. How about your parents?" she asked.

"My mom raised me. I never knew my dad," Brennan said. "She and I moved around all the time when I was little. I always wondered if maybe my mom was trying to keep my dad from finding us. She never told me anything about him. I didn't even know his name."

"Oh," Joan said sympathetically.

"Yeah. Then when I started high school, she had to leave me with my grandfather. At least Mom said he was my grandfather. I think he might have been my dad's dad, because of the last names, but I don't really know. She would call me on the phone sometimes, but after a while the calls stopped, all at once. She never came back and I never found out what happened to her. My granddad said she just disappeared."

"You poor dear," Joan said, and gave Brennan an awkward hug.

"It's okay. I'm sure everyone would say the same thing, but I know she would have come back if she could. She really was a great mom."

"What was her name?"

"Alice," Brennan said. He could not remember the last time he had said the name out loud.

"That's a pretty name. Was she pretty?" Joan asked.

Brennan grinned. "Of course she was. You about ready to get some sleep?"

"As good a time as any," Joan said. "Should we take turns? Like keep watch?"

"I think if they knew where we were, we wouldn't be having this conversation," he said. "And we both need the sleep. I think we can chance it."

"Sounds good to me," Joan said. He grabbed the extra blanket and a pillow, and she made her way over to the switch and flipped off the light.

Brennan's side ached with each jump of his pulse, but he felt drunk enough to make it tolerable. He tried not to notice Joan slide out of her jeans and under the covers.

Time passed in the dark. Exhausted and full of tequila, he listened to the steady hum of the air conditioner.

"Brennan?" Joan whispered.

"Yeah?"

"You don't have to sleep on the couch if you don't want to."

It had been a long time since he had shared a bed with someone. It wasn't that he did not want to—he could feel something stirring at the thought of it—but he had ruined her life. He was also the double of the man who had filled her nightmares for years.

We both must be pretty drunk, he thought.

"Brennan?" she asked again. "Don't worry. I'm not going to jump your bones. You just had an operation and you look like this serial killer I know."

I must be extremely drunk, he decided.

"I think it'd be better if I stayed on the couch," he said. "I have a good view of the door. In case anything happens."

"Oh, no, yeah," she said. "That makes sense. I thought it might be better for your stitches."

Brennan felt like an idiot. "The couch is actually great," he lied. "But thank you."

"Sure," she said. "Nighty night."

"Goodnight," he said, but he was too wired to even try to sleep.

Brennan lay there, listening to her heavy breathing, as he tried to decide what to do next. Those bastards had been waiting for him every step of the way. He could keep looking into the murders, but with Jennifer Cairns' files, they had access to anything he could dig up. *I already know who the killer is,* he thought. *It's my homicidal guardian angel.*

He shared a taste in music with his double. He hadn't told Joan, but a 1938 Plymouth Coupe was his dream car, and there was one sitting out in the parking lot with a trunk full of human heads.

Brennan realized he did not feel as drunk as he thought he should. He had lost blood and had not eaten anything for the better part of a day. With all the tequila he drank, he should be shitfaced, but he barely felt buzzed. He remembered what the soldier on the plane had said about the killer being able to hold his liquor.

Who was the other him? Where did he come from? The thoughts bounced around in his head, but there were no answers there. From what he had seen of the car, it belonged to someone who was an expert at not being found.

And at cutting off people's heads.

So what could I do? Stay here in the motel with Joan until someone shows up to kill us both? That was something else that had changed. They had wanted him alive before, but now they wanted him dead.

What I need is a way to take the fight to them. I have to pursue my pursuers. He was sure there would be nothing left where they had held him in New Mexico, and he was the only witness to what had happened in Kansas City. He doubted any headless bodies remained in the police station when the authorities arrived.

The heads belonging to those bodies were probably in the trunk, but he had no idea which ones. And what exactly could he do with them—just walk into the FBI field office with a garbage bag full of heads and ask if they can run dental records?

So all he had to show for his meetings with Jim and his goons was a gunshot wound and Jim's pocketknife, which he had found with his other belongings on the way out of the police station.

He pulled the knife out of his pocket and turned it in the soft light filtering in through the window. The metal was tarnished from years of use. He pulled out the blade and examined it. When he saw the words, he could barely believe it.

There, on one side, was engraved a name, '*Billy Stephenson.*' The engraving was worn almost smooth. Beneath the name, cut into the metal more recently: "'*1931–1977.*'"

Brennan smiled.

4

INSIDE THE CAR, it was cool and dark. Brennan realized with a frown that the trunk was also cool and dark, as were its occupants. He banished the thought from his head and fiddled with the radio. The rattling guitar of Skip James' "Hard Time Killin' Floor Blues" broke the silence.

"We could have waited," Joan said as she drove. "At least until you weren't so leaky."

Brennan shook his head. A week had passed, but he was still hurting. "You know that if we wait, they'll find us. They have a better idea where we're going to be than we do. The faster we move, the better chance we have. It has to be right now"

Joan smirked. "You know, you keep saying 'They' like a crazy person. '*They'll find us.*' '*They know our every move.*' You should check under the seat. Maybe our gracious serial killer host left you a tin foil hat."

"Wouldn't work with these guys. *They* are far too advanced for tin foil to block them out. *They* have lasers and psychics in special bathtubs."

Joan turned to him and raised an eyebrow. "Special bathtubs?"

"Full of mineral water and Diet Coke. Boosts their output. *They* did a study."

They laughed like old friends.

He settled into his seat and felt the cool night air rushing in through the vents. It didn't matter how dark the windows were tinted. He only felt safe out in the open when it was nighttime, when the world felt dark and underpopulated.

"Thanks," he said.

"Hmm? Thanks for what?"

He searched for the words. "Thanks for not making me go through this alone anymore."

She stared straight ahead. "It's not like I had a choice."

"You definitely had a choice. You could have left me in the street, driven to Mexico. Found someone who would give you an ID, a Mexican ID, and never looked back. Become a trucker or something."

"You don't know anything about Mexico, do you?"

"You had a choice. That's all I'm saying. You still have a choice. I slept like a rock last night. You could have slipped out the door, taken the car, and just run away."

"I am quite the runner. I did cross-country in high school, you know."

"Explains the legs," Brennan said, waggling his eyebrows as she laughed. He continued, "But you're avoiding the issue. You could leave, but you haven't."

Joan gripped the wheel, her shoulders tense. "Yeah, I guess. But it's like you said, they'd find me. And I'm ninety percent sure this isn't your fault. Plus you got shot for me."

"I did, didn't I?"

"Shut up. And that fucking twin of yours ruined my life. This looks to be a way to get some, I dunno, some closure. Or something."

"I hadn't thought about it that way."

"Yeah, well," she said, "I was stuck in a rut. Pharmaceutical sales rep? That's not what I want to do. I couldn't move forward. I'm not saying I'm glad this happened, but at least it feels like I'm doing something. I'm going somewhere." She flashed her lights as she muttered at a passing car driving with its brights. "Okay, go over it one more time."

"We've been over it a dozen times."

"One more time. Just do it. For me. It makes me feel better."

"Sure." Brennan pulled out the ratty manila folder they had put together. Photocopied pages jutted out of the edges, with paperclips clinging to every side. He flipped it open and shuffled the pages. He pulled a penlight out of his pocket and started reading.

"William Stephenson, born March 11, 1931, in Springfield, Missouri. Moved to Nazareth, Missouri, at the age of four and lived there until he died in 1977. His wife, Barbara, died in 1997. Had three sons: Trevor, Shane, and Douglas."

"Thank God for internet genealogy, eh?" Joan asked.

"No kidding. Trevor and Shane died in Vietnam; both of them were air force. Shane left behind a son and a wife. Douglas, the youngest, survived and received an honorable discharge from the army in 1973. Married Yvonne in 1974, has two daughters."

"Now get the pictures."

"Joan, we've been over this three dozen billion times."

"If we're going to invade this guy's life, I want to be totally sure it's him."

Brennan sighed and pulled out the grainy photocopies. The first picture showed a young man in an army uniform with several medals pinned to his shirt and a strained expression on his face. Underneath the picture was the caption, 'One of three brothers to return home.'

Joan asked, "You're sure it's him?"

Brennan tried to picture glasses on the haunted young man, but he could not be sure. He had penciled in frames on one copy already, and it did not help. Still, there was something about the man's posture and expression that were so familiar.

"Sure enough," he said.

"Let me see the other one again."

He pulled out an article from the previous year. It discussed a children's charity in Nazareth. Several men stood around a dunking booth at a county fair. The man seated in the dunking chair, identified as Douglas Stephenson, wiped water from his face. He was a broad man, wearing dark swim trunks and a t-shirt. Brennan held it up.

Joan gave it a quick glance. "It could be anybody," she said.

Brennan said, "It's him."

"Fine. I've never seen him, so I'll have to take your word for it. I want you to be absolutely sure before we do whatever we're going to do."

"There are no absolutes," he said. "Not anymore. But it's him. I'm more certain about that than I am about anything. It's him."

"And there's no way it's a trap?"

He shook his head. "No. He was knocked out when I took it. And it's got to be important to him, like really important. His dad probably gave it to him on his goddamn death bed. If he thought I had it, he would have made sure one of his goons grabbed it at the police department. But they never even touched my stuff. No, it's definitely him."

He reached into the backseat, and patted a small bundle in the floorboard. It had several blankets piled on top of it. There had been a three-day wait and no small amount of nail biting, but the fake ID had done its job.

"He'll never see me coming."

5

TWO NIGHTS LATER, Brennan crouched on the edge of Nazareth, hiding in the trees at the edge of a field. A neighborhood began just across the paved road.

He faced a row of attractive Victorian homes, including his target, a large white house. It stood three stories tall, with wide pillars on the front porch that reminded Brennan of a Greek temple. An enormous black Ford truck sat out front. In the yard, two trees held up a white hammock.

Nice hammock, Brennan thought. *He must nap in it on the weekends to unwind from all that torture during the week.*

Stars shone overhead, but it was dark down on the ground. A streetlight flickered a few blocks down, and only a few outdoor lights lit the outside of Jim's house. If Brennan started walking now, he could be at the back door in less than two minutes. He had been thinking about that door for half an hour, and he was sure that if he broke the glass quietly he could get right inside. Then it was only a matter of finding Jim—or rather finding Douglas Stephenson. Brennan would decide what do with him then.

He reached into his pocket and felt the comfort of cold metal. He centered himself and took a step out of the trees.

A hand fell on Brennan's shoulder, making him gasp.

"Idiot," said a voice from the dark.

Brennan reached for the gun in his pocket, but had barely made a move before he was on his face in the damp grass with his arm pulled high behind his back and the wind knocked out of him.

"Quiet," said the voice. "I'm here to help."

Brennan recognized the voice; it belonged to the other Brennan. *'The Other' is right,* Brennan thought. He had the same surreal feeling he got from hearing a recording of himself. "My doppelgänger," he said.

"Got it in one," the Other said, letting go of Brennan's arm. "Too bad you're not so clever when it comes to your reconnaissance."

Brennan stood up, wiping loose grass off his shirt. The killer stood there calmly, his clothes splattered with blood. "What are you talking about?" Brennan asked. "And what the hell happened to you?"

The Other pointed to a small bag hanging from a nearby tree. Brennan knew what was inside. "Who was it?"

"He kept an eye on your Douglas Stephenson. I found him in the house next door. I think he was there as much to keep tabs on the guy as to protect him."

Brennan felt a thick stone in his chest. "They know I'm coming."

"No, they don't. Not yet. Stephenson is high enough on the food chain to keep a few guys around. I could only find one, but there's no way he's alone. The others might be asleep somewhere. He wouldn't tell me, and I didn't have time to ask him properly."

"Shit," Brennan said under his breath.

The Other laughed. It was a quiet, empty sound. "I knew you'd panic over a little thing like this."

"A little thing?" Brennan asked, trying to whisper and not shout. "There was a guard. Now his head is over there. In a sack."

"Bowling bag."

"Bowling bag?" Brennan slowly slid the snub-nose revolver out of his pocket.

"They call it that because you usually put a bowling ball in it. I like the way those old bags look. Vinyl and piping. It was in his closet. I guess the guy was a king of the lanes."

"Shut up," Brennan said. He stepped back, and pointed the .357 at the man's chest.

The killer didn't move. He said calmly, "Whoa there, cowboy. Decide to leave the rifle at home?"

"I said shut up. You're the guy these assholes are after, right?"

The Other shrugged. "I'm the guy they think they're after."

Brennan's tried to steady his hand. "So why don't I march you in there and hand you over? Everybody wins."

"Everybody?"

"Almost everybody," Brennan said.

"Let's consider it. You take me, the guy who has been there for you every step of the way—"

"Killing innocent people."

"No one is innocent. And most are nowhere close." The Other cleared his throat. "You hand me over to Doug Stephenson, and you think he just lets you go?"

"Why wouldn't he?"

"He never lets anyone go, Brennan. And what about Joan? Does he suddenly lose his reason to want her dead?"

Brennan clenched his teeth. "No. I think Jim wanted her dead now because she saw you seven years ago. And now—damn it."

"And now, what?"

"She knows about him. She knows who he is. He'll never let her walk away with that."

"Exactly." The Other put his hand on top of Brennan's gun, pushing it toward the ground.

"Damn it," Brennan said again. His shoulders fell and he put the gun in his pocket. He looked the other man in the eye and asked, "Who are you?"

The man grinned, but not with his eyes. "Who do you think I am?"

"I think you're the devil."

The man laughed.

That laugh sounds like a soda can full of teeth, Brennan thought.

"No," the man said. "I'm the personification of your evil half, the embodiment of your darkest desires."

"What?" Brennan asked, shaking his head.

"No, you're supposed to say, 'Really?' Then I say—"

"Tell me who. You. Are."

"Fine, fine. My name is Thomas."

"Thomas who?"

"Just Thomas," he said.

"But who are you?" Brennan asked. "Who are you really?"

"You mean you haven't figured it out? Two identical men. The same DNA." Thomas looked him in the eye. "You and me. We're clones."

"What?" Brennan scoffed. "That. That is the stupidest thing I have ever heard. Why the hell would anyone clone me?"

Thomas laughed again. "That's adorable. Really."

"Damn it," Brennan said. "What—"

"Shh," said Thomas, holding up his right hand. "It's about time to run."

"Run? But—"

Thomas, still holding up his hand, shook his head and checked the watch on his other wrist. "And," he said, counting each seconds with a nod of his head, "Now."

All the lights in the neighborhood went dark.

6

BRENNAN AND THOMAS RAN IN THE DARKNESS.

"Soft feet," Thomas hissed, a living shadow. "Like a ninja." Brennan shifted his weight to the balls of his feet, and his footfalls became quieter.

"Better hurry, Brennan," whispered Thomas. "The lights come back on in thirty seconds."

"What?" Brennan asked, but Thomas had left him behind.

I was so close to the house, Brennan thought. *How did it get so far away?* His heart beat so hard and so fast, he felt sure it would explode out of his chest. His lungs burned as he gasped for breath.

Finally, he saw Thomas ahead of him, standing on the back porch. He watched as Thomas picked up a stone and sent it flying at the porch light, shattering it. Brennan dodged the falling glass, and the rest of the neighborhood lit up again. He heard a woman down the street say, "That one wasn't long at all."

Brennan put his hands on his knees and tried not to throw up. Thomas patted him on the back and whispered, "You should work out more. That was pathetic."

"Why'd you. Break the light?" Brennan wheezed. "Why not. Leave the lights off?"

"Oh, no. If the lights stay off, everyone knows something is up. A quick off and on? That could be anything. As for this one," Thomas said, pointing up at the shattered porch light, "No one will notice one light failed to come back on. No one is that smart."

Brennan fought to get his breathing under control. "If you're so much smarter, how are we getting in without someone seeing us?"

Thomas snapped his fingers, and a jagged key appeared between his clenched thumb and forefinger. "A head wasn't the only thing I took from the guard," he said, sliding the key into the lock. Thomas turned the knob, making a soft click, and they entered the house.

They stood in a kitchen. The counters were spotless and the sinks gleamed. The bland sounds of a television drifted in from another room.

"What do we do?" Brennan whispered.

"*We* don't do anything. *You* are going to go in there and deal with Jim. I have other business," Thomas said. He was out of the kitchen and halfway up a set of stairs before Brennan could question him. Brennan crept toward the television room.

The light from the old television flashed in the dark room like a tiny lightning storm. Brennan leaned his back against the wall beside the doorway. He gripped the gun tightly against his chest, the hammer digging into his skin. He took a deep breath and entered the room.

Doug Stephenson sat in a large chair holding a beer. He wore a bathrobe over a white undershirt and old boxer shorts. A bandage poked out of the neck of his shirt, covering the spot Brennan had stabbed him in the desert. He had not shaved in a while, and he had bags under his eyes. Taking a bite of his sandwich, he chewed it without visible pleasure or interest.

Stephenson looked up, and his face constricted in shock. The bite of sandwich fell out of his mouth and into his lap. He opened his mouth to yell when Brennan leveled the gun at him.

"Shut up, Jim." Brennan heard his own voice shake.

"How?" Stephenson said loudly, but Brennan motioned with the gun. Quietly, he continued, "How did you find me?"

Brennan held up the pocket knife.

A look of anger overwrote Stephenson's shock. "Son of a bitch. I should have seen it coming," he said. "Been looking for that little fucker everywhere."

Brennan shrugged. "Nobody's perfect, Jim."

"I want my knife back."

"It's too bad you're not the one with the bargaining power here."

Stephenson sighed. "What do you want, Mr. Wade?"

"What do you think I want?"

"If it were me, I'd want answers," Stephenson said.

"Look at you, with all your perspective. I want to know who sent you after me."

"Afraid I can't help you there."

Brennan cocked the gun.

Stephenson rolled his eyes. "Fine. But it won't help you. They contact me through a middle man, a different person every time. I built my team with the finances they provided. It was my job to be on call when you turned up."

"Who are they? I need a name."

"Don't got one. You don't need a name when you're the only one of something. I've heard them referred to as the Lodge, but I don't know if that's on their stationary. Curiosity, cat."

"Tell me what you do know about them."

"Are you kidding me?" Stephenson asked, examining Brennan's face. "No, you're not, are you? You're serious." He laughed. "I'll be goddamned."

"I don't think you're taking this seriously," Brennan said. "You tore my life apart. I need to know why."

"I tore *your* life apart? Son, I've seen the *people* you've torn apart."

"That wasn't me. I've never murdered anyone." He looked down at the gun, and then at Stephenson. "At least not yet."

Stephenson gripped the arms of his chair. "Fine. If that's the game you want to play, sure. I'll play. You want to know who they are, why they hired me and my boys? They're trying to stop you, you freak. They're the good guys. I'm a good guy."

Brennan wiped the sweat off of his forehead. "No. That's a lie. I saw what your men did to that police station."

Stephenson waved his hand. "Eggs. Omelet. Besides, I saw what you did to my men."

"I didn't—"

"Really? What about the men we sent after Joan Runciter?"

"Okay. That was me. But they were going to kill us."

"So you killed them first?"

Brennan shook his head. "I had to protect Joan."

"We were there to protect Joan. Protect her from *you*."

"You were there to kill her."

Stephenson smiled, but his eyes were grim. "You say tomato."

Brennan walked toward him. "You're wrong about everything. The blood you matched with mine, it didn't come from me." He was now holding the gun close to Stephenson's face. "I'm just a normal guy."

"A normal guy?" Stephenson grunted. "We both know that isn't true. I was in the desert, remember? You fought me like a man possessed. Took out my guards. I saw the aftermath of the apartment raid and the police station. I watched them rerun the test myself. There's no way that isn't your blood."

Something moved out of the shadows. "Well, now, I wouldn't say that," Thomas said.

Stephenson's eyes widened as he looked back and forth between the two men. "Impossible," he said.

"Found some rope," Thomas said, holding up a bundle of nylon cord. Nodding toward Stephenson, he said, "You know you have to kill him."

Brennan shook his head. "Not like this, I don't. I'm not like you. I still haven't killed anyone. Not in cold blood."

"Interesting clarification," Stephenson said. "Ever consider politics?"

"Shut up," Brennan said, waving the gun at Stephenson.

"If you kill him, they'll stop coming after you." Thomas said, moving behind Stephenson. "They'll stop coming after Joan." In a few quick motions, he tied Stephenson tight to the chair. He walked back around and stood beside Brennan.

"He's lying," Stephenson said. "Whoever hired us will keep coming. If you kill me, they'll be after you in force. There's no way out of it."

Thomas pulled what looked to be a fine silver thread out of his pocket. On each end was a shining metal ring. "Know what this is?" he asked Stephenson.

Stephenson glared at him. "Of course I know," he said and glanced at Brennan. "But why don't you fill in poor Mr. Wade? He looks lost."

Thomas whirled the metal ring around and around on his index finger, turning the string and other ring into a vertical translucent circle. "This is a garrote, Brennan. It's an old, old tool, and it does the job it was designed to do quite well." He stopped the motion suddenly by catching the second ring on his other index finger.

"You can make one out of anything," he said, pulling the garrote tight. It made a soft ping noise as it reached its limit. "String, wire, plastic. Piano wire is popular. I made mine out of a special industrial microfilament. You usually use a garrote to choke someone to death, but this one makes a nice, clean cut."

In his mind, Brennan saw the sudden decapitation in the police station.

Thomas returned to his place behind Stephenson. He crossed his hands over the hostage's head, and the microfilament dig into Stephenson's neck. "You claim to know things," Thomas said. "Do you know what happens to the heads?"

"Maybe," Stephenson said.

Thomas pulled the garrote tight, until it cut into Stephenson's neck. A red, beaded necklace formed on his skin.

"Yes, I know!" Stephenson said. Thomas let the line go loose, but did not remove it from around Stephenson's neck.

"Then here's the deal. You tell us who's aware of Brennan Wade and Joan Runciter, and nothing happens to your head afterward. Or the head of your wife."

Stephenson shook. "No."

"Yes," said Thomas. "I know she was just as dirty as you are. When Brennan was dancing with you down here, I went upstairs. She never even woke up. Her head's in a trash bag in the kitchen sink. Ice from the freezer is keeping it fresh."

"Oh, God," Brennan said.

"No!" Stephenson screamed, but Thomas pulled the garrote tight enough to quiet him. Stephenson squirmed. Tears welled up in his eyes.

"Tell us the truth," Thomas said. "Who else knows about Brennan and Joan?"

"I don't know. Everyone under me who knew anything was wiped out in the police station or in Runciter's apartment building. But I report everything through dead drops. I don't even know how to contact them anymore. Once I located Wade, my orders were to subdue, interrogate, and turn him over. I failed at all three. I haven't heard from the Lodge since."

Thomas smiled. "You should have made yourself sound more useful." He looked over at Brennan. "Get over here and hold this."

Brennan shook his head.

"Do it, or I let go and he calls for the cavalry." He pulled the line tighter on Stephenson, who nodded reluctantly.

Stephenson stared at him coldly "Now do it already."

"Come on, Brennan," Thomas said.

"What are you guys, on the same team now?" Brennan asked. "I should shoot you both and be done with it," He turned the gun on Thomas.

"C'mon," Thomas said. "Is that really such a good idea? Don't you think a gunshot would bring his buddies running? Take the fucking rings."

Brennan walked to him slowly. Thomas held out his hand for the gun, but Brennan only glared at him. Thomas shrugged, and handed him the rings, careful not to loosen the grip on

Stephenson. Brennan continued to grip the pistol in his right hand while he took the hold of the garrote.

"You have to kill him," Thomas said. "It's the only way to get them off your back."

"He's right," Stephenson said, tears streaming down his cheeks. "You already killed my wife. Just do it. Put me out of my misery."

"Make it a smooth, quick motion," Thomas said. "And be sure to point the body way from you. Helps avoid the splash back."

"You people are all insane," Brennan said, his hands shaking. "Completely insane."

Through gritted teeth, Stephenson said, "Do it. Just like you did to that girl, Elsie. Do it, you bast—"

And his head fell into his lap.

"Oh, my God," Brennan said. "Oh, God." He watched blood squirt up from the stump of Jim's neck, and then he went to his knees, the room spinning around him.

I had to do it, he thought. *I had to do it. He wanted it, he said so. He deserved it.* Brennan felt something snap into place, and the room stopped spinning and his stomach stopped churning. Everything felt clear, like a photograph taken at high speed, every detail leaping out.

With his increased clarity, he saw the tiny ridge in the carpet, running from the wall to Stephenson's bloody chair. Brennan scrambled to Stephenson, and grabbed the dead man's right hand. It was empty. He pried open the fingers of the stiff left hand.

In it was a small white cylinder with a button on the end. The button blinked red.

"Thomas!" Brennan called out, but Thomas was gone, along with Stephenson's head.

Brennan was not surprised. He was not even angry that Thomas abandoned him. At that moment it felt like doors were unlocking and flying open in his mind, all the way down an infinite corridor.

He felt alive.

An armed man kicked in the front door, and a red calm drifted over Brennan's mind. Without hesitation, he pointed his gun and fired three times into the guard. The man staggered backward, his rifle swinging from its strap at his side. Brennan was already there, and he could see the sweat and panic on the injured man's face. Brennan grabbed onto the rifle with both hands and planted his foot into the guard's chest, sending him sprawling as another man entered the house. The metal clips of the gun's strap made a sharp noise as they broke loose, leaving Brennan holding the rifle as the first guard collided with the new arrival. Their momentum carried them into the door. They were a monstrous conglomeration of flailing arms, legs, and terrified eyes. Brennan lifted the rifle and fired into the writhing mass, fusing it together even as he destroyed it. He dropped the smoking rifle and was gone.

7

"BRENNAN?" JOAN ASKED as he unlocked the door to the motel. He didn't bother answering; he went to her, wrapping his arms around her waist and pulling her against him. Her mouth and body welcomed his, and their loneliness melted away as they melted into each other.

It had been a long time for both of them. As he slid into her, he fell back into that red haze, and he let it erase the doubt and fear.

Afterward, they lay together gasping for breath, sheets and pillows scattered around the floor.

"I'm going to grab a shower," she said. "If you want to sleep in the bed tonight, you'd better join me."

"I know," he said. "Just give me a minute."

She stood. Moonlight glowed on the gentle curves of her body. "Fine," she said, "but don't be too long or I'll start things up again without you."

"I'll be right there," he said, and listened to the falling water when she turned it on. He found his pants on the floor and pulled a note out of the front pocket. In the same pocket jingled the rings of the microfilament garrote.

The note, written by a hand that was starting to look familiar, had been waiting for Brennan on the windshield of the

Plymouth. It read, *'If you want this to be over, you have one more stop. We have to kill the monster responsible for everything. Meet me alone. Bring the car.'* The final word was underlined with what looked like blood. Brennan guessed the blood must belong to Stephenson, his wife, or the guard with the key. Underneath those words were a set of GPS coordinates.

Joan leaned out of the shower curtain and called, "Are you coming?"

"Not before you do," Brennan said, and Joan laughed. He carefully folded the note and returned it to his pocket.

8

MIST DRIFTED around the Plymouth. Brennan had not heard a sound from the outside world since he parked off the main road. He rubbed his hands together, afraid to turn on the heater for fear of how it might affect his friends in the trunk.

He hoped Joan was still asleep back at the motel. He knew she would not have let him go off on his own again, so he left her a note stuck in a corner of the bathroom mirror:

Joan,

You probably hate me for leaving you alone. I don't blame you for that. But it's the only way.

Thomas told me one more place I have to go. To end it. There's someone at the heart of everything, and until he's gone, we'll never be safe. You'll never be safe. And that's the most important thing in the world right now.

If I make it back, and if you want me around, I'll never leave you again. My world went crazy, but you've been there for me. I don't know why, but you believe in me. And that gives me hope there's something after this mess.

Be Safe,
Brennan

P.S. You know where to go next. If someone comes back to you, no matter who they look like, the password is 'Fish Pills.' Don't let anyone in without it. If I'm not back in 48 hours, get as far away as you can and never look back.

There was no date or time on the note Thomas had left in the windshield. Brennan hoped that if he made it to the coordinates in rural Kansas, it would be obvious what he should do next. He had been sitting here for close to an hour, and the night was only getting colder. He turned on the GPS; it still said he was at the right place. He clicked it back off.

A hand slapped the window by Brennan's face. He jumped, and saw his own face staring in at him. Motioning with his hand, Thomas said, "Move over. I'm driving."

Brennan unlocked the door and slid down the bench seat. "You didn't have to scare the shit out of me," he said as his double climbed into the car and closed the door.

"Yeah, I did," Thomas said. "It's what a boogie man does." He pushed the lighter into the dashboard and pulled out a cigarette. "Need a smoke?"

Brennan shook his head. Blue menthol smoke filled the car as they drove in silence. Holding back a cough, he finally asked, "What are we doing here?"

"We are going to get you out of this mess. But there's only one way to do that. You have to kill the Old Man."

"Who is the old man and why don't *you* kill him?" Brennan asked. "I'd say you're more qualified."

"I can't." The cherry of his cigarette bounced and danced in the dark.

"Why not?"

Thomas glared at him and said, "He'll have someone keeping an eye on me. You have to trust me. If I could kill him, he'd be dead by now."

"Okay, fine," Brennan said. "Who's the old man?"

"He's us."

"What?"

Thomas threw up his hands. "He's what we came from. We're him."

"Oh shit," Brennan said, shaking his head. "You were serious about the clone thing. I thought you were screwing with me."

"I'm not screwing with you, Brennan. He's the thing we have in common. He thought you were thrown out with the bath water, but by now he has to know you're running around. You haven't exactly been low-key."

Brennan pictured the terrified face of the old woman in Joan's apartment, and the piles of dead cops in Kansas City. "That was all a bit out of my control," he said.

"Doesn't matter. The Old Man hates loose ends, and he won't stop until he ties you up. Cuts you off? I don't know. Hacks you up?"

"I get it," Brennan said. "So who is he? What's his name?"

"Doesn't really have one. It's like Stephenson said, you don't need a name when you're the only one."

"'The only one?'" Brennan asked. "You're talking about him like he isn't human."

Thomas was silent.

"What the hell does that mean?" Brennan asked. "Okay, fine. So what does that make us?"

"We don't have time for this. I've been called back. We have to get to the farm—"

"The farm?"

"Yes, the fucking farm. I'll drop you off on the way in. You've shown me you have what it takes to do what has to be done. We'd better hope I'm right. You bring my wire?"

Brennan patted his pocket. "Yeah."

"Good. The Old Man will be in the barn. You're still in his blind spot. He won't feel you coming. Sneak up behind the bastard and take his head off."

"I have the gun." Brennan said. "Why don't I use the gun?"

"A gun won't work. If it did, someone would have solved this problem a long time ago. You'd be lucky to get one shot, and if you don't kill him right off, you're done. What happens if you miss with the first shot? Just graze him? He'll take you apart."

Brennan rubbed his face. He said through his hands, "Fine. I'll use the wire. What does he look like?"

"Like you, but older. Much older. Seeing as he is the Old Man and you are a clone of the Old Man." He shook his head. "You worry me, Brennan."

"Thanks for the vote of confidence, Mr. Serial Killer," Brennan said. He clenched his fists against his thighs. "I don't even know why I'm listening to you. I don't even know why I'm here."

"You're here because I helped you. You'd be buried in the desert of New Mexico without me, and that's if you were lucky. I don't know what Stephenson's people wanted to do with you, but I can guess." He smirked. "Hell, I know I never pass up a good live vivisection. Not if I can help it."

"Oh, God," Brennan said.

Thomas spent the rest of the drive describing the layout of the farm. It was fairly simple. There were hundreds of acres of empty fields surrounded with barb wire. An old house sat near the center—"Don't go near that house, no matter what," Thomas said—with a large barn next to it.

"You'll see lights in the house. Ignore them. And don't use the small door on the side of the barn, because you'd end up looking the Old Man right in the face. There's a huge door, like for a tractor. It doesn't really close, so you can squeeze through without making any noise."

"Isn't there any security? Alarms? Cameras or something?"

"On an old farm in the middle of nowhere? Sometimes being boring is all the security you need. Here's the gate. Stay down and shut up."

Thomas got out and walked to the gate. Brennan took off his seatbelt and slid into the floorboard. Something crunched under his hand.

He picked up a candy wrapper, a Three Musketeers. It was Joan's. He crushed it in his fist, and something caught in his throat.

I'll never see her again, he thought.

Thomas leaned over the back seat and removed the bulb from the dome light before driving through the gate. Brennan continued to think of Joan while Thomas got back out of the car to close the gate and then drove down the dirt road.

Brennan was sweating hard despite the cold, and it felt like years were passing along with the miles. His leg was cramping from cramming himself into the floorboard when Thomas asked, "Ready to jump?"

"What are you talking about? You're going like fifty. Stop the car."

"No can do. How would it look if he's watching? He's expecting me, not us, and I have a delivery to make. No light will come on in the car, and I'm kicking up enough dust no one will see you. He's probably not even watching."

"Stop the fucking car, Thomas."

"Sorry. Tuck your head. Try to avoid the tires." He looked back at Brennan and said, "Good luck."

When Brennan heard that, he thought, *He means it. He really just wished me luck.* Brennan reached up, opened the door, and rolled out.

Brennan tumbled like a cat in a clothes dryer. The earth slapped him on every side, stabbing him with rocks and dirt. His long sleeves saved him some lost skin, and he managed to keep his face covered. When he finally stopped rolling, he was surprised to find himself not only in one piece, but with no broken bones. He felt like he had gone ten rounds with the champ, but he was alive and able to stand.

He could still see the Plymouth's tail lights, and farther up the road was the house and barn. His back complained as he bent down low, but he ignored it as he made his way through the tangled brush to the black barn.

The house was two stories tall with peeling, colorless paint and an orange light in the windows. It looked like it might collapse at any moment. Cars, a truck, and two motorcycles surrounded it. There had to be a dozen old cars; none of them looked newer than 1950. He only recognized Thomas' Plymouth. *The Old Man must be a collector*, he thought. As he walked past the house, his teeth hurt, like he was chewing on tin foil. He fought the urge to peek in a window.

When he approached the barn, he saw it was not truly black. The chipped and peeling red paint had grown dark with age. The windows were boarded over, as were the jagged holes where parts of the wall had fallen away.

Skin grafts over old wounds, he thought.

Brennan saw the barn's side door and gave it a wide berth. After making his way around to the large doors, he hid in the shadows and waited. There was no movement, no sign of life.

He forced himself to walk to the gap in the doors, careful not to make a sound.

As he neared the opening, the smell hit him.

When Brennan was fourteen, an old dog crawled under his grandfather's house and died there. There was no way his grandfather could have crawled under the house, so the task fell to Brennan.

He crawled under the house, flashlight in hand, through the cobwebs and rat shit. He was scared, but he owed it to Grandpa to do the job. The dog was curled in a corner, twisted and rotten.

The smell coming from the barn was the same bitter smell that had been under that old house, only so much worse, like an open air cemetery. His stomach turned, and his throat threatened to gag.

A work light blinded him as he entered. Crouching in the shadows behind a shelf, he shielded his eyes as they took a moment to adjust. What he saw made the blood freeze in his veins.

Countless metal chains hung from the rafters of the barn. They were black and red with rust, creaking as they swayed. On the end of each chain was a hook, and impaled on each hook was a human head. Skin still covered some of them, and he saw something squirming in some of their eyes. Many of them were only jawless skulls.

They all stared at Brennan, an ocean of tortured faces. The ones that still had muscles clenched their teeth, most of those with empty eyes wide in terror. Those that were further along had their mouths hanging open in silent screams. The skulls that had been picked clean just watched.

A crow flapped its wings, sending a chunk of red meat to the dirt floor. As several of the black birds them flew to the ground, Brennan realized the rafters were full of them. They fought over the piece of meat, tearing it to shreds as they snapped at each other.

The commotion shook Brennan out of his stupor. He blinked his eyes hard and looked across the barn. There, at the far end, sat a man hunched over a desk.

Brennan crept across the floor of the barn, trying to avoid the teeth and jawbones littering the dirt. He walked around the crows, which paid him no attention.

He held his breath as he walked up behind the gray-haired

old man. On the desk was one of the heads from Thomas' trunk, a young woman with brown hair. The old man wore tight gloves of black leather. Brennan watched as the man lifted two long metal rods, each with a tiny sharp hook at the end. The old man used one of the rods to hold open the woman's nostril as he deftly pushed the other deep into her. There was an audible snap and he pulled. He dug and tore, and soon pulled a pale, bloody mess from her nostril.

Something buzzed in the back of Brennan's mind, making it hard to think as he fumbled with his pants pockets. The garrote was gone. One hand went to his chest and felt the rings in his breast pocket, right where he had left them. He pulled the rings out, careful not to let them clink against each other. Slipping one on each of his index fingers, he crossed his arms as he had seen Thomas do, letting the thin wire dangle in a loop.

The buzzing in his head grew stronger. It felt like his head was full of angry wasps, stinging and stabbing his brain. He reached over the old man.

"Hello."

The voice came from behind him. He spun as the old man rose and kicked the chair aside.

A crowd of men walked toward him, crunching bones underfoot. The crows rose into the air, the beating of their wings suddenly deafening. As the men approached, Brennan found himself looking into a shattered mirror, his own face staring back at him from a dozen directions.

The hair of each was different in style, length, and sometimes in color. One man had a shaved head, and another a large scar across his face. Another had a goatee like the one Brennan had worn a few times when he was younger.

"Look who's come home," said the Old Man.

9

THEY STOOD ALL AROUND BRENNAN arguing what to do with him. It sounded like the inside of Brennan's head, the same voice echoing in conflict with itself.

"Shut up," the Old Man said, and the room was silent. Even the birds stopped cawing in the rafters.

Brennan felt dizzy as he looked into the face of the Old Man. He could see his own eyes staring back at him from behind a wrinkled brow and crow's feet. The Old Man did not look nearly as old as Brennan had expected—he was maybe in his seventies. His hair flashed gray and his grinning teeth were yellow.

"It's Mr. Wade, isn't it?" the Old Man asked. His voice was familiar, but worn with age.

Brennan stared at him. From behind, a fist jabbed at his kidney. The blow sent him to his knees as he heard his own voice say, "Answer him."

"That's right. My name is Brennan Wade," he said.

The Old Man loomed over him. "How did you find my little flesh farm?"

Brennan looked at the faces surrounding him. One of them, Thomas, looked at him with true fear hidden behind his eyes.

Brennan frowned and looked at the floor. "Stephenson told me about it when I tracked him down. He didn't know what was here."

The men murmured. The Old Man glared at them. "You smelled like one of my boys," he said. "That's the only reason you got so close. Why do you smell like one of my boys, Mr. Wade?"

The menthol smoke in the car, Brennan thought. He shook his head.

Someone kicked him in the ribs, knocking him back to the ground.

"I was at the gate when one of these guys showed up," Brennan said, gasping. "I saw him get out, open the gate. I hid in the back seat."

The Old Man pointed at Thomas and said, "You fucked up."

"I'm sorry," Thomas said. He showed his fear, but Brennan could see his shoulders lowering in relief.

"Sorry doesn't cover it, Thomas. Let this be a lesson to all of you boys. What's rule number two?"

"Don't get caught," they all said in unison.

"That's right," the Old Man said. He pointed at Thomas again. "This piece of shit showed how easy it is. Next one who fucks up that bad loses a finger. Got me?" The mob nodded.

"As for you," the Old Man said, looking back down to Brennan, "you're supposed to be dead, you little shit. How many of my boys are there supposed to be?"

Brennan looked up at him, shaking his head in confusion.

"Count them," the Old Man said. "How many?"

Brennan looked around at the faces.

The Old Man clapped his hands sharply, inches away from Brennan's face. It sounded like a gunshot. "Well?"

"Twelve. There're twelve of them."

"That's right, Wade. Twelve. I've got my twelve boys, my chosen few, my band of merry men. And I don't need no unlucky thirteen. You got me?"

Brennan stared at him, trying to force an answer out of his mouth.

The Old Man kneed him in the teeth. The movement was so quick and unexpected that it caught Brennan completely off guard. His head snapped back, and he fell into the men behind him. They shoved him back down. The Old Man bent over him, gripping his throbbing jaw in his rough, gloved hand. Brennan felt something squirming under the leather.

Brennan was still reeling from the kick as the Old Man grabbed him by the collar of his shirt and dragged him along the dirt floor. The Old Man pulled Brennan's weight effortlessly.

"The first few batches of you little abortions, I killed myself. But killing yourself over and over? That's nothing but masturbation. And let me ask you, boy, what's the point of masturbation when I can fuck up anyone I want?"

He dropped Brennan beside a large wooden trapdoor. "But everyone knows how good it feels to cut yourself. Snaps everything right into focus. Self-mutilation. That's how people talk to gods. So I thought I'd do the same with the little pieces of me that weren't up to snuff." He pulled open the trapdoor, and strange noises bounced and leapt out of the dark.

"Say hello for me," the Old Man said, and he kicked Brennan into the pit.

10

JOAN SAT ON THE MOTEL BED, knowing it would be useless to try and sleep. It had been three days since Brennan left, and she had gone on to the new meeting place as planned. She read the note for the thousandth time, knowing the words by heart that told her to leave and never look back.

But where was she supposed to go? Brennan was out there, probably dead, and whatever killed him was coming after her. Where could she hide?

Something fell against the door, making her jump. Joan listened as the person knocked on the door, so quietly she could barely hear it. She reached under the bed and grabbed the assault rifle.

She fought the urge to run. There was no other way out. She tried to slow her breathing as she opened the chained door and peaked out through the gap.

"Please," a familiar voice said. He sat with his back against the door. There was blood on his face.

"You have to—the password. You have to tell me the password," she said.

The man looked confused, and in that moment Joan lost all hope. But then he said, "Pills. Fish pills. For Christ's sake, Joan, let me in."

"Brennan," she said, ripping the chain away and opening the door.

She helped him up. His shirt was in tatters, and deep scratches covered his back and chest. His eyes were full of tears. "Joan," he said. "Joan, you waited. You weren't supposed to wait."

"There was nowhere I wanted to go."

His tears were falling freely now, and his face was distorted with bruises and anguish. "We have to leave," he said. "We have to go right now."

11

JAKE HATED WORKING AT THE GAS STATION. Everyone was such a pain in the ass. But college had not worked, and like his dad said, "You don't work, you don't eat." So he worked the register at the only all-night gas station in town.

He was trying to choose between the most recent issues of Hustler and Penthouse when an old car pulled up to the pump. It was a classy ride with a touch of chrome. The man climbed out of the passenger seat wearing a shitty old jacket, but hey, it was three in the morning, what could you expect?

The driver was a woman. Not the best one of the day—he always kept track—but not bad, either. He watched as the two of them had some kind of debate, apparently about who would go inside and pay. It looked like the man won.

Good for him, Jake thought. If Jake ever won an argument with a woman, he would probably die from the shock.

The man in the shitty jacket walked into the convenience store, and Jake thought, *He ain't looking too good.* It looked like the guy had been in a fight that night, a bad one, and had not done so well.

The man handed Jake a twenty. "For the pump," he said. Jake nodded and rang it up, and the man waved to the woman. She started pumping the gas.

The man grabbed a few bottles of water and some snacks. He piled it on the counter.

"Nice car," Jake said.

"Thanks."

"You look like shit."

"Thanks," the man said. Jake started scanning the items when the man asked, "Gimme a pack of Camel Frost?"

Jake watched the man walk back to the car. He kissed the woman, who was looking better and better to Jake. The judges held a recount and decided she was the best looking of the day after all.

"Lucky bastard," Jake said as he watched them drive away.

PHASE III

1

JOAN CARRIED HER LUGGAGE into her old apartment. Everything was exactly as she remembered. Audrey's Eiffel Tower poster still hung on the wall. Cartoons still played on the enormous television Donna's rich dad had bought for all of them to share.

She felt her muscles tightening, her body wanting to run away. She looked around, but the man was not on the couch, and his trash bag was gone. The only thing left of him was the smell of his cigarette burning in the ashtray.

Part of her hoped it would be different this time. She had dreamed of this place so many times. The details varied—sometimes the apartment was empty and the bodies were gone, sometimes they were walking around headless in the living room—but usually they were in the bathroom, dead and waiting for her. She had trouble remembering their faces, but she could remember everything else.

She dropped her bags and set down the bagels and coffee she had brought for their breakfast on the bar. Cinnamon raisin for Audrey, plain for Donna, sun-dried tomato for herself. The smell of the bagels mingled with the coffee, but she knew they would never be eaten. The coffee would go cold, and the bagels would go stale waiting for someone to throw them out.

She looked again, and on the couch sat a dark-haired man in a tuxedo, his bowtie untied and hanging loose. He was not a threat, and he watched her walk by with compassion in his eyes.

The bathroom door stood open, just a crack, and inside it was silent. It was always so silent. But she had to look—every time she had to see it—so she reached out and pushed the door.

It swung in, and she forced herself to look.

The bathroom was empty. The girls had even cleaned it, making sure it was ready for when she got home.

Sighing in relief, she realized everything would be different now. Her friends were alive. She could finish medical school, become a doctor. She could help people. The drinking would never start.

She had to tell the girls about Brennan. They were always trying to fix her up with someone. It would be hard to explain, sure, but they would be excited for her, happy she had found somebody she cared about.

The thoughts of her a life rushed through her head as she grabbed her bags and went to unpack. She opened the door to her bedroom with her free hand, and bumped it open with her shoulder.

There, lying on her old bed, was Brennan. Something had cut through him, and everything was spilling out onto the bed in a bloody, ropey mess.

"Oh my God, oh my God," she said, kneeling beside him. Crying, she took his cold face in her hands.

Brennan's eyes opened. "Joan?"

Joan woke up, startled.

"Joan?" Brennan asked again. "You okay?" Water was running in the motel bathroom, and shaving cream dripped off his face and down his neck. A red dot formed on his cheek where he had nicked himself.

"I'm fine," she said. "Fine. Bad dream."

"I'm sorry," he said, sitting on the end of the bed. "It sounded like a doozy." He wrapped his fingers around hers.

"It's okay," she said, taking back her hand. "It's nothing. Really. Finish getting ready."

"Alright," he said, disappearing into the bathroom. He called back, "You might want to get up. We need to get back on the road if we want to get to that address you found before dark."

"Can do," Joan said, but she sat in the bed for a moment longer. There was something from the dream she wanted to remember, something she needed to know, but it was gone.

Must not be important, she thought.

2

AFTER EIGHT HOURS IN THE CAR, Joan and Brennan arrived in Flatland, Texas.

"Aptly named," Joan said as she stared at the miles of empty plains surrounding them.

"You should see the sunsets," Brennan said.

"How old were you when you lived here?"

"About fourteen to eighteen, when I was in high school. I lived here with my grandpa after my mom died." He rubbed his neck. "Or with the guy I *thought* was my grandfather. After the lady died who I *thought* was my mom."

He pulled the Plymouth into a self-storage facility, Stork Storage, on the edge of town. Dozens of storage units were lined up in rows, all surrounded by a chain-link fence.

"What did the notebook say about this place?" Brennan asked.

"Nothing. Just the name of the place, the address, and the unit number."

"Lucky you found it."

"I hope so. There's no telling what a guy like Thomas wants to hold on to," Joan said. "I can't believe eleven more of him are out there running around."

"That's not totally fair," Brennan said. "I think he proved something by helping me escape."

"I don't know," Joan said. "It'll take more than one good deed to make up for everything he's done."

"Doesn't matter," Brennan said. "He's probably dead. Wait here for me." He put on his sunglasses and climbed out of the car. Joan watched as he asked the facility manager to open the gate.

Joan had patched up Brennan's injuries as best she could. *He must still be pretty sore,* she thought. When she wrapped bandages on his new injuries, she had checked out his old one.

"Looks like you're healing up nicely," she had said, tracing the scar of his gunshot wound.

"I've got a good doctor," he had said before kissing her.

The gate's chain drive squeaked and crunched to life, and Brennan came back to the car as the gate slid open.

"Which one is it?" she asked.

Brennan handed her the leather notebook. "Check the book. I can't read his damn chicken scratch."

The book's leather cover was smooth and well-worn, like a treasured journal. There was nothing on the cover to hint at its contents. On the inside of the cover, someone—presumably Thomas—had scrawled the words, *'Lose this and you are dead.'* The pages that followed were covered in thick, violent writing. She could barely read it. *It's like a crazy person's* Lord of the Rings, she thought.

She flipped through the book, catching glimpses of what looked like red-inked medical diagrams, and found what she needed on the last page.

"B-twelve," she said.

"All right. Bee-one-two." Brennan parked the car in front of the storage unit. They got out and walked up to its door. A rusted padlock held it shut.

Joan examined the lock. When she flipped it up, she saw the back was shiny and clean. She said, "This guy is crazy."

"Crazy like a fox," Brennan said. "Let's find the key."

As he was about to unlock the trunk, Joan put her hand on his arm. "Stop." She grimaced. "What about the, you know—"

"They're gone," he said. "They must have been unloaded when he got to the farm. After he made me jump."

Joan let go of his arm, and he popped open the trunk. The plastic containers were empty and clean. "Try to think like a killer," Brennan said. "I'll take the front seat, and hopefully one of us finds it before we meet in the middle."

After searching every other nook and cranny of the trunk, Joan's finger felt a bump along the lining of the roof. After she peeled back the material, a key fell out. She squealed with glee. "Nice," Brennan said. "You found it, you do the honors."

Joan snatched up the key and made her way to the deceptive padlock. She worried it would not work, but the key slid in like it had been freshly oiled. The lock popped open. Brennan grabbed the metal handles and pulled up the door, which retreated above them.

The storage unit was large, a little larger than a two-car garage. The inside was filled with cardboard boxes of all shapes and sizes and what looked like a pickup truck under a dust cover. Joan flipped on a light, and Brennan pulled the door back down.

"What'd you do that for?" Joan asked. "It's stuffy enough in here with the door open."

"There's no telling what could be in these boxes," Brennan said. "You want to risk someone driving by when we open them?"

"Point taken. Carry on."

They started opening boxes. Joan found several boxes full of old documents from something called The Fifteen Second Group, followed by a box stuffed full of twenty-dollar bills. Brennan showed her a box of knives, some of which were closer to swords. The farther back they worked, the more weapons they found—everything from guns to hand grenades to land mines. There were also several boxes of tools, clothes, and medical supplies.

"This guy should've been a Boy Scout," Joan said. "He was prepared for anything this side of Godzilla. He could have survived a zombie holocaust with this stuff."

Brennan said, "I don't think the clones of serial killing monsters get to join the Boy Scouts. But we can look into it, now that we know there's a market. Hey, found a good laptop."

"That might come in handy," Joan said as she opened a box hidden in the back. She expected to find something along the lines of a nuclear bomb, but instead it was full of old stuffed animals and other toys. She pulled a bear off the top and held it up to Brennan. "What do you make of this?" she asked.

Brennan's face melted. "Oh, man, that's Jeff. He was my bear." He took the bear from her and examined it, tracing its button eyes with his finger. "I used to sleep with this. This stuff was all in the attic at my Grandpa's, but I couldn't find it after he died. Crazy. Thomas must have taken it." He put the bear back in its box and carefully closed it. "C'mon," he said. "Aren't you dying to find out what's under the sheet?"

They took two corners of the dust cover and gave it a tug, letting it fall to the concrete floor. Underneath was a Ford pickup truck, black with two white stripes on the hood. It had a cover over its bed.

Joan leaned into its open window. "Ugh," she said. "My grandma used to say only drug dealers drove black trucks."

"At least no one will be looking for it. We can haul all the scary contraband we want," Brennan said. "But listen, you don't have to do this. You can take as much of the cash as you want. You can hole up somewhere safe or you can run away. I'll understand."

"I'm not going anywhere without you," she said. "And if you try to leave me behind again, the Old Man will be the least of your worries."

"I told you. If I'd taken you with me to the farm, you'd be dead."

"Don't care." Joan said, tossing a jangling bundle to Brennan. "Keys were in the ignition. Please be a dear and check the back for heads."

3

"I STILL DON'T SEE why you have to be the one to kill him," Brennan whispered.

The bar's neon light flashed on and off in front of the building. At the back of the brick building, Joan and Brennan were crouched behind a dumpster. Joan knew she would never get the stink of urine and beer out of her boots.

Joan looked over Brennan's shoulder, her chest to his back. "I told you. Somehow they know when you're coming after them. I think it's how they knew you were going to attack the Old Man. It's some kind of clone murder radar." She checked the pistol again. "The sound you felt in your head."

Brennan nodded. "Yeah, it was a buzzing. A really loud buzzing. Then it was funhouse mirror time."

"Funhouse mirror time?"

"Yeah," he said. "Funhouse mirror time."

"That doesn't make sense."

"Because there were so many people around who looked like me? You know, like a funhouse mirror at the fair. Carnival."

Joan shook her head. "No, a funhouse mirror makes you look all distorted. Short and fat or skinny and tall. You're thinking about a house of mirrors."

"Fine. Then it was house of mirror time."

"You've never been to the fair, have you?" Joan asked, nudging Brennan with her elbow. "You poor kid."

"I had no idea it was such a gap in my education. Not as big an omission as not knowing about the psychic alarm. Thomas dropped the ball on that one."

"He wrote in the notebook that he thought you were immune."

"I still don't want you to kill anybody," he said.

The darts contain some kind of concentrated tranquilizer, so I'm not killing him, I'm just knocking him out." She swallowed. "If it makes you feel better, the notebook says you can be the one to close the truck's bed cover. The gas inside will finish him off."

Brennan wiped his face and stared at the ground.

She put her hand on his thigh. "Brennan, you told me what you saw in that barn. I don't think the Old Man is even human. What was he doing with that girl's head? These people are like Vampire Hitlers."

"My being right here isn't enough to set off this guy's sonar?"

"Apparently not. The notebook said it doesn't matter how close another clone is, as long as they're not threatening another clone." She held up the tranquilizer pistol. "Not the one with the finger on the trigger, so to speak."

"That makes no sense, Joan."

"Oh, sure," Joan said. "And the world makes so much sense lately. It makes so much sense that I'm hiding in an alley, waiting to kill a copy paste of my boyfriend."

"Your boyfriend? I had no idea things were moving so fast. I'm going to have to think about this."

"Don't think too hard. I'd hate for your brain to start buzzing again."

Brennan smirked. "I know what would get my brain buzzing." He leaned in for a kiss.

Is he really going to kiss me when we're hiding behind a dumpster? Joan thought, but she shrugged and started to lean toward him when the back door of the bar opened. Joan put a hand on Brennan's chest and pointed.

A man walked out of the bar with a girl. The girl wore an awkward, eager look on her face. *She can't be more than nineteen,* Joan thought. *And I'm thinking more like seventeen.* The girl's companion looked like a version of Brennan with longer hair and worse taste in clothes. The man pushed the girl against the wall and lifted up her skirt.

"Freeze, police!" Joan said, jumping out from behind the dumpster.

The girl went into panic mode, but the man turned around like someone had asked him what time it was.

"Hello, Joseph," Joan said.

"You said your name was Brad!" the girl said, high pitched and angry. Joseph ignored her as he stared at Joan.

Joan said to the girl, "Honey, you better get out of here and head home before I need to check your driver's license."

The girl's eyes widened and she smiled nervously. Joan listened as frantic footsteps carried the girl away from the alley where she would have died.

"How did you find me?" Joseph asked. There was a distance of less than ten feet between them.

"We heard you were working the area. You like college bars that don't check ID. We watched you walk into this place an hour ago," Joan said. As the last syllable left her lips, Joseph lunged like a cornered animal, not for safety but directly at Joan.

Joan pulled the trigger. A sharp sound rang out, and Joseph stumbled, a plastic tube jutting from his chest.

Joseph pawed at the dart. He yanked it out and fell to the ground at Joan's feet, his head bouncing off the asphalt.

Joan kicked his shoulder with her foot. Joseph was breathing, but he made no reaction.

"Nice work," a voice said behind her, and Joan jumped. Brennan crouched next to the unconscious man and checked his pulse. "Next time don't engage him in conversation. It gives the game away a bit."

"I had to get the girl out of here. How do you think that would have gone over?"

"Touché. Let's get him in the truck. Grab his feet."

Brennan lifted Joseph up from under his arms, and Joan picked up the man's feet. His shoes looked expensive. "So you can carry, just not shoot?" she asked.

"No buzz," Brennan said. "I'm not hurting him directly."

When they reached the truck farther down the alley, Joan dropped the man's legs and tried to open the bed cover. When she touched the tuck, the alarm activated and wailed.

"Holy shit!" she said. "Turn it off!"

Brennan dropped Joseph on the pavement and turned out the pockets of his own jeans. "I don't have the keys!"

She frantically slapped her pockets. "I definitely don't have them. Oh, my God."

Brennan reached into his jacket pocket and pulled out the key ring. "Got it," he said, clicking the small red button and turning off the obnoxious alarm. He bent down and reached around Joseph's torso. "That's a really sensitive alarm."

"We need to keep that thing off or we're going to jail," Joan said. As Brennan lifted the man into the bed of the truck, she asked "Is he heavy?"

Brennan smirked. "He's not heavy, he's my brother."

Joan started to roll her eyes, but remembered what came next and frowned.

Brennan was looking at her, his face worried. He said, "I just have to close the lid. What if he wakes up? Won't his spidey-sense tell the others about us?"

"From what Thomas wrote about those darts, this guy shouldn't wake up any time soon. It won't even hurt him. And as long as he's unconscious when you seal him up, there should be no monster alarm. Thomas set this up in case he could find a way to knock one of them out on his own."

"Okay. If you're sure." Brennan reached up, gritted his teeth, and slammed the cover closed. Motors whirred, removing the air.

As they opened the car doors and climbed inside, Joan was surprised to find herself crying.

Brennan put his hand on her shoulder, but she pulled away. He said, "You know we have to do this. It's them or us. And they're as bad as they come."

Joan glared at him, her eyes red and raw. "That doesn't mean I have to like it."

Brennan's grim expression softened.

He hates doing this as much as I do, Joan thought.

He put his hand on her shoulder again, and she didn't pull away. He pulled her in close and they held each other.

"Just don't make me get him out of there," she said.

"Don't worry." Brennan stroked her hair. "I'll take care of it."

4

JOAN WIGGLED HER LEGS AGAIN to keep them from falling asleep. The bathroom stall felt smaller than it had thirty minutes earlier. Several layers of toilet paper protected her blue jeans from the toilet lid.

She suddenly feared he had left her alone. "Brennan?" The words echoed off the tiled walls.

He finally answered back, "Yeah?"

"I don't think he's going to show."

"He'll show. Everyone has their habits."

They were stalking Matt, one of Brennan's—*What? One of his brothers?* Joan thought.

The two of them had spent weeks trying to track down the clone targets, and Matt was the first they found. According to Thomas' notebook, Matt went to a movie theater's last showing nearly every night. When the opportunity arose, he nabbed a late night filmgoer from the parking lot.

No more midnight showings for me, Joan thought.

The leads in the notebook finally led them to this theater in a small town in South Carolina. Brennan thought they should follow him until he reached someplace private and wait for the opportunity to—

To what? Joan asked herself.

To murder him, she answered.

But Joan insisted they not risk losing him, and that they strike in the theater. The notebook explained Matt always drank something at the movies—beer if he could sneak it in, soda if he could not—and he always used the bathroom at some point during the movie, so it would not be a distraction if he became preoccupied with someone after the movie.

"Like you keep saying, it's all in the notebook," Brennan said again. "Thomas must have been keeping tabs on the others for a long time, creepy stalker style. Your legs falling asleep, too?"

Joan giggled. "Yeah. I can feel the ants marching."

"Ants marching?"

"Yeah," Joan said. "Ants marching? That tingly feeling when part of your body falls asleep?"

"Weird," Brennan said. "We always called it pins and needles."

The door creaked open. Joan and Brennan fell silent.

The stalls faced a row of urinals, and anyone entering passed Brennan's stall first. Joan stared through the gap of the stall door and watched a man approach a urinal.

This is just like in Porky's, she thought. *Except not. I feel like a perverted voyeur.*

Brennan opened the creaking door to his stall. The other man's body stiffened. Brennan walked up to the urinal next to the man, and they started to talk.

What the hell happened to no small talk? Joan thought. She double-checked the safety on the dart gun several times.

The two men spoke in hushed tones, but Joan heard the other man say the name Thomas.

Then Brennan turned his head slightly and gave her a nod.

Joan stood, pulled the stall door open, and stepped out with the gun raised.

Matt reacted as soon as he saw her. He spun around, and a stream of urine sprayed across Brennan. Before Joan's finger pulled the trigger, Matt's hand reached inside his jacket. Brennan grabbed Matt's wrist, holding it immobile. Matt looked at him in shock as Joan's dart hit Matt in the chest.

There was an audible rush of air as the second dart shot across the room and dug into Matt's chest. Brennan released him, and several small, double-edged blades fell out of Matt's jacket and clattered to the ground. They were shortly followed by the slumped body of Matt, urine still flying.

Brennan looked down at his wet pants. "You could have waited until he was finished."

"What? All the sudden I'm the expert at shooting guys when they're taking a piss?" Joan said, waving the gun around. "You're the one who gave me the nod."

"Touché," Brennan said, eying the gun nervously and putting his hand on Joan's arm to stop its frantic movement.

Joan looked down at his hand and back up again. "Did you just touch me without washing your hands?"

"What are you talking about? I didn't even unzip!"

"You were standing at the *urinal*." she said. "And he pissed on you."

Brennan rubbed his face in frustration, and then, catching himself, stopped. "Look, it doesn't matter. But we've got to get this guy out of here before he wakes up or someone walks in."

They looked down at the still form of a man, and then Joan looked to a door labeled *'Employees Only.'* She tested the knob, and it turned freely.

"Lucky, lucky," she said. "I have an idea."

A few minutes later they walked out the side door of the theater wearing red employee vests and wheeling a large trash barrel with its black trash bag tied off at the top. They hurried past the dumpster and continued on to Thomas' truck. Looking around, Joan opened the bed cover. She helped Brennan as they awkwardly deposited the trash bag and its contents into the back of the truck.

They looked at each other as he slammed the bed cover shut and climbed into the front seat. Joan sat behind the steering wheel. As she started the engine, she asked, "So what did you two talk about?"

"What?"

"You and your bathroom buddy. I heard you talking about Thomas."

Brennan looked uncomfortable. "I thought it would be worth a risk to pretend to be one of them and ask about Thomas. If he made it out somehow, I thought we could use the help."

Joan frowned. "I think we're doing fine without him."

Brennan shook his head and said, "Yeah, but these are supposed to be the bush leaguers. I wouldn't mind an extra set of hands."

"So?" Joan asked.

"So what?"

"So did that bastard make it out or not?"

"Oh, sorry. No, the Old Man took him. We won't be seeing him again, at least not until the others are dead. And maybe not even then."

"Good riddance," Joan said.

"Yeah, probably."

Joan drummed her fingers on the steering wheel. "You know, if—when this is all over, you need to take me to a movie for real."

Brennan looked surprised. "What? Really?"

Joan rolled her eyes at him. "Come on. Don't act like you've never taken a girl to the movies."

"No, it's not that," Brennan said, shaking his head. "It's the idea of this ever actually ending."

"We're well on the way." Joan said and started the car. "But when we get around to it, I think I'd prefer we go to a matinee showing."

Brennan put his hand on her knee as they rolled out of the parking lot. "I don't mind," he said. "They're cheaper, anyway."

5

"I'M NOT ENJOYING our little roadkill road trip," Joan said.

Joan and Brennan sat facing each other in the red vinyl diner booth. Their finished plates were neatly stacked to the side. Joan liked to do what she could for servers at restaurants; she had worked as a waitress in college, just long enough to realize how much she hated doing it. An untouched slice of cherry pie sat in front of her, its scoop of ice cream slowly melting. Brennan sipped a cup of coffee.

"I don't know," he said. "It has its moments."

"We're spree killers, Brennan. In our biopic, we'll be played by Woody Harrelson and Juliette Lewis."

"*Roadkill Road Trip*," Brennan said. "That would actually make a hell of a movie title. Sounds like it ran at a drive-in in the '70s."

"It would make a great double feature with *Cloned Killers*."

He laughed, but then frowned. "I'm sorry, Joan. I know this is not who you are or what you want to be doing. It's definitely not what I want for you."

Joan turned her plate back and forth, examining her dessert from different angles. "I wanted to be a doctor once. I worked so hard. I wanted to stand in front of everyone and take an oath, you know, 'to do no harm.' I was on the right track; my life was what I wanted. Then that monster had to kill my friends..." She sighed. "Everything just fell apart."

Brennan stared down at his cup. The creamer he poured spun and swirled in the coffee.

She continued, "It's all so fucked up. I just wish I was saving people, not killing them."

Brennan took her hands and stared into her eyes. "Those things are not people. Not after what they've done. Maybe they never were. By putting them down you're avenging everyone they've killed, and protecting, saving everyone else they would have killed. You're saving us." He gave her hands a squeeze and let them go.

She smiled at him. "It's not a total nightmare. At least I found you."

He grinned back at her, and she could see his eyes were tearing up. *He's so sweet,* she thought. *Even after everything, he's still able to be sweet.*

Joan reached across the table. Brennan jerked back at first, but he let her put her hand against his cheek, and he put his hand over hers for a moment until she pulled it away.

Time to change the subject, she thought.

"So how did you learn to defend yourself, Mr. Wade?"

"It's not so much defending myself as clumsily not getting killed."

"So no history of physical altercations?"

Brennan smiled awkwardly. "There was this one time, but it's kind of embarrassing."

She slid forward on in the booth. "Really? Do tell."

"This was back in college. I was out at the bar with some friends, and there was this girl. We were checking each other out, and my friends were giving me hell for it. You might not believe this, but at the age of twenty-one, I had no idea how to talk to women."

"Some things never change," Joan said, giggling.

"Whatever. Just as I was about to make my move—"

"Your move? Really?" Joan asked.

"You want me to tell this or not?"

"Okay, okay. Continue."

"Just as I was about to make my move, this enormous guy started giving her a hard time. It turned into a big deal real quick. He had her by the wrist, and out of nowhere, he slapped her. So I walked up to him and said, 'Hey, you! Get your damn hands off her!'"

Joan rolled her eyes. "You didn't."

"I did. He punched me right in the face. Stop laughing, it wasn't funny. It just about knocked my jaw off. The guy swung again, but he missed. I reached up and grabbed his head and slammed it into a bar stool. He dropped like a rock."

"Did your Batman act get you laid?"

Brennan shook his head, laughing himself now. "Not even close. The jerk was her boyfriend, and she called the cops on me. The guy ended up in the hospital, but witnesses all backed me up."

Joan reached out and took his hand again. "You realize we're like Batman and Robin?" she asked.

He sipped his coffee. "I didn't realize the dynamic duo were in the killing business."

"No, dummy, they're both orphans, out there fighting evil together."

"Does that go for all the Robins? Haven't there been like fifty of them?"

She shrugged. "I don't know. I bet they all end up orphans one way or another."

They sat for a moment considering it. Then she said with a grin, "So you want to be Batman or Robin?"

Brennan laughed. "You'd look better in the little green shorts, but I don't know if I can play. I'm not really an orphan."

"How so?" she asked. "You told me about what happened with your mom."

He rubbed his eyes with the heels of his hands. "We both know she probably wasn't my real mom. I don't know if I even had one. I'm more like Luke Skywalker than Bruce Wayne."

"Luke Skywalker?" She looked confused. "I don't get it."

"He thought his parents were dead? Then it turned out the big bad guy was his dad all along? Come on, this is classic stuff."

She rolled her eyes. "I don't know. I never saw *Star Wars*."

Brennan jumped like he'd been electrocuted. "You've never seen *Star Wars?* How have you never seen *Star Wars*?"

She looked at him for a moment with cold eyes, but then the expression broke and she burst into laughter. "I'm just fucking with you. Of course I've seen *Star Wars*."

Laughing, Brennan said, "You got me on that one. Which one's your favorite?"

Joan raised her eyebrow. "Empire. That's not even an objective question."

Brennan said, "I love you."

"I know," Joan said, smirking.

Brennan threw a sugar packet at her, which she dodged. Their waitress, a dark-haired woman in her late forties, happened to be walking by and picked it up. "Sorry," Brennan said.

"Don't worry about it, honey, it's been a while since anyone tossed some sugar my way," she said, and winked.

They laughed as she walked away. Brennan made a gun with his fingers and fired at Joan's pie. "Better eat that thing before we get kicked out of here."

She cut into the warm slice of pie with her fork. A trail of red goo oozed across the white plate.

6

"WHOA," **BRENNAN SAID** as a group of young men rushed across his path. Joan laughed from the stone bench where she sat waiting for him.

Joan and Brennan were staking out the campus of Carter University in Rhode Island. The older part of the campus was crisscrossed with walkways and enormous buildings that looked to Joan like cathedrals. The walkways were full of so many columns and echoes that it was easy to get lost or bump into someone around a corner.

Joan watched the college students speed around a corner. "So much for the laid-back college lifestyle."

Brennan smiled as he plopped down on the old stone bench. He opened a white paper sack and handed Joan her sandwich. "I don't think they're going anywhere important. They look too happy."

Joan peeked under the paper wrapper. "You're probably right. What kind did you get?"

Brennan popped open his can of soda. The hissing sound of carbonation filled the empty walkway. "Meatball with extra cheese. It's what I always get, ever since I was a kid."

Joan laughed. "Really? In California you got turkey and Swiss."

"I must have been off that day." He took a bite of the sandwich and spoke with his mouth full. "If our man Philip doesn't show up soon, we need to regroup. Is Dr. Lake still inside?"

She nodded. "He hasn't left his office."

Thomas' journal contained a list of researchers, focusing mostly on men and women working in the field of neurology and longevity. It was a list of targets for Philip, a clone who took out specific targets for the Old Man. The list was somewhat out-of-date, as only three people on it were still alive. Out of those three, Dr. Allen Lake was the only one currently in the United States, and he was the man Joan and Brennan had been watching. Joan had argued against using him as bait.

"He deserves to know he's in danger," she had said.

"And what do we tell him?" Brennan asked. "That the clone of a monster that looks just like me is coming for him?"

Joan rolled her eyes. "We don't have to tell him everything, dummy. We tell him someone wants to kill him. He could go to the police, get some protection."

"I told you what Thomas did to those armored guys at the police department."

Joan was flustered. "Then he can go hide somewhere!"

Brennan put his hand on her shoulders and stared into her eyes. "Philip will find Lake eventually. And in the meantime, Philip will leave the country. Or he'll go after somebody else, somebody we don't know about. Drawing Philip out is the best hope for Lake and anyone else Philip might go after."

Joan remained reluctant, but Brennan eventually convinced her. They followed him around during the day at a distance and watched his house at night as they slept in shifts. Brennan wore a cap and sunglasses and did his best to keep out of sight. The only time they let the professor see them was when they ate lunch on the bench outside his office.

That had been Joan's idea. "It's the concept of the familiar stranger," she had said. "When we leap into action, he'll trust us because he feels like he knows us."

"'Leap into action?'" Brennan had asked, grinning. This lead to a painful pinch from Joan.

They had been watching Lake night and day for nearly a month.

Now two students rounded the corner, a young man and woman. Joan recognized them as some of Lake's graduate students. Brennan put his hand on her knee and held up one finger, telling Joan with his eyes to stop talking.

Like I'm an idiot, she told him with her own eyes.

The girl continued, "I can't believe he didn't show up. I canceled a job interview for this."

"Yeah," said her companion. "It's not like Dr. Lake at all. He's the only professor here who never bails out. I don't think the guy's ever even had a sick day." They stopped at the window that looked into Lake's office.

The girl knocked on the glass as the boy pressed his face against the window. "I don't see him in there," he said.

The students walked off. The girl looked back at Joan and Brennan for a moment, and then promptly forgot about them.

After the students disappeared around the corner, Joan and Brennan rushed to Lake's window. Joan cupped her hands to peer inside. "He's gone. But I watched the door the whole time, and it's the only exit. He never left!"

Brennan tried the handle and found it locked. Without hesitation, he wrapped his jacket around his fist and smashed the narrow window beside the door. He reached through and flipped the lock.

Inside the building, Lake's office door was unlocked. Behind his desk, they found an overturned coffee cup and a stack of papers spilled across the floor. Lake was nowhere to be seen.

Joan ran to the hallway connected to Lake's office. It was an older building, and Lake's office was the only room in everyday use. There were two rooms used for the storage of lab supplies and equipment, and one used for old files. At the end of the hallway was a door marked '*Maintenance*.'

Joan frantically opened one door as Brennan opened another. "Philip must have hid inside one of these rooms until the guy showed up. Maybe they're still here."

Brennan shook his head. "Too much chance of getting caught. He would need some space, and there's too much traffic outside the window."

Joan opened the maintenance door. "I think I know where Philip took Lake," she said. A stairway was beyond the door, heading downward into the darkness. A bloody handprint marred the surface of the wall.

Flipping the light switch brought no result. Joan pulled out her key chain, which had a tiny flashlight on it. "Got a bigger light?" she asked, clicking the tiny light on and off.

"Nope, it's in the car." Brennan said. "Did you ever have to go into a dark, scary basement growing up?"

Joan nodded her head.

Brennan grinned and walked down the stairs.

Joan stopped. *Something is off*, she thought. *I don't know what, but something is wrong with him.*

Taking a deep breath, she pulled the tranquilizer gun from her waistband, and followed him down.

7

THE MAINTENANCE TUNNEL was concrete and cold. Brown stains on the walls marked the water levels of past floods. As Joan walked quietly, keeping her tiny light pointed to the ground, she could make out occasional light fixtures along the ceiling. The bulbs were all smashed.

She had explored tunnels like this one before, back in college when a few students formed an unofficial urban exploration club. Their campus lacked maintenance tunnels, but the decaying college town had plenty of abandoned buildings and drainage tunnels. On weekends her club packed up their flashlights and spent all day trespassing.

David, her first college boyfriend, begged her to come along, but she was actually dying to go. She wanted to prove she was brave, and the idea of going somewhere off limits thrilled her. This thrill translated to something else, and she and David explored more than concrete tunnels down in the dark.

She wondered where David was now; maybe he had become a lawyer like he had planned. Whatever he was doing, it was a safe bet he was not tracking a subterranean killer.

Brennan walked ahead of her, his shoulders squared and his steps confident. In her heart, she thanked him for going first, for wanting to protect her. She felt the tranquilizer gun and checked the safety. *I'll be damned if I'm going to be the girl who screws everything up because I forget to check the safety*, she thought.

Brennan paused, like he was listening for something Joan could not hear. After he found whatever it was he was searching for, he continued, with Joan following behind. He repeated this several times as they made their way through the silent maze.

Joan put a hand on Brennan's shoulder and leaned close to whisper in his ear, "How do you know where we're going?"

Brennan put the side of his finger to his mouth, and pointed down at the ground. Joan could barely make out a black dot. She crouched and touched it, creating a red smear. It was a drop of blood. She looked up at Brennan in shock; it seemed impossible he could follow a trail like that. He shrugged his shoulders and made a gesture for her to continue following him.

At the next cross-tunnel, he held up his hand and stopped. Putting his hand over Joan's light, he pulled her close to him, and whispered, "He's here."

She clicked off the small flashlight.

They peered around the corner. Surface drains and manhole covers provided a tiny amount of ambient light. As her eyes adjusted, she could make out the shape of a man crouched over the body of another man, like a wolf eating its prey.

Sorry, Dr. Lake, she thought with regret. *What the hell is that thing doing to him?*

Philip froze. He slowly straightened up and tilted his head, as if straining to hear a sound. In the dark, Joan saw something slender and wrong dancing at the end of his fingers.

Brennan pulled her back. "Interesting," he whispered. "Wait for my signal." He released her and walked around the corner. She stood waiting in the dark.

"Hello, there," said a voice oddly like Brennan's. "I thought I heard someone down here in the catacombs. It's not often I take a head that isn't on my list, but I was hoping to make an exception."

"Looks like it won't be necessary," Brennan said. "Aren't you supposed to be delivering this guy to somebody?"

The other voice said, "I don't like when any of you poke your head in my business. This man was on my list. My special list. Mine. Maybe I decided to keep him for myself, so what? He's mine!"

"You can keep him, Philip. I don't want your sloppy seconds. I need to talk to the boss. I was wondering if you knew where I could find him and his guest."

"What, you think he gives me his itinerary? Wait until he contacts you for a drop-off. Unless…"

"Unless what?"

"Unless you've found a way around the failsafe. Are you planning something?" Philip asked, grinning madly. "Never mind. Maybe I'll crack open that nut and find out for myself."

"Now," Brennan said.

Joan spun around the corner and flipped on her flashlight. Past Brennan, not a dozen feet away, a man faced her. She shined the light into his eyes, making him jerk back and shield his face. She shot at his chest with the tranquilizer, but he ducked to the side and ran toward her.

The man roared. With the back of his hand, he swatted the gun away from her. It hit the wall, shattering it into pieces. Joan shined the light into Philip's face again, but his eyes were closed.

So much for the element of surprise, Joan thought.

"Get out of here, Joan!" Brennan yelled.

"No!" she yelled, scrambling for the ruined gun. "You stay back!" *If Brennan attacks this creep or vice versa, the monster alarm will give the whole game away to the rest.*

Philip lunged for her, grabbing her ankle and knocking her off her feet. She could feel something unnatural squirming up her calf. Looking down, she saw stringy black worms protruding from the tips of Philip's fingers.

"I'm going to relish this," Philip said, smiling.

"No, you won't!" Joan screamed, and stabbed him in the neck with a handful of the tranquilizer darts. Philip fell in a twisted pile.

Joan rushed to Dr. Lake, but it was far too late. The man's head was smashed and torn open, and through the jagged hole in his skull, Joan could see the mess that had been made of his brain, as if Philip had been probing for something.

You have to eat your cereal if you want the prize, she thought wildly.

"What's going on?" she yelled at Brennan, who was crouched over Philip, making sure he was unconscious. "What the hell was he doing?"

Brennan said, "I don't know." Joan looked down at Philip's hands, but the black worms were gone.

Is that what Brennan is? Joan asked herself. She felt her lunch rising in her throat, but she fought it back down. "This is insane," she said.

"We are in agreement," he said. "I need you to get the truck as close to Lake's building as you can so I can load up Philip. Anyone who tries to figure out what happened here will make things more complicated, so I'll hide Lake and take care of the mess in his office. Hopefully no one will find the body until we're long gone."

Joan squeezed his hand and turned to leave. She glanced back over her shoulder to see Brennan dragging Lake's corpse around a corner.

She frowned and thought, *I hope that's all he's planning to do with it.*

8

"BRENNAN, WAKE UP."

Brennan continued his deep and steady breathing in the motel room. *He must have a clean conscience*, Joan's mother would have said. Joan thought that after his experience at the farm, Brennan's sleep would be more troubled than before, like back when he had slept on the couch and she took the bed. Instead, he no longer talked in his sleep, and the tossing and turning had stopped. She liked to think that lying next to her calmed him.

She sat up, leaving the safe warmth of the covers. The chill from the rumbling air conditioner crept through her white tank top. She put her hand on Brennan's cool, bare shoulder and gave him a light shake. "Brennan, wake up."

"Hmmm?" Brennan stirred. He blinked several times before sitting up quickly and grabbing her arm. "What's wrong?" he asked, his eyes darting to the window and door.

"Nothing's wrong, calm down." She bit her lip. "Okay, something is wrong, but nothing like that. We're still safe here."

Brennan sighed in relief and said, "Good." He rubbed the sleep from his eyes and checked the red numbers on the alarm clock. "Joan, it's 3:37 in the morning." He frowned and asked, "Have you been awake this whole time?"

"Brennan, it's been two days. We have to talk about what happened. Down in the tunnels."

He leaned back against the headboard and faked a yawn. "Did I already mention it's 3:37 in the morning?"

"I know you don't want to talk about it. I thought I could wait until you brought it up, but I can't wait any more. You have to tell me what happened."

"What do you think happened?" he asked.

"I think I've gone crazy," she said calmly.

Brennan nodded. "I can understand that."

"It's like the world completely gave up on making sense," she said. "Brennan, I was barely keeping track of the real world when we were on the run from the men in black and hunting clones of a serial killer. Reality and I are barely on speaking terms."

"I get it."

"Real life did not send me a Christmas card this year."

"I said I get it! Damn it, Joan. I should have put you on a plane in Florida. I was a selfish idiot for wanting to keep you with me."

"I went with you because I wanted to go with you. You saved my life. I owe you."

Brennan shook his head. "You paid me back by sewing me up. If it wasn't for you, I'd probably have bled out in the car, or died of an infection."

"Would that have really happened?" Joan asked. "I'm not so sure. I think you might have been okay. Maybe even better off. Your back sure healed up quick after you escaped from the Old Man's farm."

Brennan locked eyes with her. "What are you trying to say?" he asked.

"Nuh-uh," she said. "Nope. You are going to tell me what we saw in the tunnels."

Brennan sighed as he ran his fingers up through his hair, and then back down his face. "We saw exactly what you think we saw."

"Brennan."

"Fine. Philip was doing something to that poor guy's head—to his brains. It was a real mess." Brennan hesitated.

"And?"

"And there were these things coming out of his fingers. They looked like black ribbons or long worms, and they moved like they were alive. Philip controlled them like they were a part of his own body."

"What do you think they were, Brennan? What are they for?"

"I think they use them to do something to people's brains. I think the Old Man was about to do the same thing when I tried to sneak up on him."

"Did he have those things on his hands?" Joan asked, a shiver running through her body.

Brennan shrugged. "He was wearing gloves. I don't know."

"I checked Thomas' notebook a dozen times," Joan said. "It doesn't say anything about this."

"No, but it's there between the lines, isn't it? The trunk full of heads, the barn full of skulls. Everything they do revolves around getting heads for the Old Man. I wish we knew what he was doing with them."

"I've been thinking about that. It's one more heaping helping of crazy, but I might have it figured out."

"What have you got?" Brennan asked.

"Okay, I saw the professor's brain. It was a mess, but it looked like it was all there. So I don't think Philip was eating the guy's brain. I'm guessing here, but if Thomas and the rest of them are taking all those heads to the Old Man, that means they don't have to eat them to survive."

And you seem healthy, Brennan. As far as I know you've never dined on that delicious, oh-so-sweet skull candy, she thought.

"So they aren't brain eaters," Joan said, "and they don't need to steal life energy or whatever from them. That would be silly."

"Makes sense," Brennan said. "Then what are they doing with them?"

"Shush, I'm getting there. The Old Man cloned himself, didn't he? He wouldn't go to all that trouble if he could reproduce like a normal person. I think it also means he isn't laying eggs in people's skulls."

"Fuck!" Brennan said.

"I said shush. All the times we know about the Old Man doing this, the heads have been dead, right? Like the ones Thomas had in his car, or the professor Philip killed. So he's not putting thoughts into their heads, like a puppet master, reaching in there and flipping switches to make people his slaves. So I think maybe they can read people's minds." She swallowed.

"With those black things coming out of Philip's fingers. The things that disappeared after we dosed him."

Brennan exhaled slowly. "I dunno. It sounds crazy, but maybe it makes sense. But why—"

Joan giggled.

Brennan asked, "What?"

"Maybe the Old Man has to wear the gloves because his skin is full of saggy holes from doing it too much," she said, and then frowned. "I guess it isn't that funny."

They sat side by side in awkward silence.

Brennan was the first to speak. "Go ahead and ask me."

"Ask you what?"

"You know what," he said. "Ask me if I can do it, too."

"Well, can you?"

His shoulders slumped. "I don't know."

"Brennan, you're all copies of the Old Man. You said he was doing it, and we saw another clone do it."

"Don't you think I know that?" he asked. "What do you think I've been thinking about since we saw that freak in the tunnels?" His eyes filled with tears.

Joan put her arm around him. "Shh," she said. "It's okay. You're not like them."

"Aren't I?" he asked. "You said so yourself. We're all just copies of that thing."

"You're not 'just' anything. You're Brennan Wade. You're a good man. Whatever else you are, you're definitely that. You saved me, and I saved you. Now we're saving each other. That's something those other guys aren't capable of. You're not like Thomas."

"I guess you're right," he said. "But I probably have whatever that stuff is inside me, too. Inside me all the time."

"So what if you do?" Joan asked, hugging him tight. Her hand slipped under the waistband of his shorts. "Even if you were part monster, you'd be my monster."

"Thank you," he said as her lips found his.

9

I CAN'T BELIEVE I'M DOING THIS, Joan thought as she straightened her hair in the mirror. She checked for the third time, and her white jacket and stolen visitor's tag remained properly adjusted. With the tranquilizer pistol was tucked safely in the back of her slacks, she picked up her plastic binder, collected herself, and exited the ladies' room.

In her previous life, she had interned in hospitals all over the country, so she knew what to expect from a small hospital in Maine. Some hospitals found themselves underfunded, while others earned enough through elective surgery to spread it around. Many were well run, and just as many were headed down the toilet. But they all had much in common. There was the smell, a mix of chemical sterility and sick people. The smell made her teeth tingle after being away for so long.

Every hospital hires good people to do the impossible job of saving people from the inevitable. Once upon a time, it was a calling Joan worked so hard to be a part of, but being here now and trying to pass herself off as a doctor left a knot in her stomach.

Attempting to wear her most confident smile, she approached the nurse's station. A large Neurology sign hung from the ceiling. The slender Hispanic woman typed away at a computer; her name tag read Gaff. Joan waited for what seemed the appropriate amount of time before she said, "Excuse me."

"Can I help you," Nurse Gaff said. It was not a question.

"Yes, ma'am, my name is Dr. Voigt. I'm here for a consultation with Dr. Baynes."

The nurse raised an eyebrow. "Are you sure? Dr. Baynes doesn't usually ask for anyone's opinion."

Joan forced a smile. "Can you tell me where to find him?"

Gaff stood. "I'll do you one better, I'll lead the way. I want to see what would make Baynes send out an S.O.S." She called after a man in scrubs, "Cover the desk," and gestured for Joan to follow her.

Somewhere a man cried, and something metal crashed to the floor.

"So what can you tell me about Dr. Baynes?" Joan asked as they walked.

"Don't you know him?" the nurse asked.

"Only through email and over the phone," Joan said quickly. "I'd love to know what to expect." She took a quick look around as she transferred the tranquilizer gun from the small of her back to behind the plastic binder she held against her chest.

"Hm. I can tell you the same things anyone here could tell you. Great doctor, great man. He wants things done his own way, though. That's why I'm surprised he called you in as a consult."

"It's a special case," Joan said.

"I'll bet it is," Gaff said. "Here we are." She held the door open for Joan.

Inside the room, a shriveled man slept in a hospital bed. A man in a white coat stood at the foot of the bed, holding up a CT scan to the light. Joan recognized the doctor's expression. It was the one she had seen on the same face in the maintenance tunnel—this man looked hungry.

He finished examining the scan before looking up to see who was interrupting him.

He smiled, his teeth showing. "Nurse Gaff," he said, nodding. He looked questioningly at Joan.

"This is Dr. Voigt," Gaff said. "She said she's here as a consult."

Dr. Baynes shook his head. "I'm sorry, Doctor," he said. "I don't have a need for input on anything right now. If you would please leave, I have a delicate examination to do on this patient."

You can't let him do that, Joan told herself. She said, "You remember. We've been corresponding? About your brother, Philip?"

Frowning, the doctor said, "Nurse, if you'll excuse us, please."

Gaff sighed and rolled her eyes, not bothering to hide her disappointment as she left the room and closed the door behind her.

Joan and the doctor stood across from one another as the comatose man in the bed breathed deep, machine-driven breaths. She crossed her arms across her chest, closing her hand over the pistol hidden behind the binder.

"You must be Joan Runciter," he said.

Joan's eyes widened.

Dr. Baynes smiled. "Surprised? We know all about you. You're Brennan Wade's whore. The drunken failure. We have someone looking for you."

"They haven't found me yet, Baynes." She gripped the gun, her hand sweating.

"Call me Simon," the man said. "And don't worry your empty little head, he'll find you. It shouldn't be too difficult, since I'll be handing the only pertinent part of you over to him in a biohazard sack. He won't mind if I hold onto the rest." He smiled again, his white teeth shining.

"I don't see that happening. You're about to be as dead as the other three." It was her turn to observe Simon's shocked expression. "You should keep in better touch with your family, freak."

In a fluid, practiced motion, she pulled out the pistol and took the shot. But the three darts meant to hit Simon square in the chest instead stuck harmlessly in the wall. She landed on the floor, the back of her head cracking painfully against the tile. He straddled her chest, pinning her shoulders to the ground with his knees.

"I usually like to do this slowly," he said, pulling a tiny black bottle and a syringe from his pocket. "But you're shitting where I eat, and that breaks rule number one."

She tried to bridge her back, and clawed helplessly at his legs. She thought, *If I start to scream, will he skip the formalities and break my neck?*

He filled the syringe with solution, not bothering with pushing out the air bubbles. "I can't wait to tell your pussy boyfriend about this," he said.

Joan grunted. "You really need to call your family once in a while. Brennan escaped months ago."

He paused. "Bitch, are you crazy? He's—"

Simon's face suddenly twisted and he dropped the syringe and vial, which shattered on the floor. He clapped his palms to his ears as if to block an overpowering noise. The room's door flew open, and Brennan stood in the doorway. He fired a line of darts into Simon, two stuck in his chest and one in his neck. The doctor's face remained full of confusion and surprise even as he slid to the floor.

Brennan helped Joan to her feet. "Get out of here. I don't know how much time we have. I'll take care of things in here and follow you."

"What? I'm not—"

Brennan grabbed her by the shoulders and pressed his forehead against hers. He said, "Alarms are going off in the heads of monsters. Right now. They know where we are."

"I told you, I'm not leaving you."

He shook his head. "I'm not asking you to. Quickly but calmly get to the car and pull it around front. I'll meet you there in a few minutes." She kept shaking her head until he said, "I promised. I won't leave you behind again."

She nodded and gave herself three seconds to gain some composure before leaving the room. She heard the lock click behind her.

10

THEY FLED. Brennan ran red lights and accelerated as he rounded corners. The two of them hardly spoke. They stopped in Vermont to repack the car, throwing away or hiding everything suspicious. Joan chewed the inside of her cheeks nervously at the Canadian border, but there were no problems. The border patrol did not bother to look into the closed truck bed.

The road carried them north to Quebec City. Joan purchased food, firewood, and other supplies while Brennan purchased a camping permit. They entered the Grands-Jardins National Park after lunch.

Looking in the brochure, Joan said, "It's almost two hundred square miles of wilderness up here. We should be able to hide out for a while."

Brennan didn't answer. He flipped on the radio and sang along softly with Booker White about black cats and bones.

11

THEY DROVE until the other vehicles thinned out and the road was the last outside evidence of humanity. Brennan parked the truck on the side of the road and the two of them hiked out into the dense forest. They set up their camp and made several trips for all their supplies. When the truck and the dirt road disappeared behind the trees, they became the last two people in the universe.

"If anyone finds us, they'll find the truck first," Brennan said. "I turned on the damned alarm. Hopefully that will at least give us a little warning if someone tracks us down."

During the day, Joan read one of the paperbacks she purchased at the truck stop. Brennan disappeared for hours at a time. She did not ask where he went. At night they slept in shifts or huddled together for warmth. Meals were simple, and they brought enough food to last several weeks.

On the fifth evening, Joan was rebuilding the fire. It was a skill she had learned from her father, making it one of the activities that usually brought back welcome memories. She layered the wood and kindling, but she fostered the tiny smoking flame without emotion.

"Don't make it too big," Brennan said. "Any attention we get will be bad attention."

"I know that." Joan looked down at her dirty hands. "Brennan, I don't like how distant we are. You and me, what we have is the only thing making any of this craziness worth it."

Brennan stood beside her and put his arm around her. "There will be time for us when this is all over. I promise."

She rested her head against his shoulder. "I need to ask you a question," she said. "You need to know up front that I'm not mad."

"What?"

"The darts. They don't carry a knock-out drug, do they? It's a fast acting poison. I'm guessing some kind of neurotoxin."

Brennan sighed. "I'm sorry. I didn't want to put that on you. If it means anything, I really thought it would knock them out. Thomas' notebook was clear about that. It wasn't until we moved the first body that I realized what happened. I hoped it was a fluke, that it would work right on the others."

"I don't like being lied to, but I can understand. I don't know if I could have pulled the trigger knowing I was killing them." She looked up at Brennan. "I feel pretty messed up," she said. "I shouldn't be okay with this at all. It's like someone's messing with my mind, changing my thoughts around."

"I'm sorry," Brennan said, hugging her.

Joan hugged him back. She looked into the fire and said, "We should cook something tonight. A warm meal would do us good."

Brennan started looking through their food. "Sounds like a plan," he said.

Joan shivered.

12

JOAN AWOKE FEELING STIFF AND NUMB. The sleeping bag made that familiar scraping sound against the floor of the tent as she rolled over. Unconsciously, she reached a hand over to touch Brennan.

Her hand waved through empty space.

She sat upright, shaking the fog from her head. She looked around the dark tent, as if he might be hiding in a corner. The panic welled up inside her before she realized Brennan could be outside keeping watch. She exhaled slowly. *Way to overreact, Joanie,* she thought. *People are going to think you're a damsel in distress.*

She tried to take her time as she dressed and unzipped the tent. "Brennan?" she called.

There was only silence. The panic, which had never left, made an earnest comeback.

He might just be taking a piss, she thought. *And boys love to pee outside, so maybe he's taking his time.*

But if that's the case, what woke me up?

Even with the insanity that was currently her life, she slept soundly. She remembered her mother again, telling her she slept so peacefully because of her clean conscience.

I'm awake because something is wrong.

Her eyes darted across the campsite, looking for something, looking for anything out of place. Nothing looked touched, and she saw no signs of visitors.

There's something wrong, a voice whispered in her mind.

She left a note for Brennan, just in case, and walked quickly back to the truck. Hopefully she would meet Brennan halfway. They would laugh about her needless worry.

Something wrong.

Living in big cities for so long, she was still overwhelmed by the number of stars. Their light gave the woods an ethereal quality. The chill in the wind failed to bite through her coat. If not for that creeping fear, it would have been a beautiful walk.

Joan neared the road when the truck's alarm sounded. It blasted like an air raid siren. She stopped pretending to be calm and ran to the edge of the tree line. A scream escaped her throat as she watched flames jump out from beneath the truck.

The fire burned fast and blue. The tires burst in a rush of air, and the dark body of the truck warped in the heat. She crouched and covered her head as one of the gas canisters in the back of the truck exploded.

Wrong.

Some thing.

Then Joan saw it, a shadow under the shadows. She watched the deliberate, intelligent movement and knew it had to be a man. He was not Brennan. His eyes shined like a wolf.

She ran.

Among the trees, the moon and stars gave her enough light to not slip and break her neck. Where the branches were thick, she put her arms up to protect her eyes, but she did not slow down. The thick tree trunks flew past her, like fence posts beside the highway.

Cross country running had been her sport of choice in high school. At one time in her life, running was the only thing she loved as much as the idea of becoming a doctor. She had not trained hard in years, but a good run remained the one thing that always kept her mind off the train wreck of her life.

So although she had taken a break from running while on this cross-country killing spree with her boyfriend, she felt confident she could outrun a monster. She was not some helpless, high-heel-wearing scream queen stumbling in the woods. She was Mercury, and the wings on her ankles flapped like the wings of a hummingbird.

I left him behind, she realized, and finally stopped.

Her lungs burned, but she forced herself to hold her breath

and listen long enough to be sure she was alone. She walked, quickly but silently, back in the direction she had come. She stayed clear of the path she had taken, and kept to the shadows.

What are you going to do? she asked herself. *You don't have the tranq gun. You don't have anything.*

Doesn't matter, she answered. *Brennan's the only hope I have. I've got to help him. I have to try.*

She heard sobbing.

The sound was horrible, like the grief of a father who lost a child. She looked around and picked up a thick, heavy stick from the ground. Careful not to make a sound, she made her approach.

A dead body was strewn on the ground. She knew it was a dead because too many pieces were missing for the man to be alive. It had to be one of the clones. From what little was left, she could make out Brennan's features.

A man crouched over the body, shoulders heaving. Blood covered him.

"I'm sorry," he said to her. "I'm sorry. I thought I heard something. Didn't want to wake you. Went to check it out."

He tried to wipe the sweat from his eyes with the back of his hand, leaving a crimson streak across his face.

"By the time I realized it was Andrew, he'd doubled back. I didn't realize they'd find us this fast." He shook his head. "I failed you."

Joan walked up behind him.

"I just wanted to keep you safe, Joan," he said, "Safe like I promised. But it's all a mess. I'm sorry. I'm so sorry."

"I'm not," Joan said as she brought the club down on his head.

PHASE IV

1

EXPRESSIONLESS, JOAN WATCHED as Brennan regained consciousness. He winced at what must have been a pounding headache. His eyes popped open as realization struck; she had tied him to the chair. She had cinched his legs up underneath the seat, so his struggling nearly toppled him forward onto his face.

Joan felt his eyes land on her. She sat cross-legged on a wooden table, fiddling with the dart gun.

"I guess you owed me one of these," Brennan said, attempting a smile despite.

Joan did not react. Her face remained blank, as if she had not heard him speak.

She slowly climbed off the table. They were inside what looked to be a small house outfitted like an office. Aside from the conference table Joan had used as a perch, there were several desks, some file cabinets, and a broken ping pong table folded against the wall.

"Ranger station," Brennan said. "What, did you drag me here?"

Joan finished her assessment of the dart gun. She returned it to the table and spun it. It reminded her of a spin-the-bottle game from when she was thirteen. The wheel of fate had pointed to Jimmy Fletcher, who never found out he was her first kiss. *I wonder where Jimmy is now*, she thought. *I hope he's in nicer digs than this.*

Brennan's voice came from far away. "…went over the edge there, but I couldn't help it. He was going to kill you."

Joan raised the dart gun, aiming it at his chest.

Brennan twisted and turned in his seat. "Please don't do that. You're scaring the shit out of me. I get why you had to tie me up—"

"Shut up," she said.

Brennan shook his head frantically, pulling at the ropes. "I can explain."

"Shut up!" Joan yelled. Brennan froze.

The two of them sat there in silence. Brennan stared at Joan, and Joan stared at the ground in front of his feet.

Joan set the gun down. "I don't know how I let you do it," she said without looking up. "I don't know how I could have been so stupid."

Brennan started to say something, but stopped himself.

"You led me all over the country," Joan said. "Manipulated me. Corrupted me. And the whole time, you had me fooled. You pulled a total Clark Kent on me, you son of a bitch."

"I never—"

Joan fired, the dart whizzing to the side of his head.

"Shut up, Thomas," she said.

He sighed and closed his eyes. As he opened them, his demeanor shifted from restrained fear to cold indifference. "Nice to see you again, angel. When did you figure it out?" Thomas asked.

"I don't know," Joan said. Her shoulders trembled, but the dart gun remained fixed on Thomas. "I think part of me knew from the start."

"After the farm." He nodded.

"You were different. But after what you went through, anyone would be different. I was glad you didn't change any more than you did." She squeezed her eyes tightly closed, shaking her head. "I'm such an idiot."

"You're not an idiot."

"Shut up. Actually, on second thought," she said, walking over to him and shoving the barrel of the gun in his sternum, "why don't you tell me what really happened. I want to know what happened to Brennan."

Thomas shook his head. Joan lifted the gun, and struck him across the face with the butt of it.

"Tell me," she said. "Is he even alive? What'd you do to him?"

Thomas shook his head. "You don't understand," he said. "I saved him."

"Liar!" Joan screamed.

"It's true," he said. "Everything I told you about the farm was true. Brennan was caught and thrown into the freak pit. I cleared out with everyone else, but then I doubled back and went in after him. I thought I was going in after his body." Thomas smiled. "But he surprised me. The boy learned his lessons. He fended them off with a busted-off piece of pipe. I had to climb over a pile of the things at the trap door. But they had him cornered, like the end of a goddamn zombie movie, only with too many teeth and extra appendages.

"I cleared a path to him and half-carried him back to the entrance. He was in bad shape, and I wasn't doing much better. Helping him walk, I couldn't keep those monsters off of me."

"You're one to talk about monsters," Joan said.

Thomas grinned. "Touché," he said. "But you saw my back. They would have torn us both to shreds. I'm the one who got us both out. I'd locked the pit behind us when Brennan grabbed me. He told me where you'd be. Made me promise to protect you, no matter what. He gave me the password so you would trust me. I said he was crazy; he could do it himself. We just had to get the hell out of there.

"That's when I heard someone. I had just enough time to get out the back. Figured I could get the drop on whoever it was and still get Brennan out of there.

"So I watched from the shadows of the house as John and Peter hauled him out. I still might have tried something, but then

James showed up. And then the Old Man walked out, barking orders. I should have known, because those three bastards are always with him. The Old Man outnumbered me all by himself, so I didn't have a chance against the four of them. I watched as they loaded up and left."

"Coward," Joan said.

"Maybe," Thomas said. "I think the Old Man thought Brennan made it out on his own. It must have impressed him enough that he decided to let him live."

"Then you snuck out and came to the motel." Joan bent down in front of him and stared into his eyes. Her wide eyes shook in their sockets. "What I don't get is why you pretended to be him."

"Lady," he said, "all I've ever wanted is to be Brennan Wade."

2

THE TEENAGE BOY'S EXPRESSION was plastic, but his mind was caustic.

Thomas walked out of the Flatland Steakhouse, still tasting his rare steak. He squinted against the Texas sun and put on his sunglasses. It was July, 1992, and summer was in full swing.

His dark hair was a little longer than most young men wore in Flatland, but it was styled and neat. He wore jeans, tennis shoes, and a black t-shirt. A band's name, Mayhem, was written across the chest of the shirt in stark white; bat wings and upside crosses adorned the opposing letter Ms. Below the name, a high-contrast image of an imposing cathedral was printed in purple. At the bottom of the image read the words, '*De Mysteriis Dom Sathanas*.'

He unlocked the door to his car, a black Alpha Romeo convertible. The air in the car was stifling, but he kept the top up. People notice a convertible driving down the street when the top is down. That fabric roof was his cloak of invisibility, and he never took it down when on a job.

He pulled into the parking lot of a small motel. The sign proclaimed it to be the '*It'll Do Motel*,' and he decided this stood as a rare example of truth in advertising. He parked his car, grabbed his luggage—a canvas duffel and a leather messenger bag—and walked into the front office.

Inside sat a candy machine, the type with a clear plastic front and metal spiral holding the items in place. Tom smirked when he saw packs of cigarettes on the second row from the bottom. The only type left were menthols. Not his usual choice, but he popped in his quarters and watched as a pack dropped. He retrieved them and made his way to the front counter.

A woman in her early fifties looked up from her magazine, which had a grinning Tom Cruise on its cover. "Sorry there's only those menthols left, honey," she said. "Did you know those things can freeze your lungs solid?"

"I don't mind feeling a little cold inside," he said. "I need a room for the night. Maybe a few days."

"Maybe?"

"It all depends," he said. "That a problem?"

She frowned. "Gotta be eighteen to stay here alone, honey. You got an ID?"

"Sure." He pulled out his wallet and handed her a driver's license.

The woman held it up, comparing the picture to its owner. "Tom Smith, huh?"

"That's me."

"Sure don't look twenty-two to me, honey."

"I get that sometimes," he said as she handed him back the card.

She looked him over one more time and rolled her eyes. "Whatever. Guess I'm just getting old."

"By the way," he said, pulling a photograph out of his pocket, "Have you seen this lady around?"

The woman studied the picture. It captured a young woman, smiling as she brushed her dark hair from her brown eyes. She shook her head and handed the picture back. "Sorry, honey. She sure is a pretty thing. Why you looking for her?"

He put the picture back in his pocket. "She's an old friend of my mom's. Mom lost track of her, thought she might have ended up in Flatland."

The woman gave him a bemused look. "You track down a lot of your mom's old friends for her?"

He shrugged. "She knows I'm good at finding things."

"Good for you, honey." She nodded toward the pack of cigarettes he had bought from the machine. "You want a smoking room?"

Tom smiled. "That would be great."

He paid cash for three days in advance.

Inside his room, Tom pulled a stack of folders from the messenger bag and spread their contents across the bed. There were maps, blurry photos of a woman, phone records, receipts and his own handwritten notes. One folder was labeled "Sylvia Kindred." He sat in the middle of the bed, his legs crossed. He lit a cigarette as he pulled out the picture he had shown the woman at the counter.

"I'll figure out what you were up to," he said to the frozen image. "You cause a lot of problems for a dead bitch."

3

TOM HAD CAUGHT UP TO SYLVIA KINDRED three days earlier in Claremore, Oklahoma, the home of the J.M. Davis Arms & Historical Museum, the world's largest collection of firearms. The Old Man had been looking for Kindred since she ran off in the later days of the cloning project, but he had never found her. He gave Tom the job as a reward for the boy's enthusiastic work on similar projects.

A few messy visits to Kindred's known family and friends finally yielded results that led him to the small first-floor apartment in Claremore. Tom watched a woman, anonymous in her bland clothes, go inside around 6 P.M. He waited across the street in his car until it was nice and dark, and then he picked up a roll of duct tape from the passenger seat and trudged through the snow to a back window.

He covered one pane of glass with several strips of tape before giving it a sharp tap with his elbow. He peeled the tape and broken glass away silently and reached through to unlock the window. The lights were out, and he could see no one inside. In fact, the room was empty except for an old chair. On the floor beside the chair was a chipped ash tray overflowing with cigarette butts.

He slipped through the window feet first. The instant his feet touched the ground, he heard the unmistakable sound of a shotgun being cocked.

"Put your hands behind your head and turn around. Slowly," Sylvia Kindred said. Tom allowed himself a smirk, but he was wearing an expression of fear by the time he faced Kindred. He bounced on his feet slightly, his best imitation of fearful trembling.

Kindred looked horrible. The files had shown her to be an attractive, strong woman. But in person, her face looked like that of someone facing a losing battle with cancer. *Being on the run has not agreed with you, Sylvia*, Tom thought. She looked at him with a mix of emotion in her eyes he could not place.

He said, "Lady, I'm sorry, don't kill me. I've never done this before. It was a bet, my friend—"

"Shut up, you little monster," Kindred said, her eyes suddenly wild and blazing. "I know exactly what you are. God forgive me, I spent nine years of my life making you."

Tom laughed and lowered his arms, watching the twin muzzles of the gun shake as he did so.

"I said hands behind your head!"

Tom put his hands back behind his head, but this time in a loose, casual way. "How'd you know I was coming?"

"Someone called to warn me after one of your visits. They didn't know why, but they knew you were looking for me."

"I must have missed someone," Tom said. "Shame on me. I'll have to be more careful."

She licked her dry lips. "But you're too late. You'll never find him."

Tom cocked an eyebrow. "Him?"

Kindred, her eyes wide, took several steps backward. "Damn it. Damn it!"

Tom took a step toward her. "I think we should talk." His grin widened.

"Stay back," she said, waving the gun.

"You of all people should know I can take that from you if I want. You'll never hit me," Tom said.

"It's not for you," Sylvia Kindred said, spinning the gun around. Before he could react, she bit down on the end of the barrel and pulled the trigger.

Tom stood there for a moment, watching bits of Sylvia Kindred drip down the wall. He walked over and traced his index finger through the muck. He put the finger to his lips and licked it. "Fuck," he said. The Old Man had given him exactly one requirement for the job: bring him back the head.

I'm going to end up in the goddamn pit, he thought.

The only chance he had was to bring back something equally valuable to the Old Man. *She did mention a 'him'*, Tom thought.

Tom glanced at his watch and gave himself five minutes. Even in a shithole like this, the sound of a shotgun blast would bring the police.

He checked Kindred's body first, but there was nothing of interest in her pockets. The kitchen had a little food, but no answers. An old mattress and some blankets were laid out on the floor of the bedroom, and the closet held a suitcase worth of clothes. He found nothing but basic toiletries in the bathroom.

"Nothing," he said. The damn phone call gave her time to clear anything out that might have helped him. Tom checked his watch—two more minutes until he needed to clear out.

He was about to give up when he noticed a small vent at the bottom of the wall. The paint had been scratched away from the wall at one corner.

He pulled a large knife from his belt and pried out the vent, cracking the drywall. He felt around inside and pulled out a bulging white envelope that had been taped to the top of the vent.

A half-hour later, in his car and far away from any prying eyes, he dumped the contents of the envelope into the seat next to him. He picked up a yellowed Polaroid of a baby holding a stuffed elephant. He tossed it aside. There was a stack of paper money, which Tom estimated to be about $500, and a stack of credit cards under a variety of names.

He put everything back into the envelope except for a cheap postcard without any names. The front showed a black and white picture of an ancient movie theater with a bright neon sign. Someone had written on the back in small, ordered letters: *'All A's. Summer job. Had his first date. You'd be proud of him.'* The postmark was from a town in Texas called Flatland.

Tom grinned.

4

TOM SPENT SEVERAL DAYS in Flatland making the rounds, asking people if they knew the woman in the picture. It was a difficult balance of looking for information without being noticed himself. The obvious places to check first, like the police station or hospitals, would quickly draw attention he wanted to avoid. He had no idea what name Sylvia Kindred had gone by in Flatland, or if she had been to the town at all.

He checked other motels first, especially the cheap ones. They were the natural choice for someone trying to lay low. The upside for Tom was that many of them were family owned and operated. This meant the person who took the money stuck around for a while. He made a note of which motels had a consistent night clerk and returned to show them the picture. None of them remembered Kindred.

After hitting local restaurants, supermarkets, and the post office, it looked hopeless. He climbed back in his car after the last post office in town and pounded on the steering wheel, cursing. He must have missed something. Kindred could have planted a false lead for him to find. He would not put it past her, not after she had escaped his family for so long.

She even knew to stop me from getting her head, he thought. *That's definitely the first time that's happened.*

It was time to leave, either to try something else or head back to the Old Man and report failure. Tom put the top down and rode the highway out of town, trying to decide if he should head home right away, or have some fun first. It might be awhile before the Old Man let him out again.

On the highway east of town, Tom passed the sign for a government facility, FARM, one of Flatland's largest employers. FARM was one of only two facilities in the United States dismantling old nuclear weapons and building new ones. The name struck Tom as both hilarious and appropriate.

His low gas light came on as FARM disappeared behind him.

"Of course," he said. He looked around for a gas station, knowing they would only get scarcer the farther he got from civilization. As he was about to turn around, he spotted a place to refuel.

The gas station was so run-down he thought it might be closed, but as he pulled up to a pump, he saw people inside the small building. He topped off his tank and headed inside.

Candy bars sat on the counter in a small display, melted and deformed in their wrappers. On the wall behind the counter were a few shelves with plastic bottles of oil, and beneath them, sun-bleached car accessories hung on a pegboard. Metal fans blew the stale air around in a failed attempt to keep the temperature down.

An older man who looked like Santa Claus played checkers against another man who just looked old. Santa Claus looked up as the door opened and walked over to the cash register.

"Thanks for the business," he said, ringing up the gas. "Not too many folks pass by here."

"No problem," Tom said. "Glad you're out here, or I'd probably be walking." He handed over the money for the gas.

"Need anything else?" Santa asked. "The candy's melted, but I've got a fridge full of Cokes in the back."

"No, thanks," Tom said. He started to leave but then stopped. "Actually, maybe you could help me out. Have you seen this lady?" He pulled out the photo of Kindred and handed it to the man.

The older man looked at the picture, rubbing his beard. He shook his head. "Sorry, kid." He asked his checkers opponent, "Hey, Bill, you seen this lady?"

Bill stood up and walked over the counter with a limp. He squinted at the picture. He started to shake his head, but then his eyes lit up. "Yeah, I seen her. Remember, Frank? She came in, asking for directions out to ol' Roy West's house."

Tom could see Frank going through old mental files, retrieving the information. "Yeah, I remember now. But that was like a year ago."

"That would have been her," Tom said. "Can you tell me how to get to Roy's place?"“

Frank looked at Tom intently. "If you don't mind me asking, why might you be lookin' for her?"

Tom frowned. "It's actually a little embarrassing," he said.

"Why don't you tell me anyway?" Frank said.

Tom looked at Frank and smiled a bit. "She's actually my mom," he said, allowing his eyes to tear up. "I've been looking for her awhile."

Frank smiled kindly. "No problem, kid. I'll draw you a map."

Tom asked, "Is there a way for me to call out there first?"

"Call?" Frank asked. "If Roy West has a phone, I ain't got the number."

"That's probably for the best," Tom said.

5

TOM TOOK HIS TIME and decided to wait until after dark to visit Roy West. He parked his car on a dirt road and made his way to the old house. The lights were on inside, so he kept his movements silent and careful.

He was not sure what to expect when he looked inside. From the baby picture, he assumed the lady had stashed her kid here with a family member or some friend not on Tom's list.

In the driveway was a rusty International pickup truck, an ancient one with wooden slats in the bed. Tom crept around it and slid in between two trash cans to get a look in the window.

He saw a worn couch and recliner facing a modest television. The walls of the room were lined with bookcases. The bookcases had glass doors, entrapping books and odd knickknacks. It looked like many of the items had an ancient Egyptian theme. An older man walked in and sat in the chair. He had to be in his late seventies, if not older.

Tom examined the man for a few seconds and then sucked in his breath.

"Son of a bitch," he whispered. It looked like the Old Man would be happy to see Tom, after all. If he was right, Roy West was actually a man named Richard Henry.

The Old Man had been looking for Henry longer than Tom

had been alive, since at least the late 1940s when Henry went off the grid. Richard Henry had been the partner—"More like sidekick," the Old Man would say—of Benjamin Rosen.

Ben Rosen had been the biggest pain in the ass with which the Old Man ever contended. The Old Man claimed to have eliminated that particular problem in 1949, but no one ever found out what happened to Richard Henry.

And here he is, still kicking. Old as hell in Flatland, Texas, Tom thought. He double-checked to make sure he had his knife. He was trying to decide if the Old Man would prefer Henry dead or alive, when someone else walked into the room.

It was a boy the same age as Tom, carrying two bowls of popcorn. He handed one of the bowls to Henry and sat down on the couch. A reflection of the black and white film appeared on the glass cabinets. The boy said something to the older man, and the two of them laughed heartily.

Tom was so surprised he did not notice one of the trashcans topple over. Then he heard his own voice from inside the house ask, "What was that?"

He took off running, hoping they would think a dog had gotten into the garbage and not look out to see Tom running into the dark.

6

FLATLAND HIGH SCHOOL, "Home of the Polygons," was nearly empty most of July, and after five o'clock, it was a ghost town. Tom had never gone to school in the traditional sense, and walking through the school's empty hallways after dark filled him with an odd mix of claustrophobia and regret.

He paused at a row of trophy cabinets full of photographs and tacky gold awards for sports and academics. An old signed football and a 1950's letterman jacket depicted the school's original team nickname, the Savages. Black and white photos of smiling students stared at him from the past, judging him.

The school's alarm system was woefully outdated. *Budget cuts,* Tom thought, although he did make a mental note as he passed a room with security monitors and VCRs. Next door was the school's record room, clearly labeled with black letters on a beige sign beside the door. He glanced around to make sure the coast was clear before his gloved hand pulled out a lock-pick tool resembling a gun. He checked that it had the right bit and bumped the lock.

He walked into a gray, cramped room full of file cabinets and cardboard boxes filled with documents going back decades. He assumed the boy was in school because of the *'All A's'* bit from the postcard. Tom was gambling that Henry was not homeschooling the boy. There was also one decent private high school in town, but if Henry's modest home was any indication, he probably could not afford it. Out of the high schools in town, Flatland High School was the closest to Henry's house.

Tom tried to avoid thinking about the implications of another clone, one the others did not know about. The power balance in the group of twelve was always leaning toward all-out war, and he was in no hurry to return with the kind of news that would affect the balance of power. By checking the school records, he could possibly move forward in his investigation before checking in with the Old Man right away.

He found no students with the last name "West" in the files. He had a good guess how old the boy was—*No, really?* he asked himself sarcastically—so he pulled the files for every student who had been a freshman the year before. After a half-hour of tossing files in a pile, he found Roy West's name in the parent or guardian spot on Brennan Wade's enrollment form. West was listed as Wade's grandfather, which made Tom laugh out loud.

The first page in the manila folder included Wade's yearbook picture, taken the previous fall. He wore a plaid button-down shirt and a nervous smile. Tom looked into those nervous eyes that could have been his own, and felt an uncomfortable stirring of emotion.

The folder felt almost empty. Wade evidently kept his mouth clean and his head low. In the midst of class schedules and medical records was a stapled photocopy of Wade's birth certificate. It listed Alice Wade as the mother, with the line for the father left blank. Tom folded it in half and then in half again before pocketing it. He started to do the same with the list of Wade's other schools, but thought better of it and stuck the entire folder in his jacket.

Tom felt a knot growing in his gut. He was dizzy and felt his dinner creeping up his throat. To make himself feel better, he lit a cigarette, but his hand was shaking. It was going to take a bit more than a cigarette to distract him from the thoughts ricocheting back and forth in his head.

The generic wall clock told him it was 2:17 A.M. A hard drag got his cigarette nice and hot, and Tom dropped it in a trash can full of shredded documents. Once the fire got going, he kicked the can over into the pile of student records.

Holding Brennan's class schedule, Tom began walking through the classes from the previous spring semester: first period, Art I; second period, Spanish I; third period, Freshman English. The doors were all locked, and he did not bother tripping the locks or kicking in the doors. He could wait for an invitation.

Fourth period, Chemistry. The knob turned smoothly under his hand, and he walked inside. Student desks sat in rows in the center of the room. Lab stations with black counters, chrome sinks and pointy gas valves surrounded the room. A periodic table hung beside the teacher's desk, a holy shroud in its sacred place of honor and worship.

He opened the top drawer of the teacher's desk and pulled out a white three-ring binder. It still contained the previous semester's seating charts. Tom flipped to the chart for fourth period, and his scanning index finger found Brennan's name. There he was, in the back row, sitting behind a girl named Elsie Paroubek.

He returned the binder to its drawer and walked to Brennan's seat. He sat down and ran his hand across the cool wood veneer of the desktop. *Looks like our boy is too much of a goody goody to carve his name in his desk*, Tom thought. He kicked the metal basket of the desk in front of him and listened as it rattled.

What the hell am I doing here? he thought.

Tom's science tutor had been an older, angry man with enormous sweat stains. He fulfilled his purpose, and Tom assumed the Old Man had compensated him well. Not that it mattered; Joseph killed the man over a disagreement about the physics of *Star Trek: The Next Generation.* At that point, the Old Man decided school was out forever and handed the instructors to his children who had outperformed the others. Tom was the runner-up for math and English, but for some reason he was not disappointed the privilege of butchering the teachers went to someone else. There are plenty of fish in the sea, after all.

The smell of smoke brought him back. It was time to go. He lingered for a moment in the desk, trying to feel something that eluded him.

Tom walked to a lab station and flipped the gas valves wide open. Nothing happened. He traced the line to a tank under the cabinet and opened another valve, producing a loud hissing sound. After opening the valves at the other lab stations, he left the classroom, locking the door behind him.

He left the building as smoke alarms sounded. He had never turned the alarm system back on, which meant it would still be some time before the fire department arrived. Any video surveillance of his activities, recorded in the room right next to the fire's starting point, was already eliminated.

He sat in his car until an explosion rattled the windows of the school. He gave himself a moment to watch the fire grow. He grinned as he thought of the photos in the trophy cabinet curling and turning black.

Speeding away, he thought, *That should hold me until I can kill something.*

7

TOM SPENT THE NEXT MORNING observing the West house. Arriving early in the morning, he found his vantage point in the corn field across from the house. He watched and waited.

What are you even doing here? he asked himself again. He should have reported back to the Old Man as soon as he found out about Richard "Roy West" Henry and the new clone. He could tell himself that he was putting together a more complete report, but he knew the Old Man would be furious Tom had not immediately subdued or killed both the man and the boy and brought them in.

I have to know more about Brennan Wade, he thought. He felt this so strongly that he did not even attempt to resist. When he was satisfied, he would call in the Old Man, who would still want to spend quality time with Henry and Wade.

At 11:30 A.M., the two of them left the house by the front door and got into the pickup truck. Tom watched as they turned out onto the road, a cloud of dust behind them. He stood, dusted himself off, and made the short walk to the front door.

Getting inside was no problem, and he locked the door behind him. Standing in the living room he had seen the night before, he examined the cabinets, lingering on the collection of

Egyptian items. West—*Henry*, he corrected himself—had an impressive collection. There were ancient coins, ankhs, and scarabs. Several oil lamps, the kind that look like tiny clay teapots, sat side by side. He recognized an organ jar, with the chipped head of a jackal rising from the lid.

A metal rod, covered in the patina of time, rested on a transparent plastic stand. The thin metal twisted into two loops near the end, and the tip curved into a hook. He had seen the Old Man using a similar tool on the heads Tom brought home.

Tom checked the rest of the house. Past the living room he found a kitchen leading into a cluttered study full of books and papers. He passed a bathroom and an odd-smelling bedroom he guessed belonged to Henry. At the back of the house he found Brennan Wade's bedroom.

Brennan lived in a small room with white walls. Tom knew from Brennan's school file the boy had been in town for the past year, and from the look of the room, it appeared he had not arrived with much in the way of possessions. The room was furnished with an unmade bed, a dresser with a row of paperback books on the top, and a desk. On the floor was a small portable stereo and a few CDs Tom did not recognize. He smirked at a poster of a smiling, dark-haired girl wearing blue jeans, black suspenders, and a frilly white bra. She arched her back at a sharp angle; one of her thumbs hung on a jean pocket, while the other pulled at her suspenders.

Tom sat down at the desk, which was quite old and had a smooth leather top. Pens and pencils sat in a mason jar at one edge. He opened the top drawer and found a creased photograph of a young Brennan, probably four or five, sitting on the lap of Sylvia Kindred. The two of them sat at a table with a checkered tablecloth, and Brennan was covered in what looked like barbecue sauce. Kindred and Brennan were laughing.

Tom returned the photograph and rummaged through the other drawers. He found only school papers and random keepsakes, like movie ticket stubs and a feather. In one drawer was a Flatland High 1991–1992 Yearbook. He pulled it out and sat on the edge of the bed, the ancient bedsprings groaning in protest.

The cover of the book was a mosaic of candid campus photos scattered over an orange background, each one cut into a different shape. A human pyramid of cheerleaders was in a triangle, a shot of the band was in a square. *'Brennan Wade'* was embossed on the lower right-hand corner, the indentions filled with metallic blue. Tom scanned the cover, but did not find Brennan's face there.

Aside from the usual photos of students, faculty, sports teams, and the like, the yearbook contained several dozen signatures. Most of them were the generic *'Have a great summer'* and *'See you next year.'* But a handful said a bit more.

'Brendan—Nice getting to know you this year, man. We should totally hang out this summer. Glad you moved here! Joe Conley.'

'BEST LUNCH TABLE OF ALL TIME! NEXT YEAR WE EAT OFF CAMPUS! MIKE JENNINGS.'

'Hey!!! Thanks for the help in chemistry!!! Hope we have some classes together next year!!! Elsie Paroubek.'

He found Brendan's photo in the book, the same one Tom had taken from the school files. At the back of the book was an index listing which pages students appeared on. Brendan was not in any of the teams, clubs or other group pictures, but he was listed as being on the back cover. Tom gave it a second look and found Brennan hiding at the bottom of the page, sitting with a group of smiling boys eating their lunch in the cafeteria. Trays and brown paper bags covered the table. The boys were a motley crew, with messy hair, braces and greasy skin. One of the boys had his tongue out and was making the sign of the horns with the index and pinky finger of both hands. Tom guessed that had to be MIKE JENNINGS.

A name from one of the written messages had stuck in his head, so he gave them a second look. When he reread Elsie Paroubek's name, he remembered her from the Chemistry seating chart. He turned the pages to her picture.

Elsie's genuine smile was striking. More importantly, someone had traced the outline around the photo with blue ink.

Tom smiled as he pictured Brendan sitting behind this fifteen-year-old heartbreaker. Brendan probably told his loser friends about how he was going to ask her out, and they would tell him he never would. If her platonic message in the yearbook was any indication, his friends had been right.

Tom brought her image closer to his face. Her eyes sparkled. With his index finger, he traced the soft line of her jaw down to the gentle slope of her chest. His skin felt burning hot and he began breathing hard. He had seen what the Old Man could do, the way he could know what people were and what they knew.

She would be as good as anyone, he thought, *and more fun than most.*

He did not hear the vehicle drive up to the house, but he jumped at the sound of a truck door slamming.

He tossed the year book back in the drawer and closed it as footsteps approached the house. Tom darted out of the bedroom toward the back door, but the front door was already opening. Tom managed to slide into the kitchen before Brennan Wade walked into the house.

Brennan walked across the living room, his footsteps moving at a quick pace. Tom watched his reflection in the oven's glass window. The young man disappeared from view, but Tom could hear him rummaged around in his bedroom. The truck idled noisily outside, presumably with Richard Henry still behind the wheel.

Keeping one eye on the hallway, Tom slid a large knife out of the wooden knife block and tested its weight. It would be so easy to do the kid now. Tom could then walk out to the truck, a wolf in sheep's clothing, and take care of Henry. It would be messy, but Tom could handle messy. The Old Man could get everything he needed from them, and Tom could put a stop to these uncomfortable doubts. He nodded to himself and flipped the knife around with a quick twirl of his fingers.

The sounds in the bedroom stopped. Brennan rounded the corner. After he passed by, Tom stepped out from the shadows and lifted the knife in a swift arc. An instant before he brought the blade down into Brennan's back, he realized there was no buzz. The alarm had not been activated.

One night when Tom was seven years old, he woke up with a jolt because of a painful buzzing in his head. His eyes snapped open, and standing over his bed was his brother Andrew, holding a pillow and looking surprised. With jagged clarity, Tom realized Andrew was about to suffocate him in his sleep. Tom leaped out of the bed to defend himself, and the fight left both boys with broken bones.

Over the years, it grew obvious none of the clones could hurt each other without this warning going off in all of their heads. In the case when Andrew tried to murder Tom, intent was all it took to set it off.

Distance did not matter; Tom was across the country when Peter tried to run over Joseph with a car, and he knew immediately where the attempt took place and who was involved. The situation grew more complicated when Matt had an argument with the Old Man and tried to shoot him with a hunting rifle. Matt claimed he could not even lift the gun. The clones' headaches had lasted for weeks after that one, due in no small part to the beating the Old Man administered to Matt in return. The boys had long since decided that, while killing each other could be tricky, attacking the Old Man was impossible. It went beyond just the alarm; this was a total physical block.

But Tom was seconds away from murdering Brennan Wade, and there was no alarm. Tom's sudden hesitation caused him to shift his weight on the old wooden floor, making a loud creak.

Brennan froze. He turned, but there was nothing there. He exhaled nervously, laughing at himself, and exited by the front door. Moments later, the truck drove off.

Tom stepped out of the shadows. *Son of a bitch*, he thought. Brennan Wade was immune to the mental alarm. *A clone who is completely off the grid.*

And I'm the only one who knows about him.

It was time to find Elsie Paroubek.

8

TOM SAT ON THE CONCRETE FLOOR hugging his knees, his face buried in his arms. Blood dripped from his fingers.

Two bright halogen work lights hung from a yellow metal stand. One of the lights spotlighted Elsie's body on the warehouse floor. The blood surrounded her, highlighting her thin arms and legs. Red spatters covered her white tank top. In the pooled blood sat a ten-dollar hacksaw. Bloody handprints marked Elsie's shoulders from when Tom had clumsily separated her head from her body.

Tom rocked back and forth. *I've never regretted anything before,* he thought, but he admitted to himself that was not true. There had been times he regretted not being more ruthless. Other times he regretted not taking his time to enjoy his work. *But not this,* he thought, *this is something different.*

The other work light lit a metal table, its square surface pitted from hammer blows and rust. Propped up like a marble bust, Elsie's head sat in the middle of the table. Her face was pale and angelic, and her blond hair flowed down, the tips now dyed a dark red. There were streaks of blood on her jaw and chin. Her eyes—*Her eyes are green,* Tom reminded himself—were rolled back in her head, showing only white. A cheap metal crochet hook lay on the table. A single drop of blood had formed at the corner of her right eye and dripped down her cheek.

Two nights had passed since Tom was in Brendan's house. He located Elsie easily, but the fun was found in waiting for the perfect opportunity. Elsie spent almost every waking moment with people, but Tom knew it would only be a matter of time before he would catch her alone.

Earlier that night, Tom watched from a distance as Elsie left another girl's house, waved goodbye, and started walking home. After following her for a few blocks, he waited in the shadows as a car passed before jogging up behind her.

"Hey, Elsie," he said. She smelled like candy.

She jumped and spun around. She sighed in relief as she recognized him. "Brennan," she said, laughing. "Wow, you really scared me. What are you doing?"

"I'm not Brennan," he said, and pressed a chloroformed rag over her mouth and nose. Elsie struggled, but he had given her a heavy dose. She slumped against him. Tom gave a quick look around, but they were still alone. He threw her over his shoulder and carried her back to his car.

At the warehouse he had scouted beforehand, she woke up. This time he held the rag over her face until her breathing slowed, became shallow, and finally stopped altogether. Tom checked her pulse, and smiled to himself when he felt it stop. He had not wanted her memories of Brennan colored by his actions. What he was doing would be difficult enough.

Tom had seen the Old Man read minds, but none of his brothers, not even Peter, knew how it was done. A few had experimented, but as far as Tom knew, they had all been unsuccessful. He had worked under the assumption that if the Old Man wanted him to know, the Old Man would teach him when it was the right time. But Tom could not escape the nagging feeling this was one of the secrets the Old Man wanted to keep for himself.

He used the saw in quick strokes. *I've got to find a better way to do this*, he thought as he paused to wipe blood from his eyes with the back of his glove. Nearly finished, he tossed the saw aside.

With one hand he braced against the body, and with the other he pulled the head away, severing the remaining hookups with a hard jerk. He was drunk on his own excitement.

Feeling like Perseus after slaying Medusa, he carried the head by its hair to the work table. He peeled off his gloves carefully and picked up the crochet hook, its chrome shining under the light. Licking his lips, he went to work, trying to focus on finding her memories of Brennan.

He felt a chill on the back of his neck and a heaviness in his extremities. He gripped the hook tight and continued. At the edge of his perception, there arose a crowd of voices, thundering chaotically. A quaking began in his chest, and soon his entire body was shaking. His vision blurred.

The warehouse was gone and he was there, in her head. Memories flooded around him and through him. Every memory was a streak of color, life, and emotion. He fought against the current, looking for the image of his own face, listening for Brennan's name.

He was back in a locker-filled hallway at Brennan's school. From inside and outside—Tom was both as an observer and a participant—he watched Elsie chat with Brennan about an upcoming test. She enjoyed talking with him. She looked forward to seeing him in class because he was genuine and kind, and a part of her loved him for it. She knew nothing would ever come of it, but she was okay with that. It was nice to have just a friend.

Tom could see Brennan through her eyes, through her heart, and for the first time he felt what it was to be a real person. He truly saw Brennan, who had never been a monster and never could be. In that moment, Tom was made aware of what he himself was, and how far he was from what he could have been.

He tried to stop then, but the rest of Elsie poured through him: her family, her dreams, her first kiss. The entirety of what made her an individual was crammed into his mind. Tom had been wrong—the Old Man did not read a person's mind; he absorbed the person.

The connection broke.

Now Tom was on the floor, still rocking back and forth. His brain was misfiring, and his mouth moved noiselessly. He began to cry.

He crawled over to Elsie's body and took her lifeless hand.

I'm sorry, he tried to say. *I'm sorry, I didn't know. I thought I knew what you were, but I didn't know. I didn't know what I was.*

Tom had never known anyone before. He was raised by a monster alongside other monsters, and that was all he had ever known or cared to know. Other people were not real, not in any sense that mattered. They were there to do with as he pleased, and to be thrown away when he was finished.

Dozens of people. Tom had murdered dozens of people without flinching. He had laughed while he had done it. It was too late for all of them. It was too late for Elsie, and it was too late for Sylvia Kindred.

But it's not too late for Brennan.

"Thank you for showing me that," he told Elsie. "And don't worry about Brennan. I know what to do." He dried his eyes, and his expression grew cold again.

9

TOM GAVE THE FOLLOWING REPORT to the Old Man: Sylvia Kindred's suicide took Tom by surprise. He found something in her apartment about a city in Texas. He hoped to find something there worth reporting back to offset his failure, but nothing turned up. He killed a girl while he was there, but was interrupted before he could preserve the head to bring home.

The Old Man was disappointed about the loss of Kindred, or at least the loss of what she might know. He was still pleased to have the unfinished business taken care of, and Tom remained in his good graces. However, Tom noted without disappointment, the Old Man started using Andrew and Philip to track people.

In the meantime, Thomas made plans, watched over Brennan, and watched for his opportunity.

10

"BULLSHIT," Joan said.

"What do you mean, 'Bullshit?'" Thomas asked, still tied to the chair in the ranger station. "That's what happened."

Joan picked up the dart pistol and slid down from her seat on the dusty table. "I've been sleeping with you for months, you creep! You tricked me into having sex with you. Who even does that?"

He looked surprised. "You thought I was Brennan. Isn't that what you wanted? Didn't it make things easier?"

"You thought you were doing me a *favor*?" Joan pressed the top edge of the pistol barrel against her forehead. "Your pledge to Elsie about being a good little boy must not have meant much in the long run."

Thomas shook his head. "It did. That was when everything changed. That was what fixed me. Or broke me. Depends on your point of view, doesn't it? "

Joan laughed without humor. "You sure chase a lot of cars for someone who's been fixed."

"I don't know what you're talking about."

Joan's eyes blazed. "You're still killing! You kill everybody, you freak!"

"I kill when I have to. But I haven't killed an innocent person since Elsie Paroubek."

"Oh, really? Who decides if they're innocent or guilty?"

Thomas stared at her. "I have to. There was never anyone else to ask."

"I think you need to explain what the fuck you're talking about."

"Fine," he said. "After I found out about Brennan, I had two choices: tell the Old Man or don't tell the Old Man. If I told, Brennan would be dead. But if I didn't tell, I had to keep it a secret. If I stopped killing, stopped bringing the Old Man what he wanted, that would be it for me. Don't forget, if the Old Man got ahold of me, he would find out about Brennan whether I wanted him to or not."

"You could have run away."

"No, I couldn't," he said, shaking his head viciously. "Sylvia Kindred and Richard Henry are the only people I know of who escaped that thing for any length of time. And Henry only escaped permanently because I kept it quiet. That's why we had to take out my brothers, so we could take the fight to *him*. I thought you understood. He has access to money and resources you can't even imagine. So I kept bringing him heads, but only from the most horrible people I came across." He shrugged. "The Old Man loved the selection. He said he never got too old to learn a new trick."

Joan paced in front of him. She made no effort to hide the dart gun still in her hand. "So you kept killing after your come-to-Jesus meeting," she said, "but only people who deserved it."

"Right," he said.

"And you're the one deciding who deserves it."

Thomas frowned. "It had to be me. Who else was going to do it?"

"Let's take a look at your rap sheet. There were those men after Brennan and me."

"Hired killers," he said.

"Then there are the people Brennan told me about, the ones he read about online." Still pacing, Joan began counting with her fingers, touching one index finger to the other. "The biker guy with the tattoos."

"Killed his wife."

She pointed at her middle finger. The guy in California, the one you stuffed in a drain."

"He'd killed at least three people. But I suppose that's the pot calling the kettle black, isn't it?"

She pointed to her ring finger. "The hooker."

"Wasn't a hooker. Nurse. She poisoned dozens of patients."

She pointed to her pinkie finger. "A grandma?" she asked, raising an eyebrow.

"Her yard was full of dead kids. I think she killed her husband, too."

"You didn't think to tell the cops about that?"

Thomas looked at her, confused. "Why?"

"Oh, I don't know," she said. "Justice? Closure for families of the missing kids?"

Thomas shrugged. "Not my job."

"I've got one more instance on my checklist," Joan said, holding her hand in front of Thomas' face and pointing at her thumb with the barrel of the dart gun. "You'd better hope you have a good answer for it. What about Donna and Audrey?"

Thomas stared at her blankly.

"My friends, you bastard! Don't try telling me they were crime lords, or drug dealers, or baby snatchers. They were good people. And don't try to tell me it wasn't you, because I know it was you. I saw you."

"Yes. You saw me," he said. "But that was a special case."

"Special case!" Joan said. "I can't wait to hear this." She clicked off the safety on the dart gun.

"Okay. You've probably figured out I kept close tabs on Brennan, especially when he was traveling. It gave me an opportunity to keep an eye on him without shitting where he had to eat, if you catch my meaning."

"Way to go, hero," Joan said.

Ignoring the comment, Thomas continued. "Brennan was in Chicago, so I was in Chicago. I watched him chatting up some girls at the bar until he had to leave. After a while, I walked over and picked up where he left off, saying I decided to stay after all. They had a lot to drink, and you know I do a great Brennan. It was easy."

Joan fought back the bile rising in her throat.

"It felt good when they thought I was a person. Then I saw someone walk in the door. At first I thought it was Brennan, and that would have been pretty funny. Not ha-ha funny, but funny. Then I realized it was Justin, another clone, and that wasn't any kind of funny.

"Justin must have heard I was in Chicago from one of the others. Maybe I let it slip, or maybe someone spied on me. I don't know. Maybe he tracked me down; maybe it was all a coincidence. Didn't matter how he ended up in that place. He was there and I had to deal with him.

"He bellied up to the bar and the girls thought it was hilarious. They thought it was a gag at first, and then decided we were twins. I kept my cool, but this was a big problem. If things kept going like they were, Justin would kill at least one of the girls. He would take the head to the Old Man, because that's what we do.

"But the girls talked to Brennan. They knew his name, maybe his phone number. If the Old Man got a look at those memories, he would know they talked to someone other than Justin and me. That would be the end of Brennan. It would be the end of me, too."

Joan's throat was dry. She said, "You could have done something. You should have saved them."

"You think I didn't try?"

Joan was surprised at how hurt he sounded.

He continued. "My brain was going a mile a minute. I couldn't do anything to Justin because the others would know it. That's why I couldn't stop the others from killing on my own. It was one more thing I had to deal with if I wanted to protect Brennan.

"I played along, wracking my brain for a way out that wouldn't tip off Justin. I couldn't just yell 'Fire!' Justin would pick up on anything I said to the girls.

"I made a plan. I excused myself and got to the payphone. I called the cops and reported I had seen a guy put something in a woman's drink. I gave Justin's description and the address of the bar. I hung up when they asked for my name. It was messy, but it might have worked.

"But when I got back from the phone, the three of them were gone. I was looking around for them when a patrolman walked in the front door. He saw me and our eyes locked. Of course I fit the description I gave them over the phone, so I hurried out the back. The cop called it in and followed me, and before I knew it the street was crawling with police looking for me.

"The girls had said which street their apartment was on, but between looking at the names on all the apartments' buzzers and hiding from every passing patrol car, it took me an hour to find the right apartment building. I hit the button and Justin answered. He buzzed me up.

"When I got upstairs, he apologized. 'They were leaving,' he said. 'I didn't think you'd mind,' he said. Justin was always such a dick. He convinced them to take him home, saying I would meet them there.

"I was too late. Justin hadn't wasted any time; he was covered in blood. He said he owed me. The bastard could tell I was upset, but he was wrong about why. I told him I still wanted to be alone with them. He looked suspicious, but I said I'd take care of covering his tracks. I'd even deliver the heads.

"So he cleared out and I spent the rest of the night cleaning up his mess. I was surprised as hell when you walked in the door the next morning. I got out of there with the heads, and I made sure the Old Man could never get at the information by making sure the refrigeration system failed. Justin was mad as hell."

Joan looked into his eyes, searching for deceit. She walked behind Thomas and put the barrel of the gun against the back of his neck. His sweat caused the tip of the gun to slide as she pushed it into his spine.

"Are you telling me the truth?" she asked him.

"What?"

"Are you telling me the truth?" she repeated, pushing the gun barrel hard into his neck.

"Yes."

"You knew all along the darts would kill them, didn't you?"

"I did," he said. "It was the only way to be sure I wouldn't set off the goddamn alarm. That's one of the reasons I needed you."

Her cheeks went flush, but she kept her voice level. "The other reason?"

"I can't kill the Old Man by myself, even if I could get past the others."

"You mentioned something about that. But I don't understand why you can't take out the Old Man, if it's really so important to you."

Thomas closed his eyes. "Don't you think I've tried to find a loophole in the alarm? I've tried to poison him, plant bombs. Anything that felt indirect enough that it wouldn't tip him off or alert the others. But I just can't do it on my own. On top of the damn alarm, I think he did something to make it impossible for any of us to hurt him. I still think Brennan could do it, but he couldn't get close enough."

She said, "Alright. So you need me. And if you wanted to kill me, I'd already be dead. I'm sure of that." *Pretty sure*, she thought.

"That's a good point," he said.

"Shut up and listen," she said. "I want Brennan back. The *real* Brennan. I don't know how to do that without your help. I need to know—and you'd better tell me the truth—are you really trying to help him?"

Thomas said, "He's the part of me that's more than just a monster."

"Here's the deal," she said. "You'll tell me what I need to know, but I call the shots. We stop the Old man and we get Brennan back. Does that work for you?"

He nodded.

"But you have to promise me, no more lying. If you lie to me again, I will kill you and get Brennan back myself. I'm not going to trust you. That ship has sailed. That ship has fucking sailed right over the edge of the fucking flat earth. But I want you to promise me you won't lie to me again."

"Sure," he said.

She shook her head. "No. That isn't enough. You have to swear it on something that matters to you. Swear to me on the soul of Elsie Paroubek."

Thomas was silent. Joan tapped him on the top of the head with the butt of the gun. "Still there?" she asked.

"I'm not sure I believe in souls," he said.

"Then you better come to some quick metaphysical conclusions."

He sighed. "Okay. I swear to you on the soul of Elsie Paroubek, I will not lie to you again."

Joan bent down and untied Thomas' hands. "So what now, boss?" he asked, rubbing his wrists.

"Now you tell me if you have any more of your little safe houses scattered around. And if you tell me to check that damn journal—"

"There's one place I know that has some answers," he said. "It will be a long trip."

"Then we'd better get going. Because we're all out of darts," she said, tossing him the empty gun. He caught it, his jaw dropping in shock.

"I owed you that one," she said as she exited the room.

11

AFTER RAIDING their campsite and truck for what supplies they could salvage and carry, they hitchhiked south. The two of them snuck across the world's largest unguarded border without incident, and Joan bought a Lincoln Town Car in New York for $450 cash. They then cut a steady southwestern scar across the United States.

Joan had experienced many uncomfortable silences in her life. She had eaten entire meals with her parents in complete silence, especially during her teenage years. There was the time she turned down a wedding proposal in the middle of a party. Then there was the dean's office when she told him she was quitting medical school.

The drive from the Canadian border to Flatland, Texas, took the concept of uncomfortable to a new level. The atmosphere inside the car was heavy, like the air before a thunderstorm. Thomas made attempts at conversation, all of which Joan ignored. They spoke only when necessary, and those exchanges were short and all business.

They drove in shifts and ate in the car. Joan cried twice: once in Michigan for twenty minutes, and again for almost an hour in Oklahoma. She caught herself keeping an eye out for bars and liquor stores in every city or town they drove through.

She thought about Thomas' story. The holes were big enough to drive the Lincoln clear through, but she believed him. Not because he had convinced her, but because she knew it was the only hope she had to find Brennan.

If he's even still alive, she thought.

Thomas glanced over at her. "He's still alive," he said.

Joan said, "You don't know that." She stared out the window. "And I thought your mind reading trick only worked when you were digging through someone's gray matter with your fingers."

"I don't need to read your brain. What else would you be thinking about?" Thomas reached over and turned off the radio. "Don't worry. He's more interesting alive than dead. That's not something the Old Man comes across often. Besides," he said, tapping his temple with his finger, "the monster alarm, remember? I would have felt it."

They reached Flatland, but did not stop at the storage locker. This time Joan kept an eye out for landmarks from Thomas' story. She saw the high school, which looked none the worse for the fire. Past the city limit, she saw what she thought was Frank's gas station. The lights were off and the big plastic signs were gone, either removed or broken by the same kids who had smashed out the windows.

It was past midnight when they pulled off onto a dirt road, knocking up enough dirt to hide the lights of the city. The car's headlights fell on a house in the emptiness. Thomas parked the car and said, "Welcome to the former home of the late Roy West, also known as Richard Henry. Tours start at nine. No flash photography, please."

12

DROPPING HER BAG on a dusty couch, Joan asked, "Does the plumbing work?"

"Yeah. There should be hot water, too," Thomas said.

"Thank God. I'm taking a shower."

"Let it run for a minute. Get the crud out." Thomas pocketed the house key. "And watch out for bugs. I pay somebody to spray, but only the outside."

Joan grabbed a change of clothes and found the bathroom right where she expected it to be. She was pleased to not find any bugs, although there was a large spider-web up in a corner. Turning on the faucet in the tub produced water smelling of dirt and metal. She let it run until it looked clear before pulling the little lever that redirected the water to the shower head.

She took off her clothes, neatly folding them out of habit, and set them on the counter. Brennan had given her a hard time about doing that, asking what the point was when she just threw them in a laundry bag. Or had it been Thomas?

God damn it, she thought, climbing in the shower before the water had a chance to warm up. She sucked in her breath as the cold water hit her chest.

It had been so much easier when she and Brennan were the

only ones on the team, the only good guys. Now it turned out Brennan was a prisoner of war, and she had been sleeping with the enemy. She tried to push the disgust, betrayal, and guilt from her mind.

Joan shivered from the cold and at the thought of being with Thomas for so long, hating herself for being so blind. A small part of her even understood why he had done what he did, however wrong. Would she have gone with him at all if she had known who he really was?

That doesn't matter, she told herself. *It would have been better if he had been honest from the start.*

The doubts persisted, and she realized the water was never going to get any warmer after all.

13

ACCORDING TO THOMAS, he bought the house when Richard Henry died. Brennan was Henry's sole heir, and as far as Brennan knew, he was the closest thing the old man had to family. Brennan had been away at college and needed money to pay for school and the funeral more than he needed a house full of old furniture. After returning for a few things, he was forced to let an estate seller handle the rest. Thomas purchased the house and everything inside through a third party and had paid for its maintenance and upkeep ever since.

"It was the least I could do for the kid," Thomas said. "I thought he might want it back someday. I'm glad I did it, too. There were things in the house too valuable to lose. Things Brennan didn't even know about."

In Richard Henry's bedroom, Joan helped Thomas push aside the bed. Thomas kicked away the dust bunnies and tried to pull up a floorboard. With his knife, he popped up a section of the floor with a cracking sound. Underneath them, down in the dark, were stacks of notebooks.

On his knees, Thomas pulled out the books. Joan picked up the first, its yellow pages crinkling. On the cover was written '*1913*.'

She opened the book, which turned out to be a journal. The entry for February 17 was bookmarked. In precise, elaborate script was written:

'Today I met the most extraordinary man, one Benjamin Rosen. We were introduced by a mutual acquaintance at the art exhibition I was covering for the Eagle. Easily the most interesting man I have met since I arrived in New York, he claims his occupation as 'professional dreamer.'

'I phoned in the story and the two of us went for drinks, and I found him to be a world traveler and a fountain of thrilling anecdotes. Although my life as a newspaper journalist was far less exciting, he patiently listened to my many frustrations.

'Ben mentioned the organization for which he worked could use a man with a nose for news. He made an offhand reference to my story concerning the unusual mound excavation in Wisconsin last May. This leads me to the conclusion that our meeting was no mere coincidence, and was in fact orchestrated so I could be offered a position in his organization.

'I told my new friend I would take the sudden opportunity under immediate consideration. While I have reservations—the details stray far beyond the point of being ambiguous—Ben is just too fascinating an individual. I will sleep on it and ring him tomorrow, but I believe my mind is already made up.'

On February 18, Henry wrote one line:

'Took the job.'

Joan flipped through the rest of the 1913 volume, but nothing of interest jumped out at her. Returning the journal to the stack, she tapped Thomas on the shoulder and asked, "What if I was looking for the juicy stuff?"

"Richard Henry lived to be well over a hundred years old. With Benjamin Rosin, he chased a horrible man around the world for decades. He had experiences you don't have the words to describe. These journals rewrite the history of the twentieth century."

Joan tapped him on the shoulder again. "So what if I was looking for juicy stuff?"

Thomas stared at her, as if trying to translate her question.

He's like a robot sometimes, Joan thought. *When he was Brennan, did he pull his emotions out of thin air? Where did it come from?*

"Here," he said, handing her two journals labeled 1938 and 1991. Each one had a bookmark made from newspaper. "These two entries are pretty juicy."

Joan took the journals and carried them to the living room. She slapped the old easy chair several times, freeing clouds of dust which she waved away with the books. Satisfied, she sat down and began to read.

14

APRIL 18, 1938.

Finally back in the states, finally time to catch up a bit. The last few months have been so extraordinary; I'm not sure where to start. Perhaps it is best if I cut to the chase.

We lost all track of our quarry after the disaster in China seven years ago, and—to be quite honest—I had nearly given into the hope he was dead along with all the rest. Of course, this was not the case.

The Lodge contacted Ben to tell him one of the names on his list had popped up. I still don't believe Ben got the list of names from a dream, but this is the third time his list has helped our investigation. If he does not wish to reveal his true source, that is his business.

This time it was Stuart Ammon who turned up as a scientist on an Arctic research team. It wasn't clear what the team was researching, but the backers of the privately funded Russian expedition did not want to lose their investment.

There was a major problem from the start; the group had ceased all contact a month earlier. We immediately flew to Norway where a Russian naval ship, the *Yermak,* awaited us. I am no expert on boats, but I was assured this vessel was well-suited to the dangerous conditions we could expect at the top of the world.

It never ceases to amaze me what our agency can accomplish when it pulls its many strings.

The first part of our voyage was uneventful—but for the chilling temperature, it could have been a pleasure cruise. I took pride in my lack of seasickness; there have been ocean journeys I have been able to enjoy far less.

One short exchange on that ship stands out for me. Ben and I were on deck, leaning on the rail and watching the ice drift. We drank the most god awful coffee I have had the misfortune to come across. Our warm breath was visible, mingling with the frigid air.

I said, "Of all the places I imagined this endless chase to take us, I had not considered this frozen wasteland."

Ben stared at some vague point in the distance, as he often does. He asked, "Where else would the devil hide but in the climate where you would least expect to find him?"

After ten days on the water, our captain and his crew grew restless. I understood and was sympathetic, as these were soldiers, men of action. To play nursemaid to two Americans must have been torture, especially considering how little they knew of our mission. We continued to follow the known route of Ammon, having already passed the point when we should have overtaken him with our greater speed.

I was with the captain in his quarters, arguing over the next course of action. He wished to return the ship to port and resume his regular patrol. I attempted to explain the importance of finding Stuart Ammon without revealing information that would put the captain and his crew into more danger than they already were.

Ben stumbled into the room. He looked like hell. His dark hair was disheveled, his eyes were bloodshot and crazed. I had seen this time and time again, and it still raised the hairs on the back of my neck. I crept to the edge of my seat and readied myself for what was sure to be a tumultuous debate.

"I don't care how well you are connected, Mr. Rosen," the captain said. His English was impressive. "There is no drinking on my ship."

Ben swayed on his feet. "I haven't been drinking," he said, "I've been sleeping." He slapped a crumpled piece of paper on the table in front of the captain. Letters and numbers were scrawled across it; in some places the pen had torn through the paper in his haste. "Here is your heading. You will follow it to the research facility."

The captain's face reddened. "You do not give me orders," he began, but I gently put my hand on his shoulder, keeping him in his seat.

"Captain, please," I said. "It is not only in the best interest of my colleague and myself that I ask this of you. It is in the best interest of everyone on this planet that we find this man before it is too late."

Diplomacy won out over pride and wild-eyed theatrics. As the captain changed course, I found myself struggling once again with the secrets of Benjamin Rose. We have worked together for over twenty years, yet the true sources of his sudden information and insights remain a mystery. His answer was the same as it has ever been—"It came to me in a dream"—but I continue to question the validity of his claim.

In recent years, these incidents have been followed by increasingly erratic behavior. I suspect drugs have become involved in whatever process he employs. I long ago lost count of the number of times I have awoken to the sounds of him screaming in his sleep beside me.

Ben's heading proved to be correct, as his mystery information nearly always is. The ship's spotters located the research base situated precisely on Ben's course while we were still miles out. The captain ordered a full stop, and Ben and I boarded a lifeboat. A member of the crew accidentally kicked my pack, making a loud clanging sound. My heart stopped. I overreacted, telling him to get the hell away as I checked the pack to make sure its contents were not compromised.

Before the boat was lowered into the water, the captain

dismissed his crew and crouched to speak with us. "There is some ice, but nothing you cannot get through."

I said, "That is good to hear."

He glanced over his shoulder. "I must confess," he said to us quietly, "My superiors know much about this man you seek."

I exchanged a quick glance with Ben. We had suspected this might be the case, and it explained why the captain wanted so badly to turn back. We did not blame him; whatever he had been told would fully justify his actions. We were all madmen rushing into the fire.

"If, that is, when you make it back," he said, correcting himself, "I will make an exception to our no-drinking rule, no?"

"We look forward to it, Captain," I said.

"Take this," the captain said, handing Ben what looked like a handgun. It had three large barrels and an eagle stamped into its side. "It is my personal flare gun. When you are ready to return, fire it into the air."

Ben accepted the gift. "Thank you," he said. "We'll try to not keep you waiting."

The captain smiled, his eyes remaining grim. He barked at his crew, giving orders in Russian, and they quickly lowered our boat into the water.

We silently rowed our way across the freezing water, forced to trust our compass in the surreal stillness. If not for my goggles, I am sure my eyes would have frozen into icy marbles in my skull. A thermometer on the inner hull of the lifeboat read -67.3 degrees Celsius. I pressed my leg against the heavy canvas pack sitting in the floor of the boat to assure myself.

We were less than a mile away when the illness hit. It was a mild vertigo at first, but it quickly escalated. I was the first to vomit over the side of the boat. It felt as if my brain wanted to emancipate itself from my skull, and I could taste metal.

I was about to say we should reverse course when the hallucinations started. I saw lights swirling in the freezing darkness below us, outlining impossibly massive shapes. Then corpses began to drift by, floating just under the surface of the water. I saw a beautiful young woman, her black hair swirling around a pale face that would never grow older. Her eyes popped open, white and unseeing.

"Don't look at them," said Ben.

"You knew this would happen," I accused him. "This is worse than Botetourt. We'll be drooling idiots before we make it to the station."

"Keep rowing," he said through his clenched jaw.

Shortly after the dock was in sight, the chaos in my head calmed. It was not gone entirely, but was manageable. I asked Ben his thoughts.

"We're in the eye of a growing storm," he said. "I would hate to be our Russian friends right now."

The ice station was a small group of buildings anchored to the surface of a drifting glacial fragment. To call it a fragment is somewhat misleading, as it was nearly a thousand square yards. We tied off our boat and crept out onto the ice.

It was not long before we saw it. I thought I knew what to expect from Ammon by this point, but what I saw on the ice still took me aback. There were five male corpses, each one nude and headless. Always headless. The bodies were split in two, from the neck to the asshole. The bodies showed evidence of extensive torture, bearing almost mathematical slashes in the skin. They had been precisely placed before being separated, as the pieces had been dragged apart to create a bloody walkway to the main building. Ice crystals were forming in the open body cavities, but some of the guts spilled out onto the ice were still steaming.

We walked through the macabre welcoming committee. The main building in the camp was tall and square, with snow packed against the outside of the walls for insulation. From the intelligence reports, we knew the massive structure had only one wide entrance, which was now wide open despite the plunging temperatures.

As we approached the door, I put my hand on Ben's shoulder. "I know we probably won't make it out of this, and I've made my peace with that. If I have to charge the gates of hell, my friend, I'm glad it is with you."

Ben put his hand on top of mine and squeezed it. A loud hum began inside the building, and we entered.

The first thing I thought of was that Karloff movie. Machines lined the walls, vacuum tubes blinking on and off. Power cables as thick as my arm ran every which way over the floor, like a pit of enormous snakes. A large portion of the room was dedicated to gas generators, which were all running at full tilt. The air smelled like a hundred electric train sets. In the center of the room was a metal cylinder that looked like a massive telescope, the kind you would see in a hilltop observatory. I estimated it to be twenty-five feet tall and seven feet in diameter at either end. Instead of pointing at the stars, it was aimed at a hole in the ice about five feet across. The water down in the hole began to bubble.

Stuart Ammon moved from one machine to another, reading dials and flipping switches. Without looking up, he said, "Of course you two would show up. It's been a while."

"It has." Ben said. "Some of us thought you died in China."

Ammon pulled a massive switch, like the type that triggers an electric chair. I could see his hands were coated with the blood of the men outside. The hum, already deafening, grew even stronger, and the water beneath the device came to a roaring boil. The air between the lens and the water shimmered with heat. "I hope you didn't think so little of me, Mr. Rosen," he said.

Ben grinned, but his eyes remained grim. "Oh, no," he said. "I knew you were still kicking around, what with the world going to shit."

Ammon clicked his tongue disapprovingly. He shot me a look and said, "Your boyfriend has a bit of a mouth on him." I said nothing. "Still," he continued, "he's right. This is the time, my friends. This whole damn world—even when it's circling the drain—the whole damn world can feel it. After all these years, after all my waiting, the conditions are right."

I had no idea what the conditions were right for, but anything Stuart Ammon was excited about was bad news for the rest of us.

"What's down there, Ammon?" I asked. "What did you find?"

"Oh, Richard, Richard, Richard," Ammon said. "I never lost him. I just had to wait for the right circumstances to wake him up. The perfect circumstances. Everything finally lined up."

Ben asked, "It has to be now?"

Ammon laughed. The sound felt like something clawing at my ribs. "You chumps know as well as anyone how long I've been holding out. It's now or never."

"Then now is when we'll stop you," Ben said.

"I don't see it going that way," Ammon said. "I'm fairly sure it's only the two of you. You couldn't best me twenty years ago, princess, and the years haven't been kind. Hopefully you learned your lesson the last time and won't waste my time trying to shoot me."

From under my heavy coat, I pulled out a long metal tube. It had a grip and trigger like a gun near the front, and a second handle at the back. A rubber hose connected it to the gas tanks on my back. "We learned our lesson just fine," I said as I pulled both triggers.

Flame erupted from the tip of the flame thrower, but he moved much faster than I remembered. In an instant, he stood beside me. The flame disappeared when he ripped the wand from my hands. He pulled the heavy metal pieces apart, causing thick streams of gasoline to drench us both. Drops of fuel hissed as they hit the frozen ground. The fumes made me want to retch. I backed away out of his reach, but Ammon dismissed me as he turned back to Ben.

"This was your big idea?" Ammon asked. "I expected more out of you, Rosen."

Ben shrugged. "I don't know. We've had worse ideas." As he spoke the words, he pulled the captain's flare gun from his pocket.

Ammon looked at the gun incredulously. He knew what we had learned, that with his speed and strength, he shrugged off bullet wounds that would kill anyone else. Ben pulled the trigger and three bright red flares spiraled across the room. They collided with Ammon, igniting the gasoline fumes and his fuel-soaked jacket.

I will remember the sound Ammon made as the flames consumed him until the day I die. It was a roar of pain and fury that could have shattered the world. He rushed at us, and I tripped, falling backward. That clumsy act saved my life, as I was still leaking fuel.

I shed the gas tanks and rose to chase Ammon. Ben stopped me. "We have a more immediate problem," he said.

The device and its phantom beam were still humming that mechanical hum, and the boiling ocean water was sloshing in and out of the hole in the floor. The ice began to quake. The machine was accomplishing whatever Ammon had designed it to do. The moment of no return was quickly approaching, if it had not already passed.

"Shut it down!" Ben yelled over the increasing clamor of the device.

"How?"

"I have no idea!"

"What about the explosives back in the boat?" I asked.

"I don't think there's time," Ben said. He looked over the machines. Ben Rosen was the smartest man I have ever met, but I saw confusion in his eyes as he tried to make sense of the controls. "Start pulling cables!" he yelled.

There were dozens of the thick cables connected to the top of the device. I pulled down on one with all my strength. The connection broke loose, electricity arching and forcing me to shield me eyes. The hum continued.

I caught Ben's eye as he reached for another black cable. Our task was hopeless and we knew it. We had close to a zero chance of destroying a crucial part of the system in time to stop whatever was happening. I had no idea what was sleeping under the water, but I believed Ammon when he said it meant the end.

Ben grabbed a metal pipe from a pile on the floor and started smashing equipment. Glass dials shattered and broken connections sparked, but the beam continued its work. I studied the main device, racking my brain for an answer. It really was remarkably like a giant telescope, with a massive lens and gears to control where it was pointed. The top of the machine was immense, and looked to be the heaviest part of the whole shebang.

"Ben!" I called. "Help me!"

I found a grip high up on the machine and pulled. Ben saw what I was trying to do, and he dropped the pipe and pulled with me. The cylinder was sturdy, but the gears turned as the angle of the device changed by about 45 degrees. Wherever the beam pointed, the ice was melted clean through instantly. I tried not to think what would happen to me if I fell in the path of that invisible heat.

"It's not far enough!" Ben said. He pointed to the top of the machine. "Boost me up!"

I crouched and made a stirrup with my hands. He put a foot in my palms, and was grateful when I had the strength to help him reach high enough to grab onto the mass of cables and reach the top of the machine.

He jumped on the rear of the machine while I pulled with every muscle in my body. The mount holding the cylinder groaned. "It's working!" I called up to him.

Events progressed quickly. The device's base, designed to point at the ground, broke apart. Still connected to its mount, the heavier top swung down quickly. The part of the cylinder above the mount was longer than the part below, so as it spun, the top hit the ice hard. Ben was thrown clear, but I never had a chance to move. My leg was crushed between the ice and the heavy end of the machine. I screamed as pain exploded through my leg.

Ben scrambled over. "Richie, oh my God, are you okay?"

I tried to speak, but I only grunted. My leg felt like a pillowcase full of busted light bulbs.

Ben patted me on the shoulder. "I know it's bad, I know. But it's going to be okay. Can't you feel it?"

I held my breath and tried to block out the pain. He was right; the ice had stopped shaking. The water was calming down in the trench cut by the machine. Meanwhile, the machine's new target, the back half of the building and a fair amount of the ceiling, were gone. They had not caught fire; instead it was like the wood and metal had melted away with the snow.

"What about the sky?" I asked, my voice cracking.

The machine was pointed at about a 70 degree angle. I could only see some of the sky, but it was on fire. My mind could not cope with the idea.

"Don't worry," Ben said. "I don't think it's a big deal."

But it was a big deal. On January 25, 1938 was the greatest occurrence of aurora borealis, if that is really what it was, in almost a century. The skies burned red across the Northern Hemisphere, causing panic all over Europe, Asia, and the United States. I read in a newspaper the skies that night were so bright that firemen were out in their trucks all over the country trying to find the fire.

The machine powered down. The roaring hum diminished to a whisper, and then it was gone. Whether the device had stopped at its designated time or we had broken it, we will never know.

Ben used the piece of pipe as a lever to lift the machine high enough to drag me out from beneath it. I put my arm around his shoulder and he helped me back to our boat. I could not help noticing a set of shallow footprints other than ours. They led to the edge of the ice by the dock and disappeared into the water.

"Should we sink the equipment?" I asked. The frigid cold and no small dose of morphine from the boats first-aid pack was helping me to think and communicate more clearly, at least for the moment.

"You know the agency will want to take a look at this," Ben said. He was right, of course. I was in no condition to argue, but I still hate the thought of anyone having such a toy in their toy box. I scanned the water around our boat looking for life. I did not see anything under the red light of the sky.

Not needing to worry about making noise anymore, Ben used the boat's off-board motor to retrace our course as I drifted in my opiate-induced haze; thankfully, the hallucinations did not reoccur. The *Yermak* met us halfway. Apparently a major meteorological event is as effective a signal as a flare gun.

I heard a whistle from the deck of the ship, followed by a cheer. The crew got ready to bring us back on board. I waved sluggishly and looked over at Ben. He was looking behind us, although the research base was long out of sight.

"He's dead, you know," I said. "He's got to be. No one could survive those burns or that freezing water, not even him."

"Maybe not," he said. "But do you remember how many boats were at the dock when we got there?"

My breath caught in my throat. I had no idea.

"I think one was missing," he said.

That unfortunate bit of information ricocheted around in my head. It knocked another thought loose, so I spoke up. "You seemed to know an awful lot about what Ammon was doing out here. About what's down there in the dark."

"Maybe." Ben said.

"Where'd you hear about it?" I asked. "Somebody at the Lodge?"

Ben shook his head. The son of a bitch smiled and said, "I saw it in a dream."

15

"I HOPE THAT WAS JUICY ENOUGH FOR YOU," Thomas said as Joan set down the journal.

"Was any of that true?" Joan asked, lowering the footrest on the recliner.

Thomas looked thoughtful. He said, "As far I have been able to verify, everything in these journals is true." He sat down on the carpet beside her chair, his legs stretched out in front of him. He examined his shoes and said, "The problem is, there are few people who knew the details of anything Benjamin Rosen and Richard Henry were involved in."

"Like what?" she asked.

"Everything in the journals before 1949, for one," he said. "And the men themselves, they're like ghosts. I can't find anything about them. I couldn't even find birth certificates. Those newspaper articles Richard Henry says he wrote? I can't even find those. There are records going back to the 1960s for this Roy West identity Henry took on, but that's it."

Joan leaned over the arm of the chair, resting her chin in the crook of her elbow. Her forehead wrinkled. "Then how do you know any of it was real? Couldn't Roy have made it all up when he was bored?"

He laughed. "It's real. The Old Man hated those guys. Hated them. All of us have seen pictures of what they looked like, and pictures of what they would look like now if they were still alive. All so we could keep an eye out, maybe find them. That was how I knew it was Henry when I saw him that first time." His eyes glazed in a daydream. "If I'd delivered the elusive Richard Henry to the Old Man, I would have been the golden boy for a long, long time."

"What about this?" Joan asked, flipping through the journal. She pointed out a word. "What's the Lodge? These two guys apparently work for whatever it is, and I think I've heard someone else mention them."

"You have," Thomas said. "Douglas Stephenson—Brennan's friend Jim—worked for them or with them. At least he said as much the night he died."

Joan frowned. "That doesn't make any sense. Rosen and Henry worked for the Lodge, and they were trying to stop Stuart Ammon. Doesn't that make them the good guys?"

"The Lodge is a bigger mystery than those two men. Even Henry's journals hardly mention it. I don't know if it's connected to the United States or any other government, where it operates from. Nothing. But I have a theory that I've pieced together from what little I do know that might explain why the Lodge is operating like it is."

"Is it crazy?" Joan asked. "I'm getting pretty sick of crazy."

"It's a little crazy."

"Fine. Let's hear it."

"Okay. So the Lodge recruits Richard Henry in 1913, and he worked with Benjamin Rosen until 1949, when Rosen disappeared. The Old Man claims to be behind whatever happened to Rosen. Henry went into hiding at the same time, eventually assuming the identity of Roy West."

Joan tried to match the facts in her head. "Sounds about right. But what does that tell you?"

"If the Lodge had the knowledge and resources to go toe to toe with the Old Man, it should have been able to keep Richard

Henry safe. At least better than Henry could do on his own. So why did he run away?"

Joan sighed and said, "Get to the point."

Thomas pulled a pack of cigarettes out of his pocket. He glanced at Joan, as if remembering she was there, and put the pack away. He asked, "How about I ask you a question instead?"

"Shoot."

"How did Stephenson's group know about Elsie Paroubek?"

Joan stared blankly, thinking. "I don't know," she said. "From what Brennan said, it didn't seem like there was anything to connect hers to the other murders. And I'm guessing you told the Old Man so he could cover it up. That's how it works with you bastards, isn't it?"

"Yes, that's how it worked when we were young and always fucking up. The only two people who could connect Paroubek with the other murders were the Old Man and me."

"That is weird," Joan said.

"Exactly. But Stephenson got that information from his employers. I think the Old Man controls the Lodge, and has for a long time."

"You're right. That is crazy."

"Crazy is the only game in town, Joan. Hear me out. I think the Old Man was either behind Rosen's disappearance in '49, or he took advantage of Rosen being out of the picture. He seized control of the Lodge, but Richard Henry escaped. The poor bastard was hiding as much from his old allies as he was from his old nemesis."

"So the only people working against the Old Man—"

"Now work for the Old Man," Thomas said. "Exactly. Protecting him and furthering his damned agenda. At the very least, the Old Man has his pet agency on the lookout for evidence he or his offspring exist and sends in people to clean up any messes. It looks like he didn't count on a clone popping up he didn't know about, so Stephenson was operating on incorrect information when he followed up on Brennan's DNA match. He connected Brennan to murders he had the opportunity to commit. We were lucky I could help him get out of that cell in the desert before the Old Man showed up, or we would never have made it as far as we have."

"Speaking of the Old Man," Joan said. "Apparently he's a comic-book super villain? Named Stuart Ammon?"

Thomas stopped smiling. "Stuart Ammon was just the name he was using in 1938. In 1913 he was D. Feldman, and in 1887 he was Jean Baptiste Vincent Laborde. And I wish he was some cartoon villain. But he's much worse."

"How?"

Thomas stared at her, his eyes not blinking. "He's been around a long time. Longer than you can wrap your head around. He doesn't do the things he does for money or sex or power. He has motives and goals human beings can't comprehend, and he has had countless lifetimes to work toward his goals."

Joan said, "And you're the same thing." *Brennan's the same thing,* she thought.

"Maybe."

"Maybe?" she asked. "What does 'maybe' mean?"

"It means I don't know what I am, and I don't know what Brennan is. That doesn't mean we have to be the same. We don't have to be monsters like the Old Man."

They sat there in silence, Joan chewing on her lip and Thomas staring at his shoes.

Brennan's the same thing. The thought echoed in her head. She looked over Richard Henry's cabinets, including the one that held his collection of Egyptian items. The ancient metal rod caught her eye, the one used to remove the brain of a corpse when a person was mummified. The tip was probably just rusted, but it looked like dried blood.

Brennan's the same thing.

16

MAY 20, 1991.

I thought I was done writing in these books no one will ever read. I thought I was done with everything. I am old, so old I do not want to think about it. I have lived an entire life here in Flatland, Texas, since I lost Ben, and all I have done is wait for the end.

I still see Ben sometimes, for a brief moment out of the corner of my eye. He always looks the same, dressed to the nines for that New Year's Eve party in St. Louis, all the way back in 1922. I guess it makes sense I see him this way, as that's how I like to remember him. Young and perfect in his tux, with his bow tie hanging loose.

But now it's more than delirium tying me to the past. Two days ago I received a phone call, which was already an event in and of itself. I picked up the phone expecting a sales call or someone telling me I forgot to pay a bill. Instead, a woman's voice said, "Hello. Can I speak with Roy West?"

"This is Roy. What can I do for you?"

"My name is Ali—" The words caught in her throat. "My name is Sylvia Kindred. I'm afraid I need your help, Mr. West. I'm in trouble."

"I'm in no position to help anyone, ma'am. If you'll excuse me—"

"Wait!" she said. "Don't hang up! Please. Mr. Lampton told me to call you if I ever needed help."

"That is a name I have not heard in a long time, Ms. Kindred. Explain yourself. Quickly."

"I have been on the run for a long time from someone you are familiar with," she said. "A man of advanced age and unknown origins."

My throat dried up in an instant. "I know him," I said. Something stirred within me I have not felt in a long time. "What can I do to help?"

"I need a place to stay."

I chuckled. "It's not exactly the Hilton, but you're welcome to come here."

"It's not for me," she said. "It's for my son."

I told her how to find me, and the two of them arrived yesterday. I was not surprised she had to stop for directions on the way.

The boy is fourteen and shy as hell. From the moment I saw him, I could see the resemblance, and it terrified me.

Sylvia—I suppose I should say Alice—said, "Brennan, this is your grandfather, Roy West. He'll be taking care of you while I'm away."

"Hello, Mr. West," he said.

"Call me Grandpa," I said. Alice and I agreed on this deception over phone. I understand the importance of family and how terrible it can be when they cast you out. If the boy is going to have a chance, he needs to grow up feeling he has roots. "I'm glad you'll be staying with me. I hope you like old horror movies, because I watch an awful lot of them."

Brennan smiled politely. "That sounds great," he said.

We moved Brennan's things into my guest room and ate fried chicken for dinner. Afterward, we sat outside on the porch while Alice smoked and I told Brennan about Flatland. He listened to my bland ramblings for an impressive length of time before excusing himself and heading to bed.

When I was sure he was out of earshot, I said, “He’s not really your son, is he?”

“He is in the ways that really matter,” she said.

“I don’t understand. Did that monster find a way to become young again?”

“Not yet. Brennan’s a clone.”

“And you brought him here?” I asked. “What were you thinking?”

“Brennan’s not like him, and he’s not like the others,” Alice said. “Brennan is a good person.”

“Is he even a person at all?” I asked.

“He is to me. And I need to know you feel the same way before I can leave him here.”

“I like the boy, Alice. I really do. But I can’t promise anything until you tell me where he came from.”

She took a long drag on her cigarette. “That’s fair. When I was Dr. Sylvia Kindred, I worked in the field of genetics. I was a student of John Gurdon and other pioneers in the process of nuclear transfer. I was recruited in 1971 to work on a private project, which turned out to be the cloning of a human subject. At least, I believed him to be human at the time.

“We were instructed early on not to question the nature of the samples. The money was so good I was more than happy to turn a blind eye. The donor cells carried unique traits, and they were surprisingly, even unnaturally resilient. This allowed us to work years, decades ahead of anyone else.

“The process requires placing a nucleus from the adult donor cell into an egg with the nucleus removed, which is then placed in a surrogate mother. This results in clones that are not exact duplications due to mutation and the DNA already present in the egg. The unusual donor cells we worked with, however, transformed the eggs, making a successful clone a perfect copy of the original donor. Unfortunately, most of the embryos were still subject to mutation of a different kind.

“The project was located on a remote farm in Kansas. We used the modified barn as the lab, which was frustrating at times, but suited our needs. Our hired surrogates were kept in the house next door, at first of their own free will. Once they started dying, however, they were locked in their rooms like cattle. The things that went on in that house will haunt me for the rest of my life.

"Raised salaries and finally threats forced us to maintain a scientific detachment to the nightmare the project had become. Every clone was born looking completely normal and kept in the lab for examination. However, serious mutations became apparent before the specimens reached their third birthday. Once one of the boys exhibited abnormalities, we..." Alice started to cry. "We were ordered to lock them in the cellar beneath the barn. They survived down there somehow, and I could hear them. Sometimes they tried to get out. I never saw it, but I think that's where they started putting the bodies of the surrogates.

"Eventually the man in charge came to check on our progress. He spent time in the cellar doing things I can't even think about, and then he took away some of the children who had grown old enough without signs of problems. Older children who did not pass his inspection went down in the cellar with the others.

"During one of his visits to the barn, he noticed an infant in an incubator. 'What is this?' he asked.

"'Just a subject born prematurely,' I said. He walked over to the incubator and did something I couldn't see to the baby.

"'Get rid of it,' he said when he was done. 'It's a waste of time. Throw it in the pit with the rest.'

"I looked at the baby. He raised his tiny hand, and whatever cage held my conscience shattered. 'Sir, it doesn't show any signs of mutation.'

"He said, 'Doesn't matter. It's weak, and I don't pay you for weak.'

"'I'll get rid of it right away,' I said. 'There is just a little more data I need to collect.'

"That night I snuck him away to my apartment in town and found someone I could trust to watch him during the day. I needed to find a way to escape the project, but it was already becoming obvious we were expendable. I was sure that once the project was over, we would be locked down in the pit ourselves.

"I was trapped, and it seemed totally hopeless. Then Mr. Lampton, one of my bosses, approached me. He said he knew what I had done, and he could help me escape with a new identity. He said he had done the same for you, Mr. West, and, if I was ever in trouble, I should contact you. I've been on the run ever since.

"I've always worried Brennan would develop mutations like so many of the others, or turn out to be as evil as what he came from. But none of that has happened. He's my son, and that's all he's ever known. I love him, and I've done everything I can to give him a normal life."

Finished with her tale, Alice lit another cigarette. Moths fluttered against the porch light.

I was in shock. "That's an incredible story, Alice. But why call me now?"

Alice hung her head. "I got lonely and made the mistake of calling some family. Just to hear their voices, you know? It was a one-time mistake, and I regretted it the instant I hung up the phone. It wasn't long before I heard back from my aunt that someone had gotten to them and was coming for me."

"I'm so sorry," I said, knowing what this meant had already happened to her family. The Old Man was nothing if not thorough; I assume the same is true for his offspring.

"I'm just grateful your number still worked. I need to leave Brennan with you." She wiped away tears. "Hopefully only until this blows over."

I leaned over and took her hand in mine. "Alice, I don't know anything about taking care of a kid, but I'll protect him. He'll be safe and waiting for you when you get back."

"Thank you, Roy," she said. "Please promise me you won't tell him the truth about what he is."

"You have my word," I said.

I insisted she take my bed, and I slept on the couch. This morning I gave her all the money I could. Brennan did his best to be strong for her. The poor kid is used to change, but he has never been without his mother.

"Be good, honey," his mom said before she drove off, leaving us standing there in the dirt.

Brennan is in his room now, and I'll give him the time he needs. I admit having a delineation of that creature in my home scares me, and someday he'll have to face his true nature. But I want to believe it's not what Brennan came from that matters, but who he chooses to be.

I never had the chance to have a son, and I could certainly use a hand around here. It might help Brennan keep his mind off things to do some work. I have an old fence that needs mending out by the road.

17

THOMAS OFFERED the larger bed in the master bedroom, but Joan insisted on sleeping in Brennan's old room. Thomas remained in the living room with a stack of Henry's journals when Joan retired for the night.

The contents of the bedroom had been gutted by Brennan when he left for college, and then again after Henry had passed away. The pin-up poster was missing, presumably to keep Brennan company on those long, lonely nights in his dorm room. The leather-top desk was also gone, but the bed was still there. She found some sheets in a hall closet that were not too dusty and made the bed.

It was late in the summer, and she listened to the song of the cicadas, which she had called locusts growing up. When her parents were still alive, she once spent a week with her grandmother during summer break. The sound of locusts and the dusty, familiar smell of an old person's house reminded her of that long-ago week. The sweet and sudden vividness of the memory threatened to bring tears.

She thought instead of Brennan, and how much she missed him. Now that she knew the truth, she realized how much it had felt like he never came back from the farm. Thomas had done an incredible job imitating Brennan, but there had still been a sense of distance. At the time, she had told herself it was something they would get over together.

I hope that's still true, she thought. *Oh God, I hope that's still true.*

She tried to feel Brennan's presence there, in the same room where he had worried about his mom, fretted over friendships, worked up the courage to call girls, and cried over broken hearts. She remembered how it felt to have his arms around her, but that made her think about how many nights she had shared a bed with Thomas. Her stomach twisted in knots as she remembered how many more times she had been with a pretender than she had been with the real Brennan. Once they had Brennan back, Thomas would answer for that.

She thought she had found a true connection with someone. She had feelings for Brennan when he had left her in a motel room to face off with the Old Man, but that seed had grown in soil poisoned by a lie. The killer currently on the other side of the door had painted his own idealized picture of Brennan for her to fall in love with, and now her true feelings and allegiance were up in the air.

Before she drifted off, she came to one conclusion.

I want Brennan back, she thought. *The real Brennan. The same one Alice was forced to leave here, and the one who risked everything for me when I was just a stranger. I want him back more than I've ever wanted anything before. I don't care if he isn't who I think he is; he'll be close enough. He came out of nowhere and helped me when I only believed two things about myself: I didn't need saving, and even if I did, I wasn't worth the trouble. He was there for me at exactly the right time, and I'll do the same for him. No matter what.*

We'll sort the rest out together.

The air conditioner hummed. She curled up under the blankets, hugging her knees. She had not prayed in a long time, not since she was a little girl. But she had recently learned monsters slept under the ocean and there were men who could read your mind by eating your brain. The concept of God, while still unlikely, seemed a bit less impossible. As she drifted off to sleep, her prayers were not so much words as desires she offered up in the vague hope they might overcome divine indifference.

18

THE NEXT MORNING, Joan awoke long before the sun came up. She sat with her back against the bed and sorted through a stack of Brennan's old CDs. There was a decent assortment along with the old blues albums, including a Ramones album she used to listen to nonstop when she was fifteen. There was nothing to play it on, but she still ended up in the shower humming "The KKK Took My Baby Away" to herself. She could only remember the chorus, and she was not confident in her memory of even that. She made up for a lack of lyrics with her enthusiasm.

Thomas told her the night before there would be warm water this time, but the pilot light must have gone out again. She gave up on waiting for the water to heat up, and she was not going to let it ruin her second shower in as many weeks. Her skin was tight with goose bumps, and her nipples ached as she washed away as much of the worry as she could. It was cold as hell, but she was getting used to it.

It's crazy what you can get used to, she thought.

She tried not to think about how long the filthy bar of soap and crusty bottle of dandruff shampoo had been in the shower. She missed her own bathroom, full of her own stuff. She wondered what had happened to her apartment. Had the men from the Lodge boxed everything up? She could not imagine why they would, but it seemed like something those crazy assholes would do. She frowned at the thought of a suited man going through her underwear or putting her cat in a crate. In her mind, she saw the shadow man, thin as a scarecrow, wearing glasses with extra lenses that could be swung into position, like a jeweler or a watchmaker.

After getting dressed, Joan found Thomas in the garage, a plain looking building separate from the main house. Inside was Richard Henry's workshop. A pegboard on the wall held a variety of tools, and underneath it was a table covered in wires, electrical components, and a soldering iron. A well-used bicycle with a flat tire leaned against a metal shelf. The black convertible Thomas had mentioned in his story was there, and next to it sat a larger vehicle covered with a blue tarp. The garage was crowded with boxes, but she could tell the inventory was nothing compared to the storage locker they had visited before.

Thomas stood over the open trunk of the Alfa Romeo. Inside was a case filled with an assortment of knives. A cigarette dangled from his lips, and the smoke and the smell of menthol made Joan cough. Thomas, startled, looked up from his work.

"I thought you'd be harder to sneak up on," Joan said.

"I thought you were still asleep," he said, looking relieved. "If it had been anyone else walking in, that would be the start to a bad day for both of us."

"Why do you smoke those things?" she asked. "They smell like medicine."

"The smoke feels nice and cool in my chest," he said. "Sometimes I need to feel cold inside."

Joan kicked a canvas duffel bag. "You weren't considering leaving me behind, were you?"

Thomas flipped one of the knives in his hand, end over end. "If I was, looks like I blew it."

She took the lid off of a box. Inside were more tax documents for the Fifteen Second Group. The documents were similar to those from the storage locker, but these contained more straightforward information. She was no accountant, but the monetary amounts were extremely high, many of them in the millions.

"So this is where the Old Man gets his money?" she asked.

"That's just one company, and this is only what actually gets reported."

She leafed through the papers. "Why are they called the Fifteen Second Group?" she asked.

Thomas shrugged. "I never asked. My guess is the popular myth about how long your head stays alive after it's been cut off."

"Of course it would be that." Joan sighed.

Thomas became silent. He picked up a thick envelope and slipped it inside his bag.

"It wasn't that long ago," Joan said, "that I was helping people. I put them together when they were broken. I'd heard about serial killers and crazies before, but I had no idea how hard some people worked to tear people apart. Not until you showed up." Thomas looked at her, his expression neutral. "I know you didn't kill my friends," she said, "but you can't deny killing was something you did. Not just once, but as a routine."

Thomas frowned. "I was a prisoner of my situation. Like we are now." He accidentally caught his thumb on the blade of short knife with a bone handle. He winced. "We're still stuck on the defensive, and I don't even know where to go next."

Joan waved the thick manila folder. "How about the Fifteen Second Group? We go to their offices, bust some heads."

Thomas grinned but shook his head. "The Old Man never included me on that side of things. You have to realize, he keeps everything segregated. He kept his money over here," he said, stretching out his left arm and waving his hand. He stretched out his other arm and waved, saying, "And his progeny over here. I've never been able to track down the Fifteen Second Group's offices. There's a good chance the entire thing is a fabrication."

"There's nowhere we can go check out?" Joan asked.

Thomas shook his head.

She said, "We have to do something. As much as I'm

enjoying our little vacation home, I need to go get the real Brennan back."

She walked over to the truck and leaned in close to Thomas. She said into his ear, quietly, "I know what you must have done after I—after we killed all those guys. The heads. Did you get anything useful out of them?"

"Plenty, but not a thing that told me where Brennan is," Thomas said. "I don't have any information on his location since the farm."

"Then that's where we're going," Joan said.

"What?" Thomas asked. "That's crazy."

"Shut up," she said, jamming her finger into Thomas' chest. "In the land of the bat-shit insane, the half-crazy woman is queen. Remember, I'm calling the shots now."

"Fine," he said. "It's not like I wanted to live forever."

"Please refrain from saying things like that," Joan said. She kicked one of the black car's tires. "Is this what we're taking? If we're going nowhere, at least we'll get there fast."

"No," Thomas said. "I have something more appropriate." He pulled back the blue tarp.

"You've got to be joking," Joan said.

FINAL PHASE

1

THE 1955 INTERNATIONAL PICKUP TRUCK rolled down the Kansas interstate.

Richard Henry purchased the truck in 1962, just as he started to feel comfortable with the Roy West identity. It completed his disguise; nothing said long-time Texan like an old pickup. He had never owned his own car, but the panhandle of Texas was not New York, and a man had to get around. He found owning a vehicle empowering and found it satisfying to load the bed full of scrap metal or firewood. It made him feel like a person in control of his destiny, despite the fact he was defeated and in hiding. He used the truck to haul supplies as he built his home, and to make deliveries for a local hardware store until he got too old for the work.

Thomas' shadow company purchased the truck along with the house when Henry died. Henry's pride in the vehicle was evident in how well it still ran long after his passing, but the exterior showed its age. It had never been repainted, and the once-red paint was faded and worn away. Rust attacked the rear fender, and the wood slats in the bed cried out to be replaced. The tailgate no longer worked properly and was held closed with a chain. The bed of the truck was currently full, its contents hidden by the same blue tarp that had covered the vehicle in the garage.

Joan said there was no way they were taking the truck, but Thomas quieted her objections by popping the hood. Inside, the engine looked brand new. Thomas had never forgotten how invisible a convertible became with its top up, and the beat-up pickup was a logical extrapolation. On any road between Flatland and the farm, the old truck—driven two miles below the speed limit—would be a non-thing, a blank spot on everyone's radar.

Joan did not like how much longer it would take to reach their destination, but she did not argue with him. Thomas driving right up to their front door was probably the last thing the Old Man and his multiples would expect. They would never see him coming.

I bet no one ever sees the son of a bitch coming, Joan thought. *I sure as hell didn't.* She eyed him across the cab of the truck and shuddered.

Thomas was wearing a pair of faded blue jeans and one of Richard Henry's old flannel shirts to further the camouflage. She wore a white tank top and the same pair of jeans she had been wearing when she met Brennan for the first time. Over the radio, Bo Carter sang about the old devil.

They passed an old wooden billboard, one sitting low to the ground. The weathered, hand-painted letters read, '*Cafe, 3 miles.*' A missing board split the image of a hamburger and French fries.

"We should stop and get something to eat," Thomas said.

"Not a chance," Joan said. "You're already driving too damn slow."

"The farm will still be there. It'll wait for us."

"It's waited long enough," she said.

"I told you, there's no way Brennan is even there. It's been months, and they know we're looking for him. The only thing waiting for us at the farm is nothing or a trap."

"I don't care."

Thomas sighed. "Look at it this way. When was the last time you ate something?"

Joan opened her mouth to reply, but stopped. It must have been something purchased at a gas station and eaten in the car, but she honestly could not remember.

"Think about it," he said. "What if I'm wrong and the Old Man is waiting for us there? You'll probably pass out from hunger before he even has a chance to kill us. How is that going to help Brennan?"

"Fine," she said. "But let's be quick."

When another sign popped up for the restaurant, Thomas took the exit. They found the café on the outskirts of one of one of those small towns that hides just off the highway. The outside of the building was in the same state of disrepair as the rotting billboard, but a few older cars and a truck sat in the parking lot, showing it was open for business. The front of the restaurant looked like the porch of a country home. The steps creaked loudly as they climbed them.

A bell hung from the door, but it made no sound as they entered. A man with gray hair and a plaid flannel shirt sitting at the counter turned to look them over as they entered and, having made his appraisal, went back to his coffee and newspaper. A jukebox sat in the corner with a yellowed *'Out of Order'* sign taped to the glass. The thin waitress, clothed in a faded blue uniform, said to them, "Sit anywhere you like."

Joan sat down, and Thomas followed. The waitress, who looked to be in her late twenties, walked over and handed them menus with peeling lamination. Her nametag read "Sherri." Joan noticed again how thin she looked. Joan had worked with a few people with eating disorders in her internships, and Sherri had all the signs of a bulimic. Her hair was thin, she had the skin of a corpse, and her teeth and gums looked horrible. Joan wanted to say something, but was at a loss.

Honey, if you needed me to save you, she thought, *you picked the wrong day. I have too many to save as it is.* The man at the other table coughed, making a horrible raspy sound.

Joan ordered a cheeseburger and Thomas ordered a turkey and Swiss. Thomas also asked for a family-size order of French fries.

"In case you want to share," he said to Joan.

"Unlikely," she said.

Sherri disappeared into the kitchen. As if he were waiting for the signal, the gray-haired man folded his paper and dropped a few crumpled dollars on the table. He nodded to Joan and Thomas as he left them alone in the restaurant.

Joan fidgeted with her napkin while Thomas stared at the salt and pepper shakers.

"Private dining," Thomas said.

Joan caught herself tearing the napkin into long strips and pushing the tiny bits of paper into a pile. "Just eat quick," she said.

"Sounds like a plan."

Her skin crawled. *If he says that again, I'm going to scream.* She swallowed hard and said, "Speaking of plans, something has been bugging the hell out of me. You said that when you first met Brennan, there wasn't any psychic warning when you almost killed him."

Thomas nodded. "Right. I couldn't believe it."

"So why did it go off when he tried to kill the Old Man in the barn?"

He put his elbows on the table and rubbed his forehead, like he was trying to stop a headache. "That's bothered me, too," he said. "That first night after I found you, I didn't sleep at all. I kept asking myself that question over and over again."

"And?" she asked.

"And I don't know why," he said. "Before Flatland, I thought the monster alarm was something we were born with, something that made us the same as the Old Man. After I—after I changed, it wasn't like I could test it on Brennan again, or ask the others what they thought. Every now and then the old bastard drops hints he can put things in people's minds, change the way they think. 'I like to leave my mark,' he says. That got me thinking about music."

"Music?"

"The delta blues music. Some of us like it; a few of us love it. Even the ones who were never interested were aware of it.

How does that make sense? It's not like we were exposed to much culture growing up. But as long as I can remember, that music has struck a chord deep inside me."

"You think he implanted a love for old music in your head?"

"I'm positive he did. The Old Man has accumulated many talents over the years. The problem for him is he can steal from people, but I don't think he can improve on it, make it evolve. He's like a man who copies the techniques of the greatest painters, but has no idea what to paint. He told Philip how he made a deal down south back in the 1930s. The son of a bitch put guitar playing in some guy's head. He let the poor sucker work for a while, honing his craft on street corners and in bars. Then, when the guy was the best guitar player anyone had ever heard, the Old Man killed him and drained the know-how right back out of him. Like a fruit he'd left on the vine to ripen."

"How do you know what the Old Man told Philip?" Joan asked.

Thomas ignored her. "Even back when I was a kid—"

"Little monster in training," Joan said.

"Even then, I could tell a lot of what was in my head came from him. He could put anything in there, and I'd never know what thoughts came from me, and which ones came from him. I love cars from the 1930s and '40s, but I don't think it's because they stood out to me the year they rolled off the assembly line. I know no one told me how easy it is to snap a neck; the knowledge was just there."

"Thomas," she said, her face reddening, "I have a question for you, and you'd better tell me the truth. Did you put something in my head to make me sleep with you?" She clenched her fists under the table hard enough that her nails cut into her palms. "Did you put something in my head to make me okay with killing people?"

He slowly met her gaze. "Would it make you feel better if I said I did?"

Joan froze for a moment, but then quietly said, "No."

"Good. Because I didn't." His expression softened. "I'm sorry I slept with you when I was Brennan. I get it now, that was wrong. You're right to hate me for it. But when you helped me kill the others—that was all you."

Joan fought tears. She had found a chance at absolution, but lost it as quickly as it appeared. *I have plenty to answer for all by myself*, she thought.

Thomas continued. "After standing behind Brennan Wade in Richard Henry's kitchen, I decided the monster alarm was artificial, that it was implanted. Like that dead man's ability to play blues guitar, or whatever kept me from finding a way to kill the Old Man myself.

"So I bided my time and kept an eye on Brennan. Protecting him and waiting to put him to use. But the DNA background check set everything in motion. I had to read four of Jim's hired guns to track Brennan to the desert. I killed a half dozen more to make sure he would be alone with Jim in the cell.

"That was the first time I tested him. If we were going to have a chance, I had to know what Brennan was capable of. When he walked out of that place, starved but triumphant, I knew there was something in him I could use. He showed me a bit more when he got out of his cuffs at the police station, but he clinched it when he got you out of your apartment."

"He was really something," Joan said.

"He really was," Thomas said. "I needed to know if he could go all the way. Killing someone before they can kill you is one thing, but murdering a man in cold blood is a horse of a different color."

"That's why you made him kill Jim," she said. "It was your fucked up idea of a graduation."

Thomas tilted his head. "I guess you could say that. I knew I had to toughen him up so that when the time came, he would do what had to be done."

"But it didn't work."

"No. No, it didn't," he said, frowning. "I took Brennan and twisted him into something like me, and it was all for nothing. The instant that damn noise started up in my head, whatever plan I had went out the window. I still don't know if we were created with the alarm or—"

He stopped as the door to the kitchen opened. The waitress set down their food and drinks before hurrying back to the kitchen. *She caught me looking,* Joan thought. *She knows that I know about her problem.*

"Why do you even have the monster alarm?" Joan asked and took a bite of the cheeseburger. Her sudden hunger surprised her and she tore into the fries. "What's the point?"

Thomas laughed. "I've wondered the same thing for a long time. You've got to understand, when we were young and always around each other, it was dangerous. It wasn't like the Old Man was our dad and he kept us in line. There were times we wouldn't see him for years. The alarm was the only thing preventing us from killing each other. I thought that was all it was for, so his clan could survive."

"That must've been weird for Brennan," she said. "Suddenly having that ringing in his head."

Thomas nodded. "Maybe it helped that he had no context for it. He probably had some weird dreams. I bet Alice Wade hated hearing about those."

"Do you still think the alarm is just to keep you from killing each other? Just so the Old Man could add 'absent father' to the list of reasons your little brood is so messed up?"

"No," Thomas said, pushing his empty plate to the center of the table. "Because we can hurt each other, just not easily. The Old Man made it impossible for us to attack him directly, so he could have done the same thing with us killing each other. What it comes down to is, why did he make us in the first place? It's not like he wanted someone to play catch with. And it's not like he needs someone to take over the family business. I know it sounds crazy, but as far as I know the guy will live forever."

It does sound crazy, Joan thought. *But that doesn't mean it isn't true.*

He continued, "Sure, he'll slowly keep getting older. But even if he could get so old that he wears out and dies, it won't be for an insane amount of time. So I got to thinking, what does the Old Man get out of all this? He's been waiting for a long, long time to reproduce. For reasons I don't like to think about, he can't just find himself a concubine to pop out some babies. It doesn't work. He's not like normal people, and his biology doesn't match up. There's no mate for whatever he is, so he had to wait for science to catch up. But there still only needs to be one of him."

Joan did the mental arithmetic. "We put down five: Philip, Andrew, Simon, Joseph, and Matt. Christ, that still leaves eight of you."

"Nine," he said. "There are six more like me. Then me, the Old Man, and Brennan."

I wasn't counting Brennan as one of you, you bastard, she thought.

"If there's room for only one of you, what are the rest for?"

Thomas leaned forward and locked eyes with her. "We're his flesh and blood. We're the grapes he left on the vine to mature. His children he raised for the slaughter. Don't you get it? That's what the monster alarm was for. Once we start killing each other, not caring he and the others know it—that's how he knows we're ripe for the picking. He can tap into what no one else has even heard of, and he wanted to increase his power a dozen times over."

His eyes glazed over. "Maybe he wants to rule the world. Maybe he just wants to destroy it and everything else. Do you believe that thing he tried to raise in the arctic is the only thing out there?"

"No," she said. "I don't know what I believe anymore, but I think I believe enough to know better than that."

Joan looked down at the last few bites of her cheeseburger. It turned out she was not so hungry after all.

Thomas looked around at the empty room. "Where'd our waitress disappear to?"

"Just leave the money on the table," Joan said, scribbling the number for an eating disorder hotline on a napkin. "I don't think she's coming back, and we have an appointment."

2

THE REFLECTIVE LETTERS on a square green sign stated it was eighteen miles to Lebanon. *I thought Texas was boring,* Joan thought. *It has nothing on Kansas.* She saw no buildings as they drove through the night, only fields and the occasional tree. There weren't even fences around people's property, just flat fields and mile markers all the way to the horizon.

"Fun fact," Thomas said. "Lebanon, Kansas is the center of the continental United States. The exact spot is outside of town, and I hiked out to it once. There's a stone thing, like a cairn, with a plaque on it."

"What the hell is a cairn?" Joan asked.

"Pile of rocks."

"Then why didn't you just say it's a pile of rocks?" Joan asked.

She leaned her head against the window, which felt cool against her skin, and said, "When I was a kid, like real little, my dad used to stop at every historical marker we passed on the highway. The three of us—my dad, my mom, and me—would all get out of the car. Then Dad would pick me up so I could see, and he'd read the plaque to me. I never understood what any of them were about, not really, but we always stopped."

"That sounds nice," Thomas said.

They turned off of the main road, and he shut off the headlights. Joan had trouble seeing where they were going, but Thomas showed no hesitation. She did not say it out loud, but she enjoyed the feel of flying along in the dark. In the brush bordering the road, Joan saw the shining eyes of a predator.

Thomas pulled up to the first barb wire fence Joan had seen in a hundred miles. He got out and examined the gate. Joan looked around nervously, and jumped at the sound of the gate settling on its hinges. Thomas climbed back into the cab.

"Should we leave the truck? Walk the rest of the way?" she asked.

"At this point," he said, "I think we're screwed no matter what we do. Might as well save some time."

Through the truck's ancient transmission, Joan felt the texture of every bump in the neglected road. Thomas slowed the car as they pulled up to two buildings. Joan's eyes had adjusted to the darkness, and she recognized the farmhouse and the barn from Brennan—*Thomas*, she corrected herself—describing them to her. She looked for signs of life, but everything was still.

"I wish you had stayed behind," he said as he applied the creaking parking break. "I think this is the first thing they expect us to do."

"Not a chance. And even if they're waiting for us, that's the first rule of show business," Joan said. "Sometimes you have to give the rubes what they think they want."

Thomas shut off the engine. "Would you at least wait in the car?" he asked.

Joan motioned back over her shoulder with her thumb, pointing to the bed of the International. "With that back there?" she said. "No thanks."

"Fine. Do you have the gun?"

"Yep." She patted the small Glock pistol in her waistband. "Fat lot of good it will do, right? Too bad we used up all our darts."

"Just keep it hidden. It might surprise someone or slow them down," he said. "That might be enough."

They got out of the truck and walked over to the house.

Standing closer to it, Joan could see what terrible condition it was in. The frame of the building leaned awkwardly to one side, and some of the wood looked like it would crumble at the touch.

There was a crooked man, she thought.

A breaker box was nailed to the wall outside. With her eyes, Joan traced the wires to a large security spotlight hanging above. Thomas opened the box cover and flipped the main switch, but nothing happened.

"Looks like someone forgot to pay the bill," Joan said.

Thomas walked to the back of the truck and lifted the edge of the tarp. He rummaged around, retrieving two heavy black flashlights. He turned one on and handed the other to Joan. She turned on hers as well, creating a bright circle in the dirt. The kicked-up dust drifted through the beams of light.

"Coin flip time," Joan said. "Which one do you want to risk your life to explore first?" She motioned with her flashlight. "How about the house?"

Thomas shook his head. "If you want to leave this place, you'll go in the barn and only the barn. If the house needs checked out, I'll be doing the checking."

Joan stopped. "What's in there?"

"Nothing you need to worry about," Thomas said. "And nothing that could help us."

"Fine. So the barn is where the magic happened?"

Thomas grinned with his mouth but not his eyes. "If you want to call it that. Yeah. This is where it happened."

"It's hard to believe what scientists accomplished in some barn no one knows about," she said.

Thomas turned his back on her and started walking. "The world will be better off if no one ever knows about this place.

The barn door stood open. Joan and Thomas approached it slowly. For a moment she had the mad hope Brennan was inside, safe and sound, but this was driven out by a far more likely scenario—he was dead and hanging on a chain from the rafters. She banished the thought from her mind as she walked inside.

The barn was quiet, and she could see no one inside. Unable to resist the thought of Brennan strung up above her, Joan shined the flashlight up to the ceiling. The light startled the black birds nesting there, and their squawking scared Joan so badly she had to stifle a scream. She also stopped herself from grabbing Thomas' arm.

That's not what he's for, she told herself. *There's no comfort there.*

Aside from the birds, the rafters were empty. The hanging garden of skulls was gone, and Joan was grateful for its absence. All those empty eyes staring down at her in the dark might have been more than she could take. The only eyes staring at her now belonged to the crows. They looked hungry.

The barn was empty—even the Old Man's desk was gone. Joan stepped on something hard and tiny. Bending down to pick it up, she thought at first it was a dried corn kernel. She realized it was a human tooth and showed it to Thomas. "Looks like they didn't clean things out that well," she said. "Maybe they were in a hurry." She dropped the tooth and wiped her hand on her jeans.

"It looks that way, doesn't it?" Thomas said, but she could tell he was thinking about something else. He looked around on the ground and swept the dirt with his foot, revealing a trapdoor. Waving for Joan to scoot back, he pulled it open. Joan braced herself for what was hidden under the floor, but it turned out to be unnecessary. The hole was filled with concrete.

"Shit," Thomas said.

"I hope they at least got those things—I mean, those people out of there before they did that," Joan said.

"I don't," Thomas said. "It would at least put those poor bastards out of their misery. I guess they weren't in much of a hurry after all." He dropped the lid, sending up a cloud of dirt and dust. "I should check the house."

Joan shined her flashlight around the barn a final time, but only saw the greedy eyes of the birds. Thomas turned the knob on the door they had entered through, but it appeared to be stuck shut. He opened it by slamming his shoulder into it and swinging it outward. Joan started to step through, but Thomas put his arm across her path, making her jump. He walked out first, with her following closely behind.

When Joan had taken her fifth step outside the barn, the lights flashed on. Blinded, she shaded her eyes with her hand. The door slammed shut behind them with a bang.

A man stood facing them, looking like a bouncer but with Brennan's face. He was older than Thomas and Brennan, but not by much. She could tell he spent time at the gym and probably took steroids—his sleeveless black leather shirt was stretched tight by the absurd muscles on his arms and chest. A vein pulsed along the side of his enormous neck.

"Hello, Tommy," the cloned man said.

"Hello, Peter," Thomas said.

Joan smelled ozone and heard popping sounds to her left and right. She looked back and forth, and on either side stood two identical looking men dressed in leather and holding black batons. On the end of the baton were two copper spikes with blue sparks jumping between them.

Thomas glanced at the two men. "John. James," he said. "Looks like you got some new toys."

The two men said nothing as they rushed Thomas. His fist connected with one, and there was a crunching sound as blood exploded from the man's nose. Thomas began to advance on the injured man, but the other attacker's stun baton bit into the back of his neck. Thomas jolted and dropped to the ground.

The man with the bloody nose continued to stumble. Joan took a firm grip on her flashlight and slammed it against the side of his head. She tried to put all of her modest weight into it, and it showed. His broken nose forgotten, the man put a hand to the side of his head. His eyes burned into her, but the blow had the desired effect. He shifted his focus on her and walked toward her.

She raised the flashlight, but a quick strike from behind sent her sprawling to the ground.

"Hold still, you cunt," Peter said, advancing on her. She pulled the pistol from its holster in her waistband and fired a shot. The bullet hit her attacker in the shoulder, knocking him back. Joan did not totally understand what made the clones so resistant to firearms, but now was not the time to test it. With

Peter and the truck blocking the way in front of her and the other two behind her, she jumped to her feet and bolted for the farmhouse.

As she ran, Joan looked back to see the other two men shocking Thomas with their batons and kicking him. They kicked hard enough that the sound of it made Joan sick. The one with the broken nose kneeled down, lifted Thomas' chin, and delivered a haymaker.

When she reached the door there was a horrible moment where she knew it would be locked. But the knob turned easily and she was inside.

It was so dark she could barely see the walls, but she could make out the stairs through a doorway across the room. She started to run.

The pain hit her hard and fast. Her temples pounded like she was having a cluster headache, and her eardrums felt like they were going to burst. Nausea threatened to overwhelm her as she suddenly saw double. The whole house felt like a festering, gangrenous wound.

What happened here? she wondered.

Her eyes trembled in their sockets as she reached the stairs, and she heard Peter crash through the door behind her. She realized she had dropped her gun when the pain started, not that Peter would give her another chance to use it. Her foot sunk through one of the stairs and sharp daggers of wood cut into her leg. She barely managed to avoid twisting her ankle.

Way to go, Joan, she thought as she pulled her leg free. *You're running upstairs while pursued by a monster man. You officially deserve to die now.*

She scrambled to the top of the stairs and scanned the second floor. The floor of the hallway had caved in, leaving a pit lined with doorways she couldn't reach. She considered trying to jump for it, but the vertigo she felt made success seem unlikely. The floor inside the first room did not look stable enough to hold her weight even if she reached it.

She continued climbing the stairs to the attic. An open doorway beckoned, and she dove through it. A window at the far end of the room provided light and the possibility of escape, but she was forced to stop by her traitorous body. She hit her knees and threw up on the floor beneath the window.

The sound of Peter's heavy, unhurried footsteps filled the house below her. Joan scrambled for anything she could use to defend herself. She grasped the handle of something heavy, and she held it up to the light.

It was an ancient power drill, massive in size and solid metal. The enormous steel bit was covered in filth, but it looked more than sharp enough. She gripped the cloth-insulated power cord and frantically searched for an outlet. She had no idea if it would stop Peter, but she would put enough holes in him that he would remember her.

She had almost lost hope when she found a plug. She prayed the electricity was on inside the house. She stood with the heavy drill behind her back as Peter's shadow crossed the threshold of the room. The house's sickening effect was still strong, and she swayed drunkenly on her feet.

"Found you," said the terrible man. He walked toward her, seeming to grow larger with each step. "I saw you drop your gun, slut. That's a real shame."

He was only a few feet away now. "It's not all bad," she said.

"Why is that?" he asked, but she had already lunged at him. The drill roared to life. The spinning bit caught Peter in the cheek, tearing a horrible gash across one side of his face.

But she was not fast enough. The brute grabbed the drill and pulled it away from her. He seemed to not even feel the flapping wound on his cheek. His teeth showed through.

Definitely too many extra chemicals in him, Joan thought. She grabbed the drill by the cord and pulled with all of the strength she had left.

Peter laughed at her pathetic attempt. With one hand he gripped Joan's neck and squeezed. The world began to white out along the edges. Then Joan felt something give, and the cord broke away from the electric drill.

Peter stared at the drill dumbly as Joan jabbed the exposed wires at his heart. His torn face contorted from the shock as he released his grip on her neck. She prayed it would be enough to induce ventricular fibrillation.

Joan gasped in surprise as Peter dropped to the ground, unconscious. She carefully pulled the plug from the wall socket. A smell like burnt pork threatened to turn her stomach again.

She gave Peter a quick once over, and hardly believed it when she found no pulse or respiration. She felt like slipping into unconsciousness herself, but she remembered Thomas was still outside. She opened the window.

Thomas was facedown on the ground. John and James were taking their time with him. They were looking at Thomas with the same hungry eyes Joan had seen on the starving crows in the barn.

"You shitheads about done?" Joan yelled from the window.

John and James turned to look up at her. Thomas rolled to his back, wincing as he did so.

One of the attackers turned back to Thomas and raised a foot to bring down in the middle of the defeated man's chest. As the boot came down, Thomas grabbed it and pushed, sending the man backward.

Joan watched Thomas spring up from the ground. Once again on his feet, he spun around and behind one of the men. In his hands she could see something impossibly thin, like a spider web. The thin line stretched between his two hands as Thomas crossed his arms and brought the garrote down around the man's neck. Joan's eyes widened as Thomas used the neck for leverage and flipped his own body over the man in a wide arch.

The man's head separated from his body and flew back behind him, just ahead of a massive spray from the carotid artery. Thomas was still in the air, and his knee landed in the center of the other twin's chest. Thomas' momentum carried them down to the ground, where the other man's sternum collapsed into his chest with a deep crunch.

That man kills like a fish swims, Joan thought.

The crushed man tried to lift his arms as Thomas twisted the garrote around his neck. The man's body tried to bridge as its head rolled away.

Something moved behind Joan.

Oh shit—

She turned in time to see Peter barreling toward her. His face showed only animal rage as he grabbed her and crashed through the rotting outer wall of the house.

The crooked house refused to let her go. Joan felt a firm pull, like pale hands had reached out and grabbed her, or a rope had been threaded under her skin and around her guts. She realized that she would have never left the house under her own power.

Peter pulled her down after him as she clawed at his eyes. When they hit the ground, Peter landed flat on his back. A sickening crack signaled his spine shattering. Joan slammed into his body.

Groaning, she rolled into the grass and turned her head to see Thomas standing over them. A primal sound of pain and hate escaped Peter's contorted form.

"You don't understand," Thomas said to Peter. "I made promises."

Joan heard him say these words as the darkness overwhelmed her.

3

"YOU OKAY?" Thomas asked.

"Am I okay?" she asked, sitting up in the truck. Every inch of her body ached, but nothing felt broken. She watched the night speed by outside without vertigo or blurred vision. "I feel terrible, but I'll be okay."

"I'm just glad you're alive," he said through a busted lip. Bruises covered his face, and one ear was swollen. "The fall was one thing, but that house isn't a place for healthy people."

"You're not kidding. I know the journal said bad things happened in there, but that place was a nightmare. What really happened? It felt like something spoiled and split open."

"I don't know, and I don't want to think about it. The poor woman who gave birth to me died in that house."

Joan bit her lip. "I'm sorry. I didn't think about that."

"Don't worry about it. But are you sure you're all right?

"Nothing a week's vacation couldn't cure. What about you? Are you okay?" Joan asked. "You got the worst of it. You probably have internal injuries."

"Then it's a good thing I know a great field medic."

Joan was about to roll her eyes, but stopped herself.

"Thank you," he said.

"For what?"

"You know what."

"Don't worry about it," she said. "We still wouldn't have made it out if it wasn't for you and your deadly acrobatics. That was unbelievable. I mean, it was horrible, don't misunderstand me. But impressive."

Thomas shrugged. "You held your own. Your acrobatics might need some improvement, though."

"We're good in a spot," she said. "If it weren't for you, part of me would already be torn apart and the other part of me in a cooler for transport. Don't get me wrong: you're a son of a bitch, but you're keeping your part of the bargain."

"Thanks."

Might as well ask, she thought.

"Did you learn anything from them?" she asked.

"Not anything to tell me where he's keeping Brennan."

"Damn it. Thanks for trying."

"It's the least—" He froze.

Joan looked at him, confused. It was as if Thomas was a record player, and the needle had jumped out of its groove. She grabbed the wheel with one hand and grabbed him by the shoulder with the other. The pickup accelerated. She pulled hard on the wheel to avoid going into a deep ditch.

"Earth to Thomas!" she screamed, shaking him. "Come in, Mr. Ripper! Wake up or we are going to die!"

Thomas eyes focused again, and he came out of it. He hit the break and the truck skidded to a stop.

"What the hell was that?" she asked.

"I know where he is," Thomas said. "It was the monster alarm. The Old Man is killing one of them."

"What? Killing who?" Joan grabbed him by the collar. "It's not Brennan, is it?"

"He isn't dead," he said. "But I'm sure he's there. With the Old Man. It wasn't clear, but I felt it. And I can take us to where he is."

"Is he okay?"

Thomas frowned. "I think so."

He's lying, Joan thought.

He said, "The Old Man is keeping him close. If he wants us, he'll keep Brennan alive as bait."

But you really have no idea, Joan thought.

"You can find them?" she asked. "You can take us to them?"

"Yes," Thomas said. "It's hard to explain. It's like a neon sign, a compass needle."

"Then drive," she said.

4

JOAN HAD VISITED LOS ANGELES on three previous occasions: once on a family vacation, once on a college spring break trip, and once for a medical school interview. The two vacations had been spectacular in entirely different ways. Venice Beach could be nearly as exciting for a twenty year old as Disney Land had been for an eight year old. The last time she had been there, for the interview, was a total flop.

Joan and Thomas had hardly stopped since Kansas. Joan, her hair pulled back, wore the same jeans and white tank top she had worn at the farm. Thomas wore a white and red Kansas City Chiefs t-shirt she purchased for him at a same gas station where she had also bought supplies to patch him up. Bandages covered his burns, and superglue held together his split lip.

In rural Kansas, the rusty old truck acted as the perfect camouflage, but driving down South Broadway at night, she was surprised people were not taking pictures. Late model vehicles rolled by, their occupants staring incredulously at the International. A car full of laughing teenagers passed them, and a tan young man poked his head out a back window and waved.

"I have five words for you," Joan said.

"Are they the same five words?" Thomas asked.

"Could be."

He held open his hands, steering with the back of his hands. "Lemme have it," he said.

"Should. Have. Taken. The. Convertible," she said.

Thomas puffed out his lower lip and nodded thoughtfully. "So the same five. Again. I have to hand it to you, they are getting more helpful. Thank you. Really. And here we are."

Joan followed his gaze. A rectangular brick building, which looked to be at least a hundred years old, towered over them. A large vertical sign read *'BRADBURY'* in pale white letters. Joan counted five rows of windows as Thomas backed them into a parking space.

"Are you sure this is it?" Joan asked. Her chest felt tight and her stomach twisted into knots.

"Is anyone sure of anything?" Thomas asked her in return. "But I'm sure enough. This is where we need to go." He threw the gearshift into park and pulled the emergency break. "I'll need you to block for me while I change."

Joan stood at the tailgate as Thomas crawled under the tarp. The slick blue material bubbled and scraped as he moved around underneath it. Joan looked nervously up and down the street. Outside the traffic flow they attracted less attention, but any audience at this point would be a disaster. After several minutes he slid back out, now wearing a black leather jacket zipped up to his chin. He handed her a small black box.

The plastic box was the size of an old pocket transistor radio. On the top was a skinny, silver toggle switch and a red circular button that looked like it came from an old *Ms. Pac-Man* arcade cabinet.

"Remember," Thomas said, pointing to the switches, "You have to hold down the button, or the switch won't trigger the bomb I'm wearing. If something goes wrong, there's a wired trigger in my back pocket."

"Yeah. I got it."

"Repeat it," he said. "So I know you've got it."

"I'm not going to repeat it," she said.

Thomas sighed. "Listen." He showed his teeth, but he was not smiling. "You know what is going to happen. The least you can do is repeat my goddamn instructions."

"Fine. Hold the button down or nothing happens. And if all else fails, hit the trigger in your pocket."

"That's right," he said. "If all else fails. You ready?"

She shook her head. "Not even close."

"Good enough for me," he said. "Let's go."

Several stores and restaurants lined the outside of the Bradbury Building, but they were all closed with their windows dark. *At least we don't have to worry about innocent bystanders*, Joan thought.

A squad car drove by, slowly enough for her to lock eyes with one of the policemen. This was her last chance to call for help from the outside world, but the last time she had tried had almost gotten her killed. If it had not been for Brennan, it would have been the last mistake she ever made.

This was a train that would not stop until the end of the line, and she had boarded it a long time ago. It would end for her as it had begun, standing beside a man she should not trust.

It was amazing how fast distrust could transform into something else. Her thoughts went to that first night with Brennan, when she drank too much while patching him up. That thought knocked loose another.

"Thomas," she said, "Why do you have Brennan's gunshot scar? The one I sewed up. The one he got trying to protect me."

Thomas frowned. "I'd rather not say."

"I think we're miles past 'I'd rather not say.'"

"I did it myself. I propped up a gun and rigged the trigger. Zeroed in with a laser sight. Pop pop," he said, pulling an imaginary trigger.

"Who fixed you up?" she asked.

"I did. Who else was there?"

Joan put her hand on Thomas' shoulder, and they both stopped. She turned to him and said, "You know I never want you to pretend to be Brennan again. For any reason. Ever."

"I know. I won't."

She leaned in and gave him a kiss on the cheek. "But I'm glad you could be him for me, at least for a while."

Without another word, she walked through the entrance, which was conveniently unlocked. Here again was the absurdity of walking through the front door, but what else could they do? The Old Man expected them, and he had the high ground. Looking up, she thought, *He must be watching us right now.* She fought the nervous urge to wave.

The building's simple exterior was deceptive. Joan walked into the center court and was reminded of a print by M.C. Escher, the one with all the staircases. *It's like somebody took that picture and straightened it all out*, she thought.

The only electric lights were soft amber lamps lining the walls. Moonlight poured in through a massive skylight that ran the length and breadth of the building's central court, highlighting the dust motes dancing in the air. The first floor was brick with arched windows and doorways leading into dark offices. Above her floated walkways and staircases covered in intricate black metalwork. Everything shined, polished and beautiful, an antique vision of the future.

They walked out into the open space, their feet clicking on the tiles. Joan tried to calm her racing heart. She looked to Thomas, who appeared even colder than usual.

The sudden sound of machinery made her jump. An old cage elevator, surrounded by the same black metalwork as the guard rails along the upper walkways, descended from the top floor on its metal track. She watched the metal cables, some pulling up as others pulled down. A counter-weight traveled up the side of the shaft, and a spinning metal wheel guided it all.

The motors groaned as the cage came to rest on the ground floor. Thomas glanced at her, and she shrugged. They walked over to the waiting elevator. The latticed door caught the moonlight, transforming it into a gate of black ivory.

The gate slid open, and sitting on a tiny platform inside was a gaunt old man wearing a plain, white dress shirt and a red bow tie. He was bald, had a white, well-groomed mustache, and was thin to the point of looking unhealthy. The man smiled maniacally, pulling the skin of his wrinkly face tight.

Joan looked worriedly at the old elevator operator, but Thomas shook his head. This was not the man they had come here to find. The operator motioned for them to enter. Thomas boarded the elevator first, with Joan close behind, her heart rate climbing higher and higher. The operator, who smelt like mothballs and cancer, slid the gate shut and reached for a lever. The elevator began to rise.

This is my first time to ride in an elevator with an actual elevator operator, Joan realized. *A landmark event. Too bad it will probably be my last time on any elevator, period.*

The old man stared straight ahead, his eyes glazed and his smile frozen in place. Joan had seen that look before, back when she did clinical rotations with hospice patients. The operator reminded her of a man she had treated in his eighties, who was delusional and totally unaware of his surroundings.

She wrung her hands. Thomas stood like a statue beside her, his unblinking eyes narrowed to slits. The only evidence of life came when he swallowed, apparently with some difficulty. She wondered if his mouth and throat were as dry as hers.

The cross section of floors passed by on one side, as the main lobby's floor sank away on the other. The elevator slowed to a stop at the fifth floor landing, and the operator opened the gate.

Joan and Thomas stepped out. "Have a wonderful day," the old man said. Gazing at nothing, he closed the gate and the elevator sank out of sight.

They turned to face the only office in the building with its lights on. On the door's frosted window, fresh vinyl letters read *'The Fifteen Second Group.'* Windows looking into the office were to their left and right, but all the blinds were drawn.

Surprising herself, Joan walked up to the door and knocked loudly. There was no answer.

"Move," Thomas said. He reached for the doorknob, which turned freely. Before pushing the door open, he said to her, "Remember. Keep back. We'll both do what we need to do." Joan nodded, and followed Thomas into the office.

Dark streaks of blood cut across the stark-white walls like cracks in reality. In the center of the large room were three nude, headless bodies. They were positioned along the circumference of a circle painted in blood on the hard wood floor. In the center of the circle sat a shirtless man tied to a chair. In his lap was the head of one of the clones, one ear to the sky, trails of dried muck dripping from its nose and empty eye sockets. The other two heads sat in crimson puddles at his feet. The bound man raised his head, and Joan saw it was the real Brennan, her Brennan.

Oh, God, she thought. *Let it be him. Let him be okay.*

Like the elevator operator, his eyes looked right through her. A line of dried blood trailed from each nostril. She started toward him, but Thomas grabbed her by the shoulder.

"Thank you for arriving so promptly," a man said, stepping into view. He wore a white tailored suit, completely oblivious to the blood stains covering it.

Where did he come from? Joan thought, but she had no doubt as to what he was. He carried himself like a king, but had eyes like a shark. She could see the curve of Brennan's jaw in the man's face, Brennan's shoulders in his frame. His hair was not the complete white Thomas had described; instead, it was black with flecks of gray. The Old Man had a spring in his step.

"What did you do to Brennan?" she demanded.

"Hush, you," he said, shaking a finger. "I'm not answering questions. Especially not from livestock."

Joan backed up against the wall while Thomas took a step toward the Old Man and asked, "How about I try to guess what's been going on?"

The Old Man lifted his hands with a flourish. "Why not. Amuse me," he said.

"You never made me, made us," he said, waving at the corpses and Brennan, "to be your sons. To carry on your fucked up legacy. It was never about us at all, was it? The rest of them had it backward. We weren't going to carry on after you were gone, we were here so you could keep going."

"That's right, my boy," the Old man said, clapping his hands slowly and sarcastically. "Very good. But I'd expect nothing less from the last man standing. Tommy, my winnah and champeen!"

Thomas closed the distance between them. "You wanted me to kill the others."

The Old Man rolled his head from shoulder to shoulder causing his neck to crack loudly. "No, not quite. But hell, I can roll with the punches. You don't get to play the game as long as I have without being flexible."

"So once I started taking out the others, you had to wait it out. Either I'd come to you, or one of the others would bring me to you packed in ice. Either way, you'd get what you want."

"I was worried at first, you know, when my boys disappeared without me feeling it," the Old Man said. "I didn't expect one of you to work with a buddy. I thought I'd conditioned you against that, right along with the failsafe that kept you all from a little patricide. None of you can spend much time with the *hoi polloi* without your instincts taking over." He mimed slitting his throat with his finger. "I can't tell you how relived I was when I found out I always had a man on the scene. Preserving my fruit, keeping it fresh. All so you could bring it on home to me."

"How'd you know?" Thomas asked. "That whatever it is you need from us, that it would transfer second-hand?"

"I had a gut feeling. You've felt the difference in eating one of me and eating one of them. My kiddos carry a lot more juice. I've been around long enough; I can feel it without having to get my chompers in you. Nothing I need is lost in translation. Besides," he said, straightening his tie, "I already tested it on Nathan and Jude and Justin. It's like those little Russian dolls that stack inside each other, except they all stay the same size." He nodded toward Brennan. "You know, I always thought one of you would end up coming after me somehow, mental block be damned. I never expected the first to be the fucking runt of the litter."

He approached Thomas and put his hands on Thomas' shoulders. The Old Man said, "But not you. You shine like a fucking beacon, Tommy. There's your power, which is damn good all by itself. But then you went out and took it upon yourself to eat eight of your brothers. Eight. Even I'd be scared of you, if you wouldn't give yourself an aneurysm just trying to lay a finger on me."

Thomas put his hands on the Old Man's shoulders as well. They looked like a statue of two ancient wrestlers. "That's why I'm not going to try and hurt you," Thomas said.

The Old Man reached out and grabbed Thomas' jacket, pulling it open. Under the jacket, Thomas was wearing a flak jacket covered with squares of C-4 explosive, wired up in rows. Glistening rows of thick, heavy nails were strapped over the C-4.

"Joan!" Thomas yelled.

Joan already had a hand around the remote in her pocket, and she pulled it out. She dropped to the ground as she mashed the red button and flipped the switch.

Nothing happened. Joan flipped the switch back and forth once more before dropping the worthless remote. She sprung to her feet and ran toward Thomas, reaching for the wired trigger in the pocket of his jeans.

The Old Man was between them in an instant. He struck Joan with the back of his hand. The force of the slap sent her sprawling.

"I don't think I like where your mind's at, Tommy," the Old Man said, rubbing his hand. "I don't remember raising any pantywaists. Seems to me any way we slice it, you were planning to give up the ghost for some stupid bitch and the retard. Your big plan was what? Blow yourself up, take out the whole floor? Unusual method for a rescue mission."

Thomas tapped the steel plate on his chest with a knuckle. "Targeted blast. Like a claymore." He forced a smile. "Only the best for you, sir."

"Tsk, tsk, tsk, shame, shame, shame," the Old Man said. "Too bad you don't know as much about our special talent as you think you do. Ingesting. Did you know modern conveniences like radios and cell phones actually weaken the whole experience? Spoil the flavor. Tone down the orgasm. It cost a pretty penny to get this place up to spec, but it was well worth it." He walked over to where Thomas was picking himself up off the floor. Moving unnaturally fast, the Old Man's foot shot up and caught Thomas in the teeth. Thomas' head flew back, and a tooth clattered against the hardwood floor. The Old Man lifted his arms, gesturing around the empty office. "This room's a dead zone, you little shit. The better to eat you with."

"What are you?" Thomas asked. "What are you really?"

"There isn't a name for what I am, boy," the Old Man said and lunged at him.

Joan knew Thomas could do nothing for her; from the look of things, the indoctrination prevented him from even defending himself against his progenitor. As soon as the Old Man finished off Thomas, he would deal with Joan. She had the Glock tucked into the back of her jeans, but could not decide if she should take the chance of firing on the Old Man. At most, she could provide a momentary distraction, and at worst it would only remind the Old Man she was there.

She heard a sound. Turning, she saw the head roll out of Brennan's lap and hit the floor with a soft thud. Brennan groaned again.

Fighting the pain in her head, she ran to him. He looked at her as if he had awakened from a deep sleep. "Joan? What are you doing here?" he asked. "Is that Thomas? What—?"

"I'm getting you out of here," she said. *If we don't die first*, she thought.

"Something happened," he said. He sounded drunk. "I can't, something's wrong."

"I know," she said, surprised at how calm she sounded. "But we have to get out of here right now." Now that she was behind him, she could see he was not even tied to the chair. "Oh, honey," she said. "What did he do to you?" She tried to help him up, but it was like trying to lift dead weight.

He leaned against her. "Said I was—he said I was a botched abortion. Said he would set me straight. Then, I don't. I don't know. What are you doing here, Joan?"

Tears stung her eyes as she held his face in her hands. "You saved me at my apartment, remember? You didn't even know me, but you saved me. And you were trying to save me when they got you and took you away from me. The least I can do is save you back."

Brennan looked to where Thomas was struggling with the Old Man. Thomas was fighting hard, but it was obvious who would win. "I have to help," Brennan said.

"Brennan, you can't," Joan said. "Thomas knew before we came in here that he wasn't leaving. All of the clones were brainwashed so they can't fight back against that thing."

"Not all of them," Brennan said. "I flunked out of monster school. You need to get away from me now."

"I'm not leaving you here," she said. "I—"

"Get back," Brennan said again.

Something in his voice made Joan step back. She looked down at his arms, which were shaking. *No, they aren't shaking*, she thought.

"There's something wrong with your skin," she said quietly.

Tiny black specks formed on his hands, like a dark rash. The dots grew until they were smooth tunnels in his flesh, like he had been stabbed numerous times with an ice pick. There was no blood in the squirming punctures, only darkness.

Brennan stood up, but Joan's eyes were still locked onto his hands. Something black was poking out of each of the widening holes, like little hairs. Her heart pounded in her ears as Brennan walked across the room to the Old Man.

"Look who finally decided to wake up," the Old Man said casually, but his eyes widened as Brennan raised his hands. Slender black chords shot out of Brennan's skin, wrapping themselves around the Old Man's face, head, and neck. The Old Man wailed and reached for Brennan, and Joan cringed as she saw Brennan's black feelers digging into the Old Man's eyes.

The Old Man's suit tore. Jagged, thin black bones emerged from the pores of his chest and shoulders. His ancient claws ripped and pulled at the sleek black tendrils squirming from inside Brennan.

"Brennan!" Joan screamed, but he was beyond hearing.

5

BRENNAN FOUND HIMSELF in an oddly familiar hallway. The cinder-block walls were painted a shade of yellow that was almost white. A windowless door was located on each end. He wore a pair of black slacks and a white undershirt, but no shoes, and he had no memory of how he had arrived there. Confused, he stood slowly, trying to piece things together.

He put his hand against the cold brick wall and realized the hallway was familiar because he had once walked through dozens exactly like it. This was the hallway he had been trapped in after Jim drugged him back at the Dallas airport, a million years ago.

How the hell did I get here? he thought. His head felt empty and weightless, and it was hard to think. He felt a tickle on his nose and brushed at it with his hand. As he pulled his hand away, he saw his nose was bleeding. *What is going on?*

Joan, his mind said. *Joan's in trouble.*

Brennan rushed to one of the doors, knowing it would prove useless. He took a deep breath as he prepared himself for another endless series of empty corridors.

The knob turned and Brennan found himself in the entryway of a house. He stood in his bare feet on an old mat, wet from the storm outside. Inside the doorway, a black suit jacket hung from a coat stand. Beneath the jacket was an expensive-looking umbrella with a curved bone handle. He lifted the jacket and put it on as he peeked around the corner into a kitchen that smelled of baking cookies. A magnet held a blank piece of paper to the door of the refrigerator

This is Jennifer Cairns' house in Chicago, Brennan realized. His muddled thoughts tried to put together why this felt wrong, but the misshapen pieces would not fit. He continued down the hall to another door, hoping he would find Jennifer sitting on her red leather couch so he could explain himself.

Instead, he walked into a large, dimly lit parlor. Surprised, he spun around to see Cairns' house gone, replaced by a different room.

In the parlor, the oil lamps' sparse, flickering light revealed a room full of people. The men were dressed in tuxedoes, the women in beautiful gowns. Everyone in attendance wore a mask, and the variety was striking. Brennan spotted a Phantom of the Opera half-mask, a black cat, and a man in a top hat, who also wore a pale mask with a long, pointed beak. Many of the women wore elaborate Venetian masks covered in gold, lace, and feathers. A small man passed by wearing a white suit and a white mask with empty, squinting eyes and a tiny pinhole mouth. Most of the people gathered in clusters, engaged in lively conversations.

Brennan worried for a moment he would be asked to leave because his face was not covered, but he realized he already had something on his face. He pulled it off and found he had been wearing a red devil mask. It looked to be custom molded to fit over his forehead, eyes, nose, and cheeks, but with the addition of two horns jutting out from the top of the forehead. He replaced the mask and continued to explore.

Still intent on reaching Joan—*She's in some kind of trouble, she needs me,* he thought at random intervals—Brennan shouldered his way through rooms of partygoers. They offered little resistance, and seemed only dimly aware of his existence.

He found a group gathered around a white chaise lounge where a panting woman wearing a white silk slip and the face of a white china doll straddled a man wearing only a military gas mask. The top of her slip had been pulled down to reveal firm, pale breasts. She shuddered, digging her fingernails into the man's chest. Brennan walked away as the onlookers descended on the couple.

In the dining room, Brennan joined another crowd, this one watching a cloaked magician in a white and gold mask. The mask jutted out above and below his face, like a crescent moon. A guest whispered the performer's name: "Darius the Diabolist." The silent magician stood behind a velvet table and manipulated three silver cups lined up in a row. Three small cork balls disappeared and reappeared as he lifted or stacked the cups, much to the amusement of his audience. Each time he tapped them with his slender wand or they touched each other, they produced a beautiful, almost musical sound.

The magician moved faster, and now the colliding cups truly did make music, a lilting, sweet melody. When the song reached its climax, the three cups were once again lined up in front of him. The magician lifted each cup one by one, revealing the cork balls he had vanished in his hands with a tap of his wand. He swept his cape back dramatically and lifted the cup on his right; beneath it was an ivory carving of a human skull. The opposite cup was lifted to release a live crow. With his wand, he tipped back the final cup to reveal a beating, oozing human heart.

The small audience applauded, and Brennan clapped along with them. A hand fell on his shoulder and he jumped.

"Calm down, buddy," a man said.

He was wearing a tuxedo, but the top few buttons of the crisp white shirt were undone and the black bowtie hung, untied, against his chest. His dark hair was thick and curly, and his eyes were covered by a simple black domino mask. "Can we talk?" he asked.

"Sure," Brennan said automatically, and he followed the man to a secluded corner. The man took off his mask and said, "You okay? You look a little out of it." Without the mask, Brennan saw he had a handsome face and large, intelligent eyes.

Brennan removed his own mask. Instantly the conversations around the two grew louder. "I'm a bit lost," he said.

"That's to be expected," said the man. "Brennan, do you know who I am?"

"Not a clue," Brennan said. "But it sounds like you might know who I am."

"I do." The man lit a hand-rolled cigarette with a match. "A long time ago, I was a close friend of your grandfather."

"Is that right?" Brennan asked. His voice was soft and relaxed.

"Is your head still a bit cloudy?" the man asked. He took several puffs on the cigarette. "Are you still just going with the flow?"

"Could be," Brennan said drunkenly.

The man took Brennan's hand and, like it was the most natural thing in the world, pushed his cigarette into the back of Brennan's hand.

"Son of a bitch!" Brennan cried, quickly pulling back his hand.

Around them, all conversation immediately stopped, and all eyes were suddenly on Brennan and his companion. The guests quickly turned back to their conversations.

Brennan blew on his hand as he frantically waved it.

"Feeling a bit more focused?" the man asked.

"Yes," Brennan said, "but I wish you had used another technique."

"I know. It hurts like the dickens, but you can't argue with the results." He took one drag on the cigarette, grimaced, and tossed it in a discarded whisky glass. "Do you know where you are?"

"A party. A masquerade, I guess."

"Do you remember how you got here?"

"Jennifer Cairns' house. Before that was a hallway, I think."

"How about before that?" the man asked.

Brennan's looked down, his brow furrowed. Suddenly his eyes widened. "The Old Man in the white room. Joan and Thomas came for me, but something went wrong."

The man smiled. "Now we're getting somewhere."

"How do I get back?"

"Slow down; you have to understand some things first. If you're going to have a snowball's chance in hell, that is. Time moves along at a strange pace here. You should be all right for a minute."

"What are you talking about? Who are you?"

The man grinned. "My name in Ben Rosen. Like I said, I knew your grandfather, and the two of us waged a war on the Old Man for over thirty years."

Brennan laughed. "Sure you did. You and my grandpa, I'm sure it was exciting."

"Listen up, and don't be a smart ass. Just because I look younger than you right now doesn't mean I have to take your shit." He lit another cigarette. "I had a peculiar talent when it came to dreaming. When I was sleeping, I could go on little jaunts to hither and yon, tracking down information, people, what have you."

"Like sleep walking?" Brennan asked.

"No, not like sleep walking. My consciousness, my soul maybe, would leave my body so I could travel to and fro in the earth and elsewhere. This was extremely useful in my line of work, which dealt in no small part with finding and destroying this entity you know as the Old Man." He looked around, nostalgic. "In fact, this party is a memory of the first time I met him. That's probably why I could bring us here so easily. That was years before I was recruited by the Lodge."

"The Lodge?" Brennan asked angrily. "Those are the bastards who tracked me down, tried to kill me. They tried to kill Joan. You're with them?"

Ben waved his hands and shook his head. "No, no, I'm not with anyone. The Lodge, the organization I was a part of, no longer exists, at least not in any form I would recognize. But the threat it was most concerned with is still a problem. I'll ask you again, do you know where you are?"

"I have no idea. You said something about it being a memory, but I don't know what that means."

"Brennan, because of what you came from—what you are—you can access information in a different ways than a normal person. I would go as far as to say you can reach another level of reality. Do you have any idea what I'm talking about?"

Brennan recalled vague images of the Old Man doing something to his mind, but nothing was clear. "I think so," he said.

"Right now, you're experiencing one of the Old Man's memories. I'm here with you because once, many years ago, I found the Old Man after a prolonged search, one of my dream trips. I was exhausted, and I overestimated my own ability, so I became trapped in the—oh, I don't know—you could call it the gravitational pull of the Old Man's mind. I could not escape, so I wander from memory to memory, mind to mind, while my deserted body surely withered away. It would be hell, and in many ways it is, but at least I have plenty of company."

"You're stuck in his head? With all the other minds he's devoured?" Brennan asked.

"That's correct."

Brennan looked around the room at the partygoers. "Are these all—?"

"No," Ben said. "At least not that I can tell. Like I said, this is a memory of the Old Man I played a small but memorable roll in, a memory of the night I stopped a man in a devil mask from killing my friend, a senator. But what is important now is that you understand what you are up against." He pulled Brennan toward the window and said, "Look."

Outside the window, the sky was black but without stars, a swirling nothing. Brennan saw an ocean, but unlike any he had ever seen. The water churned as something sinister and monstrous moved in its depths. Under the surface, an enormous, fractured eye full of dead light blinked open and disappeared.

"That's the world the Old Man came from," Ben said. "An empty world of chaos and darkness. He is not a person and never was. You have to stop him, because if his plan succeeds, the nightmare out there will look like a paradise compared to what he will do."

I'm not a person, Brennan thought. *I'm so far from human I'm not even on the map.*

"That's not true," Ben said. "You're more than the sum of your parts, boy. You've proven you have it within you to defy your nature and stop that thing. Where so many have failed, you can bring that bastard to an end."

"But what can I do against something like that?" Brennan asked.

"I don't know. We tried to kill him a dozen different ways, but nothing stuck."

"Then what chance do I have?"

"I have a theory I pieced together from the Old Man's mind. We could never put him in the ground, but you're a copy of him. Whatever he's made of, you're made of the same stuff. When we were up against him, it was like we were trying to fight a ghost. No, it was like we were the ghosts, and we were going right through him. But you're on the same playing field. You can attack him here, where the otherwise untouchable part of him lives, while you're struggling with him in what we questionably call the real world. "

Brennan slumped against the wall. "There's no chance."

"Yes, there is. If there wasn't, why would he put the failsafe in the rest of the clones? If they were no threat, why did he make it impossible for them to hurt him? The Old Man knew they would be able to kill him. He just didn't count on you surviving and coming for him."

"He's been digging around in my head. What if he already did it to me, too? What if I can't hurt him, either?"

Ben shook his head. "No. As far as I can tell, he was only reading you. He didn't put anything new in there."

"As far as you can tell? That's the best you can do?"

"This isn't about the best that I can do." Ben suddenly looked around the room.

Brennan followed his gaze, and saw the masked partygoers were staring at him again. The crowd closed in around them.

"Get out of here, Brennan," Ben said. "Good luck."

Brennan cried out "Wait!"

It was too late. Ben was gone, and the mob was on top of him. A man in an owl mask grabbed Brennan by throat, and Brennan struck him in the face hard enough to push him back and split his mask in two. Brennan lifted a chair and swung it, knocking down one mindless drone after another. There was no end to them in sight, so he turned to the window. Outside, the bottomless ocean and its enormous denizens waited for him. He raised his arms to protect his face and jumped through the glass.

Brennan landed on a dirt floor. Looking back, he saw his pursuers were gone and he was surrounded by darkness. He stood up and brushed away dust and shards of glass. Feeling a bump beneath his bare foot, he bent down to pick it up. Holding it up to the light, he saw that it was a human molar.

Brennan looked up.

6

"BRENNAN!" Joan screamed again.

The Old Man slammed Brennan into the wall, and Brennan slumped to the ground. The black tendrils covered them both now, making it difficult to see. Brennan struggled to his feet, but he looked to be in a daze. The Old Man grabbed him by the throat and lifted him several feet off the ground. Joan watched in horror as the jagged black segments burrowed into the skin around Brennan's face. Brennan's feet kicked helplessly in the air, but he reached out and pushed a thumb into the Old Man's eye, forcing him to release his grip.

The black tendrils shot in every direction. They now filled the room like jungle vines, or a living spider web. Being touched by them sent a horrible chill down her spine, but Joan put her head down and fought her way through them, trying to reach Brennan and the Old Man. The two of them moved like they were in a trance, but it was obvious the Old Man controlled the situation.

Joan's heart pounded, and reality pulsed to the frantic rhythm in her veins. She pulled out the gun, and tried to find an angle where she could shoot the Old Man but not hit Brennan. As she took aim, a sharp, bony feeler shot out and knocked the gun from her hand. She dropped to her knees and searched, but it had disappeared among the writhing mess on the ground.

Brennan fell to the ground, the Old Man holding him by the throat with both hands. Brennan, a glazed look in his eyes, had one hand between his throat and the Old Man's grip, his other hand pushing against the Old Man's face. Joan suddenly saw Thomas on the ground behind them, not moving.

Slapping and tearing at the black filaments blocking her path, Joan rushed to Thomas. The Old Man had done a real number on him—his face was a battered wreck. She managed to keep her footing while dragging Thomas as far from harm's way as she could.

Thomas was not breathing. She put her finger to the side of his throat and found no pulse. Automatically, her hands found the correct location on his sternum and administered chest compressions.

The frantic activity around her took on a surreal quality. As she counted the compressions, it seemed the black jungle around her disappeared and was replaced by odd-looking people chatting and laughing. She looked up, but saw only Brennan straining as he tried to hold off the Old Man.

Joan moved quickly, checking Thomas' airway for any obstructions. She tilted his chin upward with one hand as she pinched his nose closed with the other, and then she breathed twice into his open mouth, ignoring the blood from his injuries.

You probably thought we'd shared our last kiss, didn't you, Thomas? she thought.

Resisting the urge to recheck his pulse, she started the compressions again and cursed herself for being so out of shape. That familiar burn screamed in her shoulders. Joan knew the chances of success with CPR outside of a hospital setting, but she would not allow herself to lose hope. They had come too damn far.

"You'd better wake up, asshole," she said to Thomas. "We still need you."

She glanced back to see Brennan's face nearly engulfed in the dry, cracking tentacles of the Old Man. Brennan made a guttural sound that made Joan's blood run cold. He continued to scream as the darkness covered him and he disappeared from view.

7

BRENNAN LOOKED UP. Above him were the rafters of the Kansas barn, but they stretched out forever. Instead of dry skulls, human heads hung from the rusted chains with their flesh still attached. He was grateful their eyes were closed. As he stared upward, a drop of blood escaped from a ragged neck and struck him in the middle of the forehead like an ancient torture machine.

The number of lives cut short by the monster overwhelmed Brennan. There were thousands, hundreds of thousands, millions of faces. The Old Man had been doing his job for a long, long time, and he relished every kill.

As Brennan took in the terrible scene, one of the victim's beautiful blonde hair began to move, blown by a breeze he could not feel. The others' hair followed suit, and the heads themselves swayed on their tethers. Blood fell like rain from a tree shaken after a storm.

Brennan shielded his eyes from the grisly downpour. To his horror, the eyes of a Middle-Eastern boy opened and locked with his. Eyelids fluttered open for miles in every direction, like ripples spreading outward in a pond, and he was their sole focus. Their eyes burned into him from eternity, some accusing him of crimes committed thousands of years before he existed. The child who had started the chain reaction now opened his mouth and screamed, his naked terror echoing back in every conceivable voice.

The chains lengthened, and the staring, screaming heads descended on Brennan. He howled right along with them, caught in the crushing grip of their anguish. As they reached him, he saw the rotten roof of the barn breaking apart. Instead of falling down, the crumbling pieces fell upward into the sick, swirling sky.

Every chain flowed into a single core floating high above: the Old Man, who looked younger and stronger with each passing moment. The uncountable chains attached to him, holding him aloft.

The son of a bitch looks like he's hooked up to life support, Brennan thought.

Face to face with the horde, he expected the screams of the damned to be feel cold, but they were hot and rich, like a compost heap. The chains spun around him hypnotically. He broke free of the spell and fled.

Brennan crashed through the locked door of a smoky room full of people, mostly Asian, lying on the floor and on makeshift beds. Some of them looked up as he entered, while others continued smoking long, skinny pipes. He tripped over sleeping bodies, blankets, and cushions as the wall behind him splintered and tore apart.

Stumbling blindly through the opening, Brennan scraped his knuckles on a rough, stone wall. He felt his footsteps slow and his sprint took on the dull, underwater sensation he knew from his nightmares. In this room, men in robes gathered around a dissected corpse. A man pulled at the dead intestines like a sailor gathering a rope. His own body still moving in slow motion, Brennan watched as the man carefully placed the organ in an urn. On top he placed a lid with the head of a bird and picked up a slender metal hook, like a knitting needle. As the man shoved the hook into the corpse's nostril, Brennan realized he was watching a shadow of the Old Man. The man looked at Brennan, showing rows of jagged teeth.

Brennan's momentum caught up to him, and he slammed into a chair. Shocked, he realized he was in the back of a classroom, seated at a desk. Young students surrounded him. The silent children sat at awkward angles, and he did not want to see their faces. Before he could move, the girl seated in front of him leaned back in a cat-like stretch, and rested the top of her blond head on his desk. She smiled at him, her green eyes bright and alive. The other children disappeared.

"E-Elsie?" Brennan asked. The girl turned in her desk to face him, and it was her, forever fourteen and shining with potential never to be realized. Brennan's heart broke. "Oh, God, Elsie, I'm so sorry."

She dismissed his statement with a wave of her small hand, like he had apologized for bumping into her in the hallway. He smelled something burning and realized they were surrounded by growing flames. The chalkboard cracked from the heat, pieces falling like dirty green glass.

The high school is burning down again, he thought.

Elsie took his hands and locked eyes with him. "Brennan, you are not alone in here. But you need to find a way to stand your ground and fight or it's all over."

In the next instant she stood at the doorway, but now she cradled her own head in her hands, her neck an empty stalk. Her eyes were closed, but the flush in her cheeks made it look like she was sleeping peacefully. A halo surrounded Elsie's face. Then she was gone.

Stunned, Brennan took a moment to hear the rattling behind him. He turned in time to see the chains—their skewered heads burning away in the fire—hook into the wall and pull it down. The red hot metal chains dropped out of site, and Brennan watched as he himself, cloaked in fire, emerged from the flames. The Old Man stood before him, now as much a reflection of Brennan as Thomas was.

Brennan tried to leap from the desk, but got tangled up. He fell, taking the desk with him, and struck his temple on the hot tile floor, hard enough to see stars. The Old Man laughed, but Brennan only heard Elsie's words echoing in his head. He rose and exploded into a run. Brennan tackled his pursuer, and the two of them plunged through the hole in the cinderblock wall and into empty space.

8

THE TWO GRAPPLED AS THEY FELL. The Old Man was stronger, but Brennan fought with renewed hope. They landed on the ground face to face, and the Old Man threw Brennan with enough force to break bones. Brennan rolled as he hit the ground, sliding into a crouch on the stone floor, his fingers leaving four trails in the dust.

They were now in a large, round room. The walls were lined with carved limestone pillars and stone benches, and two more pillars stood in the center of the room to support the high roof. On the central pillar closest to him, Brennan saw a carving of a headless man with an erect penis riding on the back of a giant bird.

The Old Man slowly stood up. He now wore the charred remnants of his white suit. "They worshipped me here, you know. Before the pyramids, before Abraham walked the earth. My prey built this for me, because they knew, if I so chose, I would take the best of them into myself, where they would live forever."

"That's not life," Brennan said. "It's a nightmare. A living hell."

"Beggars can't be choosers, boy," the Old Man said. "And I think it's about time you started begging. If you really lay it on thick, I might let you remember who you were."

Brennan readied himself. "You won't be doing anything, you piece of shit. You'll be dead."

"I've been many things, but I've never been that." The Old Man laughed. Then, as if wracked by pain, he bent over. The muscles in his neck, shoulder, and arms quaked. He screamed, and heads grew from his back. Another layer sprouted from those, and the process continued.

Brennan ran toward the Old Man, but a hard slap sent Brennan down again. The lowest ribs on his right side cracked, and pain radiated throughout his body.

I'm not really here, this is all in my head, Brennan told himself, but he knew it was a lie. *Whatever this is, it's real. It's the most real thing I have ever seen.*

The heads formed revolving circles, one on top of the other, each one larger than the one beneath it. They reached the ceiling and pushed through. The Old Man roared, and the rest of the ceiling exploded outward. The massive stack of grinding, sentient gears formed a tower reaching to the heavens, the top of it so wide it blocked out the sky. The Old Man's damned horde formed the engine powering his endgame, and the energy kept ramping up.

Brennan picked up a wooden board from the ground and tried to plant it in the Old Man's skull. The Old Man dodged the strike effortlessly and grabbed Brennan by the collar. The Old Man threw Brennan into a limestone pillar, shattering it. Shaking his head, he tried to regain his footing, but fell back down, barely catching himself with his hands.

If I'm going to stop this, it has to be now, he thought, but he had no idea how to hurt the Old Man if could not reach him. The Old Man divided his attention between raising the tower and protecting himself from Brennan, making it impossible for Brennan to act.

He saw sudden movement out of the corner of his eye. Seeing another person approaching the Old Man, Brennan forced himself to not react. The interloper lifted up a stone piece of the ceiling and crept behind the occupied Old Man. He brought the heavy rock down on the Old Man's head, knocking him prostrate. He was still, and the tower still jutted from his back, but the revolutions slowed. The man turned to Brennan and grinned.

"Jim!" Brennan yelled. "What the hell are you doing here?"

"I told you not to call me that," Stephenson said. "And you know how it is. Better late."

"I can't believe this. You've got to help me finish him off. He's stronger than ever."

"No can do, kiddo," Stephenson said. "When he wakes up in a second, he'll never let me or anyone else near him again. If you want a chance, you've got to find a way to cut him loose."

"I'll try. And thanks."

Stephenson shook his head. "Don't worry about it. I still have a lot to make up for."

Brennan planted a foot in the Old Man's back and pulled at the souls rising from it. They would not budge. "This isn't working," he said, but Stephenson was gone.

The Old Man stirred, and Brennan stumbled back. The screaming human gears picked up speed.

"This was fun," the Old Man said, "but it's time to wrap things up."

Brennan prepared for the worst. If he had to go down, he would go down fighting. As he raised his fists, he thought suddenly, *Why am I fighting with my hands?* He realized he had been thinking like a man, but that was not his true nature, not really. *I'm a monster*, he thought.

Closing his eyes, he opened his fists. The pores of his skin opened, and the darkness rocketed out in long, thin lines.

Opening his eyes, he saw the Old Man slicing at the strings, but there were too many. The Old Man's face grew taut and fire burned behind his eyes. He tried to swat Brennan away, but his arms were tangled in the dark tendrils. They climbed the tower like creeping vines, slowing the spinning gears and tearing them apart. Heads began disappearing sporadically from the tower, leaving gaps like missing teeth. This occurred slowly at first, but increased in intensity with each passing moment.

Brennan made no attempt to draw the power into himself. He let it flow over him and past him. He quickly realized this was the only way he would survive the transfer; it had taken the Old Man millennia to acquire this many souls, and they would have burned him out in an instant. Brennan avoided being overloaded by freeing the Old Man's slaves.

He caught brief glimpses as the minds passed through him, thinking excited thoughts in a thousand languages. Here was a British soldier from 1917, then a Bavarian prison guard. He could have learned new ways to murder if he had tried, or how to craft a poem. He heard soft notes of music and saw splashes of brilliant color.

As the heads fell from the tower, they grew bodies. Brennan watched as men, women, and children were made whole again. They disappeared as quickly as they popped into existence, going on to whatever had been stolen from them at their unnatural ends. Brennan watched as Benjamin Rosen, smiling, drifted with the others to freedom. He gave Brennan a quick salute and faded away.

The tower toppled, the living gears splitting into broken sections as they tumbled. The pieces transformed into more falling bodies that faded from sight. The spinning abomination was gone, leaving the broken temple and the two men. The Old Man lay facedown in the dirt, his clothes in shreds. Brennan approached and flipped him over with a sharp kick. He expected the Old Man to be a burned-out husk, but he fell back as he saw the Old Man still looked young and strong. The Old Man's eyes popped open, and he stood.

"You'll have a long time to regret that!" the Old Man yelled. "The part of you I keep alive so it can scream!" His eyes were ravenous, and his teeth flashed like a wild animal. The Old Man's erratic movements revealed an odd blurring effect. Brennan blinked, expecting his vision to clear, but it continued.

"Don't worry, I held onto the ones I need," the Old Man said. Brennan realized with horror the Old Man's form overlapped three others, the clones he had ingested in that nightmare room on the top floor of the Bradbury Building. The movement of the images made the Old Man look like a hydra or a Hindu god.

The Old Man continued, "The only power that's important is still in here. You may have ripped up my stamp collection, but there's always a supply. Maybe you slowed me down, but it's not like I have to hurry. You're still outclassed, boy, and with what I'll get from you and Thomas, I'll be unstoppable." He laughed. "Actually, once I finish off Thomas and the haul he brought with him, you're pretty superfluous. I wanted to at least keep you around to watch me play with your little girlfriend, but I think after all this I'll feel better if I just kill you and be done with it."

Brennan remembered how the Old Man had tossed him like a ragdoll into the pit in the barn. At that point, the Old Man had looked to be in his seventies. Now he was back in his prime with three ruthless killers in tow. Brennan knew he had no chance; it was over. *Still, I won't go quietly,* he thought.

"I hope you're ready to work for it," Brennan said.

"Trust me, I won't need to," the Old Man said, advancing. "Not with three of your betters on board. I outclass you four to one."

"That's not how it looks from here," said a voice from the darkness.

They turned to see Thomas approach. His injuries were gone, and Brennan was surprised to see he was smiling.

"What are you here for? Moral support?" the Old Man asked. "Did you get tired of choking on your own blood, and now you want me to finish you quick? You know you can't do anything to me."

Thomas moved instantly from the perimeter of the temple to the center, slamming into the Old Man with his shoulder. The Old Man hit the dirt ground, grunting in pain and surprise. The next second, Thomas was on top of him, hitting him in the face with brutal, solid punches.

"I've been in here for a while, you bastard," Thomas said. "I ran into an old friend of yours. Ben Rosen. He helped me get my head straightened out. You might have three of those sick fucks in your head, but I have eight. Who's outclassed now?"

The Old Man snarled and threw a handful of dirt in Thomas' face. Thomas let him go as he rubbed at his eyes.

"Brennan!" Thomas yelled, but Brennan was already behind the Old Man. He put his hands around the Old Man's neck, and tiny black lines extended from the tips of his fingers. The black wire tightened around the Old Man's neck, cutting into his skin.

Thomas dug his fingers into the Old Man's scalp, and Brennan watched as black tendrils slid out of Thomas' fingers and burrowed into the Old Man's head. The Old Man's eyes bugged out of his head as Thomas strained.

As Thomas pulled again, Brennan yanked the living garrote tight, cutting through flesh and bone. The Old Man's head twisted and his body dropped to the hardwood floor.

9

JOAN RAN to Brennan and Thomas. The black jungle surrounding them began to retreat. Brennan's eyes looked straight through her.

Oh, Brennan, she thought. *We were too late. You're gone.*

His head turned, and she saw him come back to her. She knew that whatever he was, he was still human, still Brennan. He screamed and black threads were pulled back into his body. Brennan fell to his knees, the holes in his skin already shrinking and closing up. There was blood on him, and a detached part of Joan's mind realized it was from the Old Man, whose body had collapsed in a heap in front of Brennan. The monster's head was a ruined mess.

She rushed to Brennan, who was staring at his hands. He looked up at her. "What am I?" he asked her.

Joan wrapped her arms around him and started to say something, but she had no idea what to say.

"You're good," Thomas said. One eye was already swollen shut, and his lips and chin were covered in blood from his broken nose. "You did good." He turned to Joan. "You need to get him out of here, right now. No hospitals, you got that?"

Joan nodded. She pulled Brennan's arm over her shoulder and helped him to his feet.

"You saved me," Brennan said to no one in particular.

"You saved me first," Joan said. She said to Thomas, "What about you?"

"I'll stay behind and clean up."

"Thomas, come on," she said. "We're all getting out of this together. Don't be a jerk!" she said.

He grinned. "I'll always be a jerk," he said. "Now get out of here. I left you something in the truck. Everything you need will be there."

"What are you talking about?"

"Go," he said. "Just because the Old Man is dead doesn't mean there's no danger here. Get Brennan somewhere safe. Whatever you do, don't wait for me."

Joan wanted to argue, but Brennan was barely conscious. So she walked him to the door. After she opened the door, she said to Thomas, "It's true for you, too, you know."

"What?"

"What you told Brennan," she said. "You're good."

"We'll see," Thomas said.

Joan got Brennan to the elevator, but the operator was gone and the elevator was stuck on the ground floor. She was thankful Brennan was walking almost on his own by the time they reached the stairs, and they hurried down the four flights. When she looked at his hand, an image of those worm-like extensions flashed across her mind, but she pushed the thought away. She finally had him back, and nothing was going to get in the way of that.

They walked out the front door unmolested. Brennan's jaw dropped at the sight of the truck, but he climbed in without asking where his dead grandfather's truck had come from. Joan got into the driver's seat and started the engine.

"Wait," Brennan said. "What about Thomas?"

There was a loud explosion above them. Glass rained down onto the street and the top of the truck. The entire top floor of the Bradbury Building was decimated.

"I don't think he's coming," Joan said.

EPILOGUE

SIX MONTHS LATER.

Joan awoke to the smell of coffee and eggs. She paused to take it all in before wrapping herself in a bed sheet and walking out of the bedroom. Brennan, wearing a bathrobe, was hovering over the stove in what they jokingly called the kitchen. The flat was not large, but they had all the room they needed.

"Good morning, sleepyhead," Brennan said as he shook the eggs out of the frying pan and onto two plates. "I was about to come in after you."

"Then I should have stayed there," Joan said. She posed, holding the sheet with one hand while she put the other hand behind her head. "How do I look?"

Brennan paused from fixing the toast to lick a bit of jam off of his thumb. "You look like a hooker who had her clothes stolen. Ouch!" he said, as she kicked him in the shin.

He poured two cups of coffee and they sat down at the table together. "You're sweet, but you didn't have to make breakfast," she said around a mouth full of food. "It has to be my turn by now,"

"It's the least I can do," he said. "With you starting classes at Saint George's tomorrow, this might be the last time I see you."

After they had driven away from the Bradbury Building, Joan found a key and a note in the glove compartment. The note had the address of a post office in New Jersey, and the key opened a post office box. It contained a package from Thomas. Joan had no idea when he had sent it since they had been together the entire time. Inside the package were identification papers, including passports, for her and for Brennan. On paper, Brennan was now Jeffrey Archer, and Joan was Linda Bohlen.

There were also details to a bank account in Joan's new name. After weeks of debate, they decided to risk looking into it. They were shocked to find it contained over three million dollars.

They both had their fill of traveling back and forth across the United States, so they used their new passports to make their way to the United Kingdom. Thomas had fabricated Joan's past with enough detail she could apply and be accepted to St George's, University of London. She knew starting medical school all over again would be difficult to say the least, but it could not compare to what she had survived with Brennan.

She was sure the school would uncover their lie, but Brennan had convinced her Thomas knew what he was doing when he created their false history.

Joan had drifted off, and Brennan was grinning at her. She knew he had caught her worrying again. "You know it will be okay," Brennan said.

"I know, I know," she said. She raised her glass of orange juice. "To Thomas," she said. "He was a son of a bitch, but he was our son of a bitch."

"To Thomas," Brennan said, and their glasses made a clinking sound as they connected.

There was a knock at the door. They stopped breathing, and she wondered how long they would panic every time someone was at the door.

"Stay put, Bed Sheet Barbie. I'll get it," Brennan said, cinching up his robe. Joan, still holding the sheet, went back into the bedroom. She watched as Brennan walked to the door and looked through the peephole. "What the hell?" he said quietly and opened the door.

"Who was it?" she asked.

"Delivery man. Didn't wait, just left this envelope." He held up a large envelope, covered in a plastic sleeve. "It could be a problem."

"Who's it from?"

He looked at the label. "Doesn't say. But it's addressed to both of us."

"What's the problem with that?"

"It uses our real names."

Brennan handed it to her. It was strange seeing their names in print again. She sat back at the table and opened the envelope with a butter knife. Inside she found a single sheet of off-white paper with a letterhead reading, *'The Fifteen Second Group.'*

'Congratulations on the new life,' she read. *'Thank you for saving me.'* She looked up at Brennan, whose eyes were wide and unblinking. *'Sorry I had to lie to you one more time. Best of luck. I'll be watching out for both of you.'*

"Oh, my God," Brennan said. "We left him up there."

"With what was left of the Old Man."

She dropped the paper, which floated gently down to the cold tile.

You're good, she remembered telling him.

We'll see.

AFTERWORD

I began writing this book following the birth of my son. Staying home seemed like the perfect way to spend time with him and work on a novel. Surprising no one but myself, it turned out any writing took place in rare moments and in the middle of the night.

It was this sleep-deprived delirium that shaped the book you have just read. The idea of an affluent serial killer and his army of clones has bounced around in my head for over a decade. It was reading too much Philip K. Dick—*Ubik* waited with me in the hospital when my son was born—that influenced me to make Brennan one of the clones. But it was falling asleep at the kitchen table with my laptop that added the horror.

I woke up to find I'd typed a page of gibberish in my sleep. One line read, '*nothing else mid all the faces.*' Brennan and Thomas had reached the barn, and that unconscious phrase told me what they found inside. But why so many skulls? All of a sudden I had a story chock-full of monsters.

It took me two years of late nights to write *Nothing Else Mid All the Faces,* and it took me another year to edit it into *Monsters All the Way Down.* It's the first book of a loose trilogy, and my hope is you will join me for at least two more trips to Flatland.

This book exists because other works inspired me. Philip K. Dick gave me his doubts in reality and identity, and the paranoid feeling of being on the run is pure PKD. It's no coincidence we end up at the Bradbury Building.

H.P. Lovecraft supplied the nature of the horror and the

theme of a terrifying lineage. Lovecraft once wrote a letter describing the dream that inspired his Nyarlathotep character, and that letter inspired my own immortal monster. I owe *At the Mountains of Madness* for the Arctic journal entry, and Ben Rosen is basically a secret agent version of Randolph Carter.

Stephen King and Neil Gaiman influence every story I create. They are my heroes.

The road trips in the story come from too many marathons of the TV series *Supernatural*. Sax Rohmer inspired Ben Rosen and Richard Henry by way of Hamilton Drew and Ben Luddy from James Robinson's *Starman*. And if you hate how I write my dialogue, blame Joss Whedon and Brian Michael Bendis—I learned it from studying them.

As for music, I am indebted to Jim Steinman, especially Meat Loaf's *Bat Out of Hell*. Its title track helped me know Thomas, as did the song "You're a Wolf" by Sea Wolf. I played The Mountain Goats' *Heretic Pride* so much I'm surprised the record isn't worn smooth. Every song on that album inspired elements in this book, and it's playing in my office tonight as I type.

I couldn't have written this book without the love and support of my beautiful wife, Tricia, my two children, and the rest of my loving family. My friends, especially those from TINTBEGITWNTIJAT, were more encouraging than they could know. My beta readers—Dustin Taylor, Ryan McCracken, and Olaf Alexander—are gentlemen of the highest caliber. They survived an early draft so you didn't have to. My critique group—Bernice Simpson, Mike Akins, and Amber Jones—came along at the right time to help me publish this book. I love and thank you all, and I thank everyone else who believed in me.

Thank you for reading, and I hope to see you here next time for a story about a dead man's comic books and the nature of reality. Until then, stay out of the barn.

~Ryan McSwain
Amarillo, Texas
July 15, 2014

ABOUT THE AUTHOR

Ryan McSwain lives in Amarillo, Texas, with his wife and their two children. Ryan spends his days caring for his children, writing, and looking for that next novel, comic book, TV show, film, or album that will give him the brain tingles. It is unlikely he is standing behind you this very instant, but you should turn around just to check.

You can keep up with Ryan and his work by visiting www.ryanmcswain.com.